PATRICIA WEN... ᴗ...
ANNE BELINDA

PATRICIA WENTWORTH was born Dora Amy Elles in India in 1877 (not 1878 as has sometimes been stated). She was first educated privately in India, and later at Blackheath School for Girls. Her first husband was George Dillon, with whom she had her only child, a daughter. She also had two stepsons from her first marriage, one of whom died in the Somme during World War I.

Her first novel was published in 1910, but it wasn't until the 1920's that she embarked on her long career as a writer of mysteries. Her most famous creation was Miss Maud Silver, who appeared in 32 novels, though there were a further 33 full-length mysteries not featuring Miss Silver—the entire run of these is now reissued by Dean Street Press.

Patricia Wentworth died in 1961. She is recognized today as one of the pre-eminent exponents of the classic British golden age mystery novel.

By Patricia Wentworth

The Benbow Smith Mysteries
Fool Errant
Danger Calling
Walk with Care
Down Under

The Frank Garrett Mysteries
Dead or Alive
Rolling Stone

The Ernest Lamb Mysteries
The Blind Side
Who Pays the Piper?
Pursuit of a Parcel

Standalones
The Astonishing Adventure of Jane Smith
The Red Lacquer Case
The Annam Jewel
The Black Cabinet
The Dower House Mystery
The Amazing Chance
Hue and Cry
Anne Belinda
Will-o'-the-Wisp
Beggar's Choice
The Coldstone
Kingdom Lost
Nothing Venture
Red Shadow
Outrageous Fortune
Touch and Go
Fear by Night
Red Stefan
Blindfold
Hole and Corner
Mr. Zero
Run!
Weekend with Death
Silence in Court

PATRICIA WENTWORTH

ANNE BELINDA

With an introduction by
Curtis Evans

DEAN STREET PRESS

Published by Dean Street Press 2016

Copyright © 1927 Patricia Wentworth

Introduction copyright © 2016 Curtis Evans

Cover by DSP

First published in 1927 by Hodder & Stoughton

ISBN 978 1 911413 15 8

www.deanstreetpress.co.uk

Introduction

BRITISH AUTHOR Patricia Wentworth published her first novel, a gripping tale of desperate love during the French Revolution entitled *A Marriage under the Terror*, a little over a century ago, in 1910. The book won first prize in the Melrose Novel Competition and was a popular success in both the United States and the United Kingdom. Over the next five years Wentworth published five additional novels, the majority of them historical fiction, the best-known of which today is *The Devil's Wind* (1912), another sweeping period romance, this one set during the Sepoy Mutiny (1857-58) in India, a region with which the author, as we shall see, had extensive familiarity. Like *A Marriage under the Terror, The Devil's Wind* received much praise from reviewers for its sheer storytelling élan. One notice, for example, pronounced the novel "an achievement of some magnitude" on account of "the extraordinary vividness...the reality of the atmosphere...the scenes that shift and move with the swiftness of a moving picture...." (*The Bookman*, August 1912) With her knack for spinning a yarn, it perhaps should come as no surprise that Patricia Wentworth during the early years of the Golden Age of mystery fiction (roughly from 1920 into the 1940s) launched upon her own mystery-writing career, a course charted most successfully for nearly four decades by the prolific author, right up to the year of her death in 1961.

Considering that Patricia Wentworth belongs to the select company of Golden Age mystery writers with books which have remained in print in every decade for nearly a century now (the centenary of Agatha Christie's first mystery, *The Mysterious Affair at Styles*, is in 2020; the centenary of Wentworth's first mystery, *The Astonishing Adventure of Jane Smith*, follows merely three years later, in 2023), relatively little is known about the author herself. It appears, for example, that even the widely given year of Wentworth's birth, 1878, is incorrect. Yet it is sufficiently clear that Wentworth lived a varied and intriguing life that provided her ample inspiration for a writing career devoted to imaginative fiction.

It is usually stated that Patricia Wentworth was born Dora Amy Elles on 10 November 1878 in Mussoorie, India, during the heyday of the British Raj; however, her Indian birth and baptismal record states that she in fact was born on 15 October 1877 and was baptized on 26 November of that same year in Gwalior. Whatever doubts surround her actual birth year, however, unquestionably the future author came from a prominent Anglo-Indian military family. Her father, Edmond Roche Elles, a son of Malcolm Jamieson Elles, a Porto, Portugal wine merchant originally from Ardrossan, Scotland, entered the British Royal Artillery in 1867, a decade before Wentworth's birth, and first saw service in India during the Lushai Expedition of 1871-72. The next year Elles in India wed Clara Gertrude Rothney, daughter of Brigadier-General Octavius Edward Rothney, commander of the Gwalior District, and Maria (Dempster) Rothney, daughter of a surgeon in the Bengal Medical Service. Four children were born of the union of Edmond and Clara Elles, Wentworth being the only daughter.

Before his retirement from the army in 1908, Edmond Elles rose to the rank of lieutenant-general and was awarded the KCB (Knight Commander of the Order of Bath), as was the case with his elder brother, Wentworth's uncle, Lieutenant-General Sir William Kidston Elles, of the Bengal Command. Edmond Elles also served as Military Member to the Council of the Governor-General of India from 1901 to 1905. Two of Wentworth's brothers, Malcolm Rothney Elles and Edmond Claude Elles, served in the Indian Army as well, though both of them died young (Malcolm in 1906 drowned in the Ganges Canal while attempting to rescue his orderly, who had fallen into the water), while her youngest brother, Hugh Jamieson Elles, achieved great distinction in the British Army. During the First World War he catapulted, at the relatively youthful age of 37, to the rank of brigadier-general and the command of the British Tank Corps, at the Battle of Cambrai personally leading the advance of more than 350 tanks against the German line. Years later Hugh Elles also played a major role in British civil defense during the Second World War. In the event of a German invasion of Great Britain, something which seemed all too possible in 1940, he was tasked with leading the defense of southwestern England. Like Sir Edmond and Sir William, Hugh Elles attained the rank of lieutenant-general and was awarded the KCB.

Although she was born in India, Patricia Wentworth spent much of her childhood in England. In 1881 she with her mother and two younger brothers was at Tunbridge Wells, Kent, on what appears to have been a rather extended visit in her ancestral country; while a decade later the same family group resided at Blackheath, London at Lennox House, domicile of Wentworth's widowed maternal grandmother, Maria Rothney. (Her eldest brother, Malcolm, was in Bristol attending Clifton College.) During her years at Lennox House, Wentworth attended Blackheath High School for Girls, then only recently founded as "one of the first schools in the country to give girls a proper education" (*The London Encyclopaedia*, 3rd ed., p. 74). Lennox House was an ample Victorian villa with a great glassed-in conservatory running all along the back and a substantial garden--most happily, one presumes, for Wentworth, who resided there not only with her grandmother, mother and two brothers, but also five aunts (Maria Rothney's unmarried daughters, aged 26 to 42), one adult first cousin once removed and nine first cousins, adolescents like Wentworth herself, from no less than three different families (one Barrow, three Masons and five Dempsters); their parents, like Wentworth's father, presumably were living many miles away in various far-flung British dominions. Three servants--a cook, parlourmaid and housemaid--were tasked with serving this full score of individuals.

Sometime after graduating from Blackheath High School in the mid-1890s, Wentworth returned to India, where in a local British newspaper she is said to have published her first fiction. In 1901 the 23-year-old Wentworth married widower George Fredrick Horace Dillon, a 41-year-old lieutenant-colonel in the Indian Army with three sons from his prior marriage. Two years later Wentworth gave birth to her only child, a daughter named Clare Roche Dillon. (In some sources it is erroneously stated that Clare was the offspring of Wentworth's second marriage.) However in 1906, after just five years of marriage, George Dillon died suddenly on a sea voyage, leaving Wentworth with sole responsibility for her three teenaged stepsons and baby daughter. A very short span of years, 1904 to 1907, saw the deaths of Wentworth's husband, mother, grandmother and brothers Malcolm and Edmond, removing much of her support network. In 1908, however, her father, who was now sixty years old, retired from the army and returned to England, settling at Guildford, Surrey with an older unmarried sister named Dora (for whom his daughter presumably had been named). Wentworth joined this household as well, along with her daughter and her youngest stepson. Here in Surrey Wentworth, presumably with the goal of making herself financially independent for the first time in her life (she was now in her early thirties), wrote the novel that changed the course of her life, *A Marriage under the Terror*, for the first time we know of utilizing her famous *nom de plume*.

The burst of creative energy that resulted in Wentworth's publication of six novels in six years suddenly halted after the appearance of *Queen Anne Is Dead* in 1915. It seems not unlikely that the Great War impinged in various ways on her writing. One tragic episode was the death on the western front of one of her stepsons, George Charles Tracey Dillon. Mining in Colorado when war was declared, young Dillon worked his passage from Galveston, Texas to Bristol, England as a shipboard muleteer (mule-tender) and joined the Gloucestershire Regiment. In 1916 he died at the Somme at the age of 29 (about the age of Wentworth's two brothers when they had passed away in India).

A couple of years after the conflict's cessation in 1918, a happy event occurred in Wentworth's life when at Frimley, Surrey she wed George Oliver Turnbull, up to this time a lifelong bachelor who like the author's first husband was a lieutenant-colonel in the Indian Army. Like his bride now forty-two years old, George Turnbull as a younger man had distinguished himself for his athletic prowess, playing forward for eight years for the Scottish rugby team and while a student at the Royal Military Academy winning the medal awarded the best athlete of his term. It seems not unlikely that Turnbull played a role in his wife's turn toward writing mystery fiction, for he is said to have strongly supported Wentworth's career, even assisting her in preparing manuscripts for publication. In 1936 the couple in Camberley, Surrey built Heatherglade House, a large two-story structure on substantial grounds, where they resided until Wentworth's death a quarter of a century later. (George Turnbull survived his wife by nearly a decade, passing away in 1970 at the age of 92.) This highly successful middle-aged companionate marriage contrasts sharply with the more youthful yet rocky union of Agatha and Archie Christie, which was three years away from sundering when Wentworth published *The Astonishing Adventure of Jane Smith* (1923), the first of her sixty-five mystery novels.

Although Patricia Wentworth became best-known for her cozy tales of the criminal investigations of consulting detective Miss Maud Silver, one of the mystery genre's most prominent spinster sleuths, in truth the Miss Silver tales account for just under half of Wentworth's 65 mystery novels. Miss Silver did not make her debut until 1928 and she did not come to predominate in Wentworth's fictional criminous output until the 1940s. Between 1923 and 1945 Wentworth published 33 mystery novels without Miss Silver, a handsome and substantial legacy in and of itself to vintage crime fiction fans. Many of these books are standalone tales of mystery, but nine of them have series characters. Debuting in the novel *Fool Errant* in 1929, a year after Miss Silver first appeared in print, was the enigmatic, nautically-named *eminence grise* Benbow Collingwood Horatio Smith, owner of a most expressively opinionated parrot named Ananias (and quite a colorful character in his own right). Benbow Smith went on to appear in three additional Wentworth mysteries: *Danger Calling* (1931), *Walk with Care* (1933) and *Down Under* (1937). Working in tandem with Smith in the investigation of sinister affairs threatening the security of Great Britain in *Danger*

Calling and *Walk with Care* is Frank Garrett, Head of Intelligence for the Foreign Office, who also appears solo in *Dead or Alive* (1936) and *Rolling Stone* (1940) and collaborates with additional series characters, Scotland Yard's Inspector Ernest Lamb and Sergeant Frank Abbott, in *Pursuit of a Parcel* (1942). Inspector Lamb and Sergeant Abbott headlined a further pair of mysteries, *The Blind Side* (1939) and *Who Pays the Piper?* (1940), before they became absorbed, beginning with *Miss Silver Deals with Death* (1943), into the burgeoning Miss Silver canon. Lamb would make his farewell appearance in 1955 in *The Listening Eye*, while Abbott would take his final bow in mystery fiction with Wentworth's last published novel, *The Girl in the Cellar* (1961), which went into print the year of the author's death at the age of 83.

The remaining two dozen Wentworth mysteries, from the fantastical *The Astonishing Adventure of Jane Smith* in 1923 to the intense legal drama *Silence in Court* in 1945, are, like the author's series novels, highly imaginative and entertaining tales of mystery and adventure, told by a writer gifted with a consummate flair for storytelling. As one confirmed Patricia Wentworth mystery fiction addict, American Golden Age mystery writer Todd Downing, admiringly declared in the 1930s, "There's something about Miss Wentworth's yarns that is contagious." This attractive new series of Patricia Wentworth reissues by Dean Street Press provides modern fans of vintage mystery a splendid opportunity to catch the Wentworth fever.

Curtis Evans

Prologue

JOHN MAURICE WAVENEY came round the turn of the path and looked down into the valley. The side of the hill fell sheer away. A little zigzag track ran to and fro amongst the roots of the great, bare beech trees and dropped at last to the valley.

John Maurice looked at the track, whistled through his teeth, and then made the best of his way down it. Leg or no leg, he wasn't going to turn back now. He had come to have a look at Waveney, and he wasn't going back without that look. He climbed down slowly and very carefully, as befitted a man only three days out of hospital. Every now and then he sat down on a beech root and rested.

The year was 1917, and the month was May. After wet, squally weather there had come half a dozen days of pure enchantment. The pale blue sky was so brimmed with the sun that all the shadows looked warm and soft. The valley was the valley of a dream, full of still, golden light and a green mist of breaking leaves. John Maurice looked at it, and found it worth the climb.

He slid the last couple of yards and began to walk rather haltingly along the so-called level, which was not really level at all. The path followed an erratic thread of water, sometimes dammed into a pool, sometimes falling like a single thread from a real waterfall, sometimes burying itself in a little marsh of moss. John Maurice found it very attractive. He drank from one of the baby pools, and felt an absurd secret thrill because he and the stream bore the same name. This was the Waveney. He was on ground which had belonged to his forefathers for more generations than he could count. From this valley Sir Anthony Waveney had gone out to ride with Richard Cœur de Lion on Crusade.

John Maurice wondered whether the Crusader's helmet was as uncomfortable as his own tin hat. Then he grinned and went limping on his way, singing in a funny toneless whisper:

"Augustus Fitzlucius O'Ryan
Was the loftiest soul on the earth.

His mother was Susie O'Brien,
And his wife was a Jones by birth."

The path rose abruptly and climbed a sort of rocky bastion, leaving the little Waveney far below. John Maurice was panting when he got to the top. He flung himself down on a drift of beech leaves and looked about him. The blighted path, having climbed all that way up, was now going to climb all the way down on the other side.

He got his breath and observed the view. The rocky cliff on which he lay dropped sheer to the thread of water. Ten feet away the other half of the cliff reared itself, its crumbling face screened by a little birch tree in its first leaf. The sun made the green of it tremble like green fire. How many hundreds of years, how many ages, had it taken for the little stream to cut its way through the rock and leave the twin cliffs parted?

John Maurice had some queer thoughts. He whistled to himself and let his thoughts make pictures for him. The sun shone, and the beech leaves were soft. He watched a spider with long, thin legs run delicately across the red-brown leaves. He heard a thrush begin to sing, and break off with half his song unsung. Someone said, "What are you doing here?"

John Maurice sat up. In front of him, looking down on him from the other cliff, there was a girl of about fifteen. She held a branch of the birch tree aside and looked at him out of dark blue eyes. She had long, falling plaits of dark brown hair. She wore a very much stained brown holland overall; there was a green smudge on one of her smooth, pale cheeks.

"What are you doing here?" she said in quite an accusing voice.

John Maurice scrambled to his feet, made a horrible face, and dropped again to a sitting position.

"Sorry," he said.

"What for?"

"I forgot about my leg—I have to go easy with it."

"What's the matter with it?"

"Oh, it's practically all right. I'm going back next week."

The girl continued to hold back the branch and to look at John Maurice. Her plaits were so long that she had pushed them under the leather belt which held her overall.

"France?" she said. A curious fleeting expression just touched her eyes, her voice.

John Maurice nodded.

"You're on leave—with your people?"

The curious something came again, and again was gone. John Maurice wondered what it was.

"I haven't any people."

"None? None at all?"

"Nary one, except a great-unclish sort of cousin whom I've never seen in my life."

The odd look went away. It was like a cloud going away; the sun shone very suddenly and sweetly. The dark blue eyes brimmed with a smile. The girl said:

"I'm so frightfully glad. Aren't you?"

"Why? Because I haven't any relations?"

"Of course."

"Balmy," said John Maurice to himself. "Balmy but nice—nice but balmy." Then he said aloud, "Do you mind explaining why?"

The girl let go of the branch. Then she climbed up a couple of feet and sat down cross-legged on a mossy stone. She had nice slim ankles and terribly shapeless old shoes.

"You said you were going back next week?"

"Yes."

"Well, if you haven't got any people, it doesn't matter."

"Doesn't it?"

"No, of course not. I mean it doesn't matter to *you* if you're killed."

John Maurice burst out laughing; there was such an earnest thrill in her voice, the dark blue eyes were so solemn, that for the life of him he couldn't help it. When he laughed, the girl flushed scarlet.

"Why should it matter to you? I don't see that it does a *bit*. I'm not sorry for the people who are killed—not a single bit. They're all right. I expect it's all frightfully interesting and exciting for them. I'm not going to waste my time being sorry for *them*. I don't care what anyone says; it's the people who are left—the people who can't go because they're too old or too young. How would you like that? How would you like to be a girl at home, when your brothers had gone and you couldn't go?"

"I don't know that I've ever wanted to be a girl," said John Maurice candidly.

The long dark plaits jerked with the vehemence of her nod.

"Of course you didn't. No one ever does."

John Maurice looked at her with amusement, and something else. She was a pretty kid—this from the height of his twenty-three years. Comic too, with her solemn eyes, and the smudge on her cheek, and her earnest assurance that his being killed wouldn't matter in the least. The whole thing tickled him; but he was young enough to feel a little aggrieved.

"That's all very well, you know. There's something a bit chilly about feeling that no one's going to care a blow."

"That can't be helped." But she frowned a little and her colour rose. "Haven't you got anyone, really?"

He shook his head.

She had locked her hands about her knees—long, slim hands, very brown; they looked strong. There was a queer little mole between thumb and forefinger on one of them; it was shaped like a heart. It caught John Maurice's eye as he shook his head.

"Not a soul. The cousin would be rather bucked than otherwise."

The dark blue eyes took on a deeper shade of earnestness.

"*I* should be sorry—I should be sorry about anyone," she said. And as she said it, a distant "Cooee" came floating down the valley.

"That's for me," said the girl.

She unclasped her hands, stood up, and scrambled down the rough face of the cliff. She jumped the last few feet, began to run, and then, turning, looked up at John Maurice.

"I promise I'll be sorry," she said.

Chapter One

THE CAR DREW UP in a drizzle of rain, and a young man sprang out. He stepped over the tortoise-shell cat which lay asleep on the top step of the village shop, and penetrated to the counter. To the left there were saucepans and trousers; to the right some marled bacon and two mouldy cauliflowers; overhead a ham, some balls of tarred twine, a packet of flypapers, and a miscellaneous collection of leather straps.

The young man banged on the counter and whistled between his teeth. Mr. Murgleton emerged, smoothing his grey whiskers and blinking his greenish eyes; he had the air of a dissipated elderly mouser.

"I want to know the way to Waveney Hall. I'd be awfully obliged if you could tell me how to get there."

Disappointment lent austerity to Mr. Murgleton's voice.

"Up the 'ill and second to the left." Then he added, "There ain't no one livin' there."

"There's a caretaker, isn't there? I was told there was a caretaker."

Mr. Murgleton gazed morosely at the fly-papers.

"There's Mrs. Mossiter," he conceded, "*and* her daughter—*and* her daughter's babby, for that matter." He sniffed, and the village spirit asserted itself. "It's time someone took the place in 'and. A year since Sir Anthony died, and nothin' seen to nor kep' up—goin' hall to bits is wot I should say if I was talkin' to the King 'isself, or to Sir John Waveney. May I ask if you know 'im?" The green eyes blinked inquisitively.

John Maurice Waveney did not answer the question. He had no desire to be hailed as the returning heir; he wanted to see the old place without any fuss and to make up his mind whether he wanted to live in it. He therefore backed away from the counter, scratched the back of the tortoise-shell cat's head, said "Second to the left and up the hill? Thank you very much," and went out humming:

"Cassidy was a gentleman,
Cassidy said to me—"

The rest was lost in the whirr of the starter.

The second turning to the left was a narrowish lane. It went up a hill, and then came down again. At the very bottom there were great stone pillars and high iron gates. The pillars were covered with moss. The gates were shut.

John got down and opened them. They swung very stiffly on rusted hinges. He got back into his car and went slowly up the drive. No new gravel since the year one; weeds everywhere; trees unlopped and cluttered up with dead boughs; bushes untrimmed; and again weeds, and weeds, and weeds.

"Cheery sort of home-coming!" said Sir John Waveney with imperturbable cheerfulness.

The car slid out from under the dripping trees, and he saw Waveney, all grey in the rain. Even so, it gave him an odd, romantic thrill. The oldest part of the house was out of sight. What he saw was what Maurice Waveney had seen when he brought his cousin Claude there as a bride in the year of the French Revolution—a Queen Anne front with a terrace before it. But in Maurice Waveney's time the door had stood open for his welcome, and there had been firelight and candlelight in the rooms. Now every window showed shuttered or curtained, and the only light came from the weeping sky.

John got out and pulled the iron bell with a will. He could hear it ring; and presently he could hear the sound of the ringing die away. He pushed his hand down into his pocket, took out a folded paper, and rang again. Once more he heard the distant echoes die. He had rung a third time, when the door opened. A stout woman with a gloomy expression looked past him at the rain.

"I have an order to view the house," said John.

He unfolded his slip of paper and proffered it. Mrs. Mossiter looked at it morosely.

"What's this?" she inquired.

"An order to view. It's all right—signed by Sir John Waveney's solicitors."

"The house isn't to let," said Mrs. Mossiter, adding as an afterthought, "Not that I've heard of."

"It's really all right. You're Mrs. Mossiter, the housekeeper, aren't you?"

"I've not heard anything at all about the house being to let." There was suspicion and resentment in every note of the heavy voice.

"Well, it isn't to let yet. But it may be, in certain circumstances; and I've an order to view," John was cheerful, but a shade impatient.

Very slowly Mrs. Mossiter stepped back and made room for him to pass into the hall. She reminded him of a brindled bulldog who had bitten him years ago in Durban—the gloomy eye, the same waddling dignity, the same air of having encountered the dregs of creation.

"The dining-room," said Mrs. Mossiter, turning to the left and throwing open a door.

John peered into the darkness. With every shutter closed, the dining-room was just gloom and the corner of a dining-table. Mrs. Mossiter trod heavily to the window, opened two inches of shutter, and let in a spectral greyness.

The late Sir Anthony had had a lively taste in carpets. Even in this grey light, John found a scarlet ground lavishly patterned in Reckitt's blue a trifle crude. The long dining-table stretched away into the shadows. Dark panelled walls looked down upon it.

Mrs. Mossiter closed the shutter with a click. John backed out into the hall, which seemed quite light and cheerful in comparison.

"The droring-room," said Mrs. Mossiter.

She had waddled past him with her bulldog gait and preceded him into another closely shuttered room. When a little ray of light had been admitted, John Waveney felt himself invaded by a most unwonted depression. All the chairs were in shrouds, and the chandelier in the middle of the room in a horrible white cotton bag that made it look like the carcase of something hung up in a butcher's shop. A drugget hid the carpet. He tried to fancy the room with its white panelling all lit up, or with the sunshine slanting in through the long window that looked to the west. He strode past

Mrs. Mossiter and opened another shutter. Falling rain, and low clouds, heavy and black with more to come.

He turned from the window.

"Beastly day to see a house, isn't it? I expect you find it a bit lonely. I say, who's that?"

On the right of the fireplace hung a portrait of Claude Waveney in a white dress.

"Lady Waveney—wife of Sir Maurice, fourth baronet—taken just after her marriage," said Mrs. Mossiter. "That's Sir Maurice on the left."

John looked with interest at his great-great-grandfather and his great-great-grandmother. Claude Waveney held herself gallantly and looked straight out of the picture with steady blue eyes. Sir Maurice gloomed a little from his side of the fireplace; he had not taken kindly to having his portrait painted, but he made a very fine figure of a man.

They left the drawing-room and went from room to room, a pilgrimage at every moment more dismal. The kitchen, with its bright fire and a younger edition of Mrs. Mossiter crawling on the floor after a fat, rebellious child, alone had a human air. Of anyone less forbidding, John would have craved a cup of tea. As it was, he left the kitchen regretfully and followed his guide to the upper storey.

By the time he had inspected half a dozen bedrooms, all darkened until they suggested funerals, John was quite certain that he couldn't ever live in the place. And yet all the while something in him wanted to live in it.

At the end of a long corridor they came into the room which had been Claude Waveney's. The window looked out across the garden to the wooded valley into which John had climbed painfully nine years before. He thought back to that stolen visit whilst he was at home wounded. He remembered the bright warm day, the crystal thread of the Waveney breaking over the stones and losing itself in moss, the funny earnest kid who had promised to be sorry if he was killed.

He stared into the soaking rain, and strangely, suddenly, his mood darkened. He hated this place of which he was the unwanted, unwelcomed heir—hated it, and felt it draw him as if it would never let him go. It was not so much that the place was his as that he belonged to the place, and whether he loved it or hated it, it had a hold on him which no other place had ever had or could have. He swung round, and his look startled Mrs. Mossiter; it was so bleak.

Without paying any attention to her, he walked down the room, pausing by the foot of the big four-poster bed, which still carried a heavy obsolete canopy of crimson damask. The walls of the room were of the same dark crimson, faded almost everywhere to a shade between brown and magenta. Over the mantelpiece a sharp oblong of deeper colour caught the eye. John looked at it and, still looking, spoke shortly:

"There was a picture there. What's happened to it?"

Mrs. Mossiter bridled. But she answered: "There's pictures in the house that goes with the house, and there's others that don't." The note of impertinence became a little clearer as the sound of her own voice heartened her.

John turned on her.

"And this picture?"

"It don't go with the house"—she gave back a step—"it belongs to Lady Marr."

Marr—yes, one of Sir Anthony's daughters had married Nicholas Marr. But why on earth had this Mossiter woman looked so furtive all at once?

"What picture is it? Has it been taken away? Has Lady Marr taken it?"

The questions followed each other so sharply that Mrs. Mossiter found herself answering quite respectfully:

"No, sir—not yet, sir."

"Where is it?"

John was persistent, partly because his mood was an overbearing one, partly because the woman's sullenness had irked him from the beginning.

"Where is it?"

"It don't go with the house."

"Is it in here? The dressing-room? Is it in the dressing-room?"

Her face changed; she looked startled, then sullen again. John walked to the dressing-room door and threw it open.

It was a good-sized room, but it looked small because the furniture was so large. A mahogany wardrobe covered one wall from ceiling to floor. A huge, dark tall-boy confronted the wardrobe. The very washstand was immense, holding a hideous double set of Victorian crockery. There was a boot-cupboard that would have held the shoes of a family.

John had the oddest sense that he was intruding; the room was so evidently Sir Anthony's room. He glanced about it, and was on the point of drawing back, when Mrs. Mossiter spoke at his elbow, breathing heavily.

"The picture don't go with the house, and you've no call to meddle with it. It belongs to Lady Marr—it don't go with the house at all."

"Ah!" said John. "Yes, you said that before, didn't you?"

He followed the direction of her angry gaze, and saw the frame of the picture jutting out a bare inch on the far side of the tall-boy. The frame was a gilt one, and the picture leaned, face hidden, against the smooth mahogany. As he put his hand on it, he was aware of alarm as well as anger in Mrs. Mossiter's voice:

"You've no call to touch it! It don't go with the house—it belongs to Lady Marr." And there she stopped, because John looked at her, and there was something in the look that stopped her.

He turned the picture to the light.

The canvas was about three feet by two. It showed a very young girl looking at herself in the glass. That was the first impression—a girl in white, with short fair hair, looking at herself in an old mirror with a walnut frame. Her head was bent a little forward, her face in profile; the light just touched her hair and showed the exquisite line of head and neck. But the face that looked back from the mirror was the face of the child who had told John Maurice nine years ago that she promised to be sorry if he was killed. On either side of the face in the mirror there hung the long dark plaits which he remembered.

The picture startled whilst it charmed, and charmed whilst it startled. Some vague recollection of having heard of this picture as Amory's masterpiece just touched the outer surface of John's memory. He looked at the two faces, and then at the neat black lettering which crossed the gold of the frame below:

"Jenifer Anne and Anne Belinda, twin daughters of Sir Anthony Waveney."

Chapter Two

WHEN A FIRM of solicitors has been established for a hundred and fifty years or so, it may very well happen that the names which appear on the brass door-plate do not to-day reveal the identity of a single one of the partners.

It was Messrs. Garden, Longhope, Longhope and Mortimer who had informed John Waveney of his succession to the entailed Waveney property; but the benevolent old gentleman whom he interviewed on his arrival in England bore the name of Carruthers, and mentioned that, should Sir John Waveney require any information or assistance during the next month, "Mr. Smith, my nephew and partner, will be available—I myself am taking a short holiday." There was, apparently, no Longhope, no Mortimer, no Garden. The past into which they had receded was decorous and honourable in the extreme. Its flavour clung about the dark, narrow stair and panelled walls of the old Georgian house.

John Waveney, asking for Mr. Smith, was shown into one of those high rooms with narrow windows, in which so much legal business is transacted. Outside, the sky was dark with the threat of rain. A lamp with a tilted shade stood on the desk at Mr. Smith's elbow. The light touched the top of a cropped red head; then, as he looked up, shone full on sharp features and surprised blue eyes.

With a jerk that nearly upset both chair and lamp, Lewis Smith was on his feet.

"Maurice! Hullo! My dear chap, where on earth did you spring from?"

John dropped his hat.

"Good Lord! It's Lulu!"

"But you—how on earth—where on earth? I say, you're not—Where's that card? You're not Waveney? Don't tell me you're Sir John Waveney!"

"John Maurice Waveney. I dropped the Waveney when I enlisted. Just as well I did, though I didn't know till afterwards that I was going to find myself in Tom Waveney's company."

"Sir Anthony's second son?"

"Yes. Jolly good fellow—killed at Loos."

There was one of those little pauses which fall suddenly when people meet who have not met for years—on one side of the gulf every step so familiar, so full of intimate detail, so crowded with memories, strange, odd, comic, and horrible; on the other, a new country, in which the two who were so closely associated are each cast for a different rôle.

The little silence fell, and was broken by the sudden laughter of Mr. Lewis Smith:

"By gum, it's funny!" He smote John on the shoulder. "You—why, the last I remember of you is damning you into heaps because you'd pinched the tin of Keating's—only it wasn't Keating's, but a special bug-slayer which my Aunt Louisa had sent me for my birthday."

John grinned.

"I wanted it more than you did. It was good stuff. Besides, old Ananias Brown had half of it."

"The blighter!"

"Where do you suppose I ran into Ananias last year? Java, of all places in the world, where he's a highly respected member of a highly respected engineering firm. I've knocked about all over the place these last few years, and it's astonishing what a lot of fellows I've run into. You remember Fatty Higgins? I bumped into him in Rio. He told me that Kennedy—you know, Rat Kennedy—had made no end of a pile and was setting up as a landed proprietor. D'you ever come across Morrison?"

"We briefed him for the Burlsdon Bank Case only last week. He'll be taking silk one of these days."

"And Purdie?"

"Gone under, poor devil."

The pause fell again; and again it was Lewis Smith who broke it.

"What on earth have you been doing with yourself? And why on earth didn't you come home a year ago, when Sir Anthony died?"

John sat down on the arm of the big chair sacred to clients. With a swoop he retrieved his hat and cast it into the capacious leather seat. He answered the last question first.

"I didn't come home, because the place without any money was more than a bit of a white elephant, and I was in the thick of old Peterson's book."

Lewis Smith got back into his chair, crossed his long legs, and said:

"Peterson?"

"Old Rudolphus Peterson. Don't tell me you've never heard of him—the snake man—tremendously famous."

"Snakes? Yes, I've got him. But where do you come in?"

"When I got demobbed I went back to Canada. I'd been out there two years when the war started, so I thought I'd go back. I hadn't any people over here, and Sir Anthony—well, he'd given me pretty plainly to understand that he didn't want to set eyes on me. I don't blame him, poor old chap; it must have been a most frightful knock for him, losing both his sons and feeling that I'd got to come in instead of the daughters. I must say it's a pretty rotten law, and I don't wonder he never wanted to see me."

"I think he ought to have seen you. The whole thing would have come easier if you hadn't been an absolute stranger."

John made a quick, impatient gesture with his right hand.

"I wasn't keen myself. Hanging around waiting for dead men's shoes is a beastly job. But I'd a pretty rough time over there." He jerked his head in the supposed direction of Canada. "First I got cheated out of my gratuity like the veriest tenderfoot. It makes me sick to think what a mug I was; and it used to make me a great deal sicker when I was absolutely on my beam ends, doing any sort of beastly odd job to get a meal."

"As bad as that?"

"Worse, because I didn't always get one. That's how I ran into Peterson. I wanted to carry his bag for him; and he wanted to carry it himself, and went on saying 'No' in his funny cracked voice. And then, all of a sudden, he said, 'You are hungry? No? Yes?' And I said, 'Damned hungry,' and the old man looked at me as solemn as an owl and said, 'It is wrong to swear, but it is damn wrong to be hungry. Come and eat, young man, come and eat at once. Carry my bag, and come and eat with me, and tell me why you are hungry. You are not a drunkard—no?' Well, I went along with him, and about twelve hours later I woke up in a decent bed and thought I had dreamt the whole thing."

"And had you?"

"It was rather hard to realize that I hadn't. I remembered a frightfully good dinner, and being asked where I was at school, and what I'd done in the war—'the so much to be regretted and calamitous world catastrophe,' as the old man called it. And the last thing I remembered was being engaged as his secretary to go round the world with him and correct his English whenever I wasn't taking photographs of snakes. You must admit that it didn't seem very probable."

Lewis Smith leaned back in his chair and roared with laughter.

"Was he mad?"

"Not in the least—one of the best—one of *the* very best. We knocked about together for five years, petting material for his book on snakes. Pretty hot work some of it. I assure you the trenches aren't in it when it comes to slithering on your tummy through a crawling swamp, trying to get a close-up of a puff-adder in the bosom of his family, or stalking one hamadryad whilst another one stalks you. Old Peterson was a wonder. He was too fat to crawl himself, but his pluck and endurance were amazing. We were in the thick of his book when I saw your advertisement; and, naturally, I couldn't have left him then. Besides, I had no money to keep the place up on—and of all beastly jobs in the world, I should think the beastliest would be to sit down in a mouldering old place and wait for it to fall about your ears. I would rather tout for jobs in the street again—there's more life in it."

Lewis Smith looked puzzled.

"Aren't you going to stay over here now? My uncle seemed to think—"

John shifted his position rather abruptly.

"Well," he said, "I haven't made up my mind. I've got the money now. That ripping old chap just lived to see his book come out, and when he was gone I found he'd left me every cent he'd got. I don't believe he knew himself how much it was—money didn't interest him. Well, I've got plenty."

"What a stroke of luck!"

John's eyes went bleak. That he would have given the money twice over to hear old Peterson say "My boy," with his funny accent, was a thing which Lulu Smith couldn't be expected to understand. He leaned forward with a sudden change of voice and manner.

"Well, that's that. About Waveney—I haven't made up my mind. I got an order to view from your uncle and went down incog. to have a look at the place."

"What did you think of it?"

John wasn't going to say. He laughed, and drummed with his heels against the side of the chair.

"The housekeeper's the grimmest female I ever met—absolutely. Now look here, Lulu, I want to ask you some questions."

"Fire away."

"Well, the estate comes to me. But most of the money went to Sir Anthony's daughters?"

"Daughter."

"What?" The word came out very short and sharp. John felt, in fact, as if he had been hit.

"Daughter," repeated Lewis Smith.

"But there are two, aren't there?" He still spoke quickly. "I saw a picture of them down at Waveney."

"Yes—twins. But the money went to Lady Marr."

"All of it?"

"Yes, all of it."

John stared at the carpet, but he didn't see the pattern; he saw a girl looking into a mirror at a reflection which was yet not a reflection—fair, short hair cut close to the neck; and long dark plaits hanging down until they were lost in the shadow. Jenifer Anne and Anne Belinda—which of them was Lady Marr? He looked up with a frown and said the words aloud:

"Jenifer Anne and Anne Belinda—which of them's Lady Marr?"

"Oh, Jenifer. They call her Jenny."

"And which is she? One of 'em had fair hair, cut short the way everyone's wearing it now; and the other one had long dark plaits." His voice changed ever so little. With all his conviction that it was the fair-haired girl that was Lady Marr, he waited impatiently for Lewis to say so.

"I don't know that I noticed. We drew up the marriage settlement; but my uncle attended to it mostly. I only saw the sisters together once, and they were awfully alike—what you'd expect of twins. Lady Marr was in here about a month ago, and I saw her then, because my uncle was out."

"Well?" The impatience was in John's voice now.

Lewis laughed. "You can't see anyone's hair nowadays. She'd on one of those sort of extinguishers women wear, just let you tell how much lipstick they use. But now I come to think of it, I *could* see one of her eyes; and it was brown, if that's any help."

John felt a quick relief. Impatience and relief were both quite out of proportion to the incident.

"Oh, then she's the fair one. The other one had blue eyes."

They came up before him vividly—dark, solemn eyes like dark blue water. The eyes, and the long plaits, and the oval face were Anne Belinda's. From that instant she ceased to be the funny kid of nine years ago, the dim reflection in her sister's mirror; she became an astonishingly realizable creature; she became Anne Belinda.

"Where is she?" he said, and was, not unnaturally, misunderstood.

"Lady Marr? Oh, they've a place down in Sussex—Waterdene."

"No, the other one—Anne Belinda."

Chapter Three

THERE WAS JUST the very slightest pause before Lewis Smith said, "I don't know." As soon as he had spoken, he pulled his chair up to the table and reached for pencil and paper.

"By the way, I've made an awful break. You've just reminded me. That picture you saw at Waveney—Lady Marr wanted it removed before you came over; and it went right out of my head. I've been pretty busy with all my uncle's work to see to."

"Why didn't she take it away before if she wanted it? It's a year since Sir Anthony died."

"She doesn't want it. As a matter of fact, she wanted us to have it destroyed."

John made a sharp sound of protest. Lewis swung round in his chair.

"Yes, I know. She changed her mind when I told her that it was probably worth at least five thousand pounds. There's been a boom in Amorys, and this is considered one of his best."

"She wanted it destroyed? Why? Why on earth?"

Lewis Smith began to be conscious of indiscretion. He drew in the corners of his mouth and hesitated before he answered.

"I don't know. Don't ask me."

John's glance took in the hesitation; his mind refused the spoken words.

"Destroyed? That picture! She must have had a reason."

"She probably thinks it doesn't do her justice," said Mr. Smith suavely.

"Rot! Why did she want it destroyed?"

Lewis turned to his scribbling-block without answering. John was leaning forward, elbow on knee, chin in hand, eyes very intent. Where was Anne Belinda? Why had Sir Anthony left all his money to Jenny Marr? Why had Lulu dried up like that all of a sudden? And—back again to the first question—where was Anne? Where was Anne Belinda?

"Look here, Lulu," he said, "what's the good of being so poisonously discreet all at once? You know something; and I want to know *what* you know. It's all in the family, anyway. I want to know why Sir Anthony left all his money to one of his daughters—and the one who didn't need it. Nicholas Marr's rolling, isn't he? I was at school with a cousin of his, and he used to talk about Nicholas and say he'd got money to burn—that's how I know."

"He made a very generous settlement on Lady Marr. Sir Anthony was still alive then, of course."

John's expression hardened a little. Lewis wasn't writing, though he was pretending to write. The writing-pad showed a meaningless scribble.

"Yes, I'm not feeling anxious about my cousin Jenny," he said drily; "I'm thinking about my cousin Anne. Why did her father cut her out of his will? Where is she? What is she doing? And what is she living on? More particularly, what is she living on? I've had a shot myself at living on nothing a year. There aren't any points about it at all. Where is my cousin Anne?"

"I don't know."

"Look here, Lulu, I mean business. What *do* you know?"

Lewis Smith pushed his pad away.

"I really don't know anything."

"Then tell me what you do know. I won't give you away."

"I tell you I don't know anything. I can give you a few disconnected facts, most of which are public property."

"That's better."

"They don't amount to much. We drew up Lady Marr's settlement, as I told you. She came in once to sign some papers, and brought her sister with her. Sir Anthony wasn't able to come to town, so my uncle went down to see him once or twice."

"Yes?"

"There's really nothing I can tell you."

"Go on! Get it off your chest!"

"Lady Marr was married in April—at least I think it was April—last April year. She was married in London, from an hotel. Her sister wasn't at the wedding."

John's "Why?" was a sharp exclamation. When he got no answer, he repeated the word in a more ordinary voice.

"Why wasn't she?"

Lewis Smith shrugged his shoulders.

"Illness, I think. I know next time I saw Lady Marr she went out of her way to tell me that her sister had gone abroad for her health."

There was a pause. Then John said:

"What about the will? Where does that come in? When did Sir Anthony make the will that left everything to one daughter?"

"He made it within a month of Lady Marr's marriage. My uncle went down to see him. I don't mind telling you that he came back a good deal distressed. He hoped, I know, that the dispositions were not final—he said as much to me. Of course, this is all very confidential."

"Of course."

"He told me he hoped Sir Anthony would change his mind. But there was no time for that; Sir Anthony died just a week after he signed the new will."

John got up and walked to the window. He stood there looking down into the wet street. An interminable procession of shiny, dripping umbrellas passed, crossed, and jostled each other.

"Why did Sir Anthony change his will?" said John, watching the umbrellas.

"I don't know, Maurice—really I don't know."

"Does Mr. Carruthers know?"

"I don't think so. He was distressed; and I remember his saying that he couldn't understand it, and that Sir Anthony was not in a frame of mind to listen to reason."

John turned round. He could watch the street and throw a glance at Lewis too if he leaned like this against the window jamb.

"Did Sir Anthony send for him suddenly?"

"Yes, very suddenly—he telephoned."

"And Mr. Carruthers found him excited?"

"I suppose so. He said he wouldn't listen to reason."

John turned a sharp look on him.

"What d'you make of it? *Honest*, Lulu."

Lewis Smith looked up quite coolly.

"Do you really want me to say what I think?"

"Yes, I do."

"I don't want to hurt your family feelings."

"Fire away."

"Well, it seems to me that it's one of two things—the girl may be off her head; or else she came a cropper of some sort and Sir Anthony found it out. In either case, it would probably be as well to let sleeping dogs lie."

Just for a moment an extraordinary, scorching anger flared in John. It surprised him very much, and it was gone as suddenly as it had come. He said:

"That's all very well. You mean it's no business of mine. I suppose it isn't, personally. But I can't help feeling responsible all the same. I mean I've stepped into her brother's place, and in that way I think it is my business. Hang it all, Lulu, the girl can't live on nothing."

Lewis Smith lifted his eyebrows.

"Well, there's Lady Marr."

John looked out of the window. He counted eight black umbrellas and a green one. Then he said:

"What's Lady Marr like?"

"Very pretty—knows it too."

John jerked impatiently.

"I don't mean that. What's she like? You know how some people are—if anyone comes a cropper, they just wipe 'em off the map. Is she that sort?"

"My dear chap, I don't know her; I've only seen her. She's pretty, she's smart, she's prosperous. She has an adoring husband and a fat, thumping baby—a boy. So she's inordinately proud of herself. She told me so."

"'M," said John. "Look here, I want to meet her."

"She wants to meet you. She told me that too. I can write and say you've been in, and that there are one or two family matters you'd like to discuss with her."

John nodded.

"I don't know any of them. It's a bad handicap. I don't know who their friends are, or who'd be likely to know anything. That's where I want help." He spoke in a reflective undertone. "Yes, that's where I want help. Would Mr. Carruthers know?"

"He might. I'll ask him. He's by way of taking a holiday, but he hasn't gone away. I shall be seeing him to-morrow. I'll ask him about the whole thing. But I expect he'll say that you'd do better to leave it alone."

"I'll leave it alone when I've found Anne Waveney. She mayn't be in need of finding, in which case everyone curses me for butting in. Little things like that don't worry me—I rather like scrapping. You go ahead and get me some introductions to people who may know where she is. If they're friends of the family, it's quite natural that I should want to know them. I'll do the rest." He drummed on the window-pane and hummed:

"Cassidy was a gentleman,
Cassidy said to me,
'Don't you go in with Jimmy McBride,
Nor yet with Tim Magee.
You come in on a ground-floor, rock-bottomed, stone-cold cert
     with me.'"

Chapter Four

THE VICARAGE LAY on the village side of Waveney. John drove up a sweep that had ceased to be gravelled; there was moss on it, and there were weeds. The enormous garden looked frightfully neglected; but the apple-blossom was coming out, and there were daffodils under the trees.

He rang the bell, and was aware of a scurry in the hall, fierce whispering, and rapidly retreating footsteps. Presently he rang again. This time nothing happened at all. He watched the sunshine on the daffodils with resignation, and presently pulled the bell for the third time. As its loud ringing died away, there was a small patter of feet. The opening door disclosed a little angelic person with flaxen hair, forget-me-not eyes, and smudged pink face. It looked at John, and nothing happened. John was moved to speech.

"Hullo! Is Mrs. Thompson—is your mother at home?"

The little girl nodded. Her eyes never left John's face.

"Can I see her?"

"I—don't—know." The words dropped slowly; the blue gaze persisted.

"I'd like to if I can. Will you go and ask her if she'll see me?"

He produced a card, pressed it into the plump, grubby hand, and waited. After a moment a door opened and shut, and a little lady came flying along the passage.

"Oh, Sir John, I'm so sorry—you've had to wait—I was in the garden. *Do* come in. I'm so very sorry."

She ran in front of him into a large bleak room, where each piece of furniture seemed to be a very long way from the next.

"So kind of you!" she fluttered. "So dreadful to keep you waiting—your first visit! And now, where will you sit?"

John took the nearest chair—none of the chairs were very near—and found himself at some distance from his hostess. She was a small person with a high, hard colour and a good many hairpins stuck at odd angles into the heavy knot of fair hair which rather overweighted her little head. Once upon a time she must have been exceedingly pretty. Her eyes were still very brightly blue, but the face from which they looked was terribly lined.

John had told himself all the way down that it was no more than his duty to call on the Thompsons. It had seemed a pretty good idea. He would call on them, do his duty, and gather information, "all under one" as his old nurse used to say. Now, struggling through the polite preliminaries, he began to wonder why he had come. Mrs. Thompson fluttered. How on earth did one talk to a woman who fluttered? And he was probably disturbing her just when she most particularly didn't want to be disturbed; she had the air of a person who is always doing something very important at the highest possible rate of speed, and she would go on talking about his having been kept waiting. He made a determined effort, and stemmed the flow of apology.

"It doesn't matter in the least. It's very kind of you to see me. I'm such an absolute stranger, and I thought—"

The door was banged open abruptly. John had an impression of flaming red hair, a turned-up nose, freckles, and enormously large hands. Then there was an exclamation of "Bother!" and the door was shut again with a bang.

"Oh, Cyril!" protested Mrs. Thompson.

John repeated his last words firmly:

"I'm such an absolute stranger, and I shall be most grateful to anyone who will make me feel a little less strange—tell me something about the place and the people, you know."

"Oh, *yes*," said Mrs. Thompson.

The door opened again. A long, ramshackle girl came half-way in and stood twisting the handle. She wore a desperate frown. The outgrown sleeves of a faded grey jumper showed some six inches of a bony wrist and arm.

"What is it, Delia?"

Delia went on twisting the handle. She had a high, bony nose, red and wind-bitten. She spoke through it now.

"The Clothing Club accounts—Mrs. Anderson's sent Annie, and she says that if she can't have them at once, she can't possibly do them before Saturday." She finished with a sniff.

"Oh, my dear child, how inconvenient and—This is my eldest girl, Delia, Sir John. Delia, pet, let go of the handle and come and say 'How d'you do?' And—dear me, let me see—yes, the accounts are in the left-hand corner of the third long drawer of my bureau—or if it isn't the third drawer, it's the second—and it's the blue book with the torn label and 'Library Account' crossed out."

Delia drifted from the room. Mrs. Thompson turned again to her guest.

"Ah, *yes*," she said—"yes, of course—it must all feel very strange to you. But anything I can do—It's very nice indeed to have you taking so much interest, and I hope we shall all get to know you quite soon. Now, there's Mrs. Anderson—you heard Delia mention her—one of our most helpful workers, a war widow with one little girl—"

"I'm afraid," said John, "that I was beginning by being interested in my own family, though, of course, I hope I shall soon get to know all the other people round here. You knew my cousins?"

There was a rattling, scrambling sound outside the window; the head and shoulders of a boy of nine appeared. John identified the red hair and the freckles which he had seen for a moment through the half-opened door.

Mrs. Thompson whisked round in her chair and said "Oh, Cyril!" in exactly the same tone as before.

Cyril burst into speech:

"Annie says that Jim's come to-day instead of to-morrow. And her mother says can Tin and I come to tea?"

"Not in those clothes—My second boy, Cyril, Sir John. And tell Augustine to take the new nail-brush and scrub his hands, and then come and show them to me—and you too."

There was a smothered "Bother!" a renewed scramble, and, as Cyril disappeared, Mrs. Thompson said brightly:

"Ah, yes, your cousins—such dear sweet girls! You know them?"

"I've seen Anne—" He got as far as that and stuck; he had the most ridiculous sense that he was confiding in Mrs. Thompson. Resisting it, he said, quite loudly and firmly: "I don't know either of them, but I've seen Anne Belinda."

"Dear, sweet girl," said Mrs. Thompson a little vaguely. "Dear, sweet girls, both of them. But perhaps we knew Anne best. She was here more—Jenny used to visit her godmother, Mrs. Courtney. And she was so very kind to Delia, lending her books—though I don't know that it's really wise to encourage such a passionate love of reading. What do you think?"

"Where does Mrs. Courtney live?" asked John.

"She has a flat in town—in Queen's Gate, I think. She's a cousin of the late Lady Waveney. She was a Miss Courtney, as, of course, you know. And they were at school together. But somehow Jenny's always been her favourite. To be sure, she's her god-daughter, but then—"

John sat forward in his chair, waiting for a break in the rapid, tangled sentences. He thrust in now with a blunt question:

Where is Anne Waveney? Do you know?"

As he spoke, the door opened about a foot; the small blue-eyed person who had let him in sidled through the opening, advanced shyly a few steps, and then made a rush at her mother. She wore a blue cotton frock, and trailed a mutilated doll by its one remaining leg.

"My youngest little girl, Daphne," said Mrs. Thompson. "Daffy, darling, say 'How d'you do?' nicely."

Daphne took no notice. She began to speak very slowly and deliberately.

"Christabel says if I come in the kitchen, she'll go home. She says she can't do with a clutter of children."

"Oh, Daffy!"

"She says—"

"Hush, darling! Go and play in the garden."

"She says—"

"Darling, go and play!"

Daphne turned, swinging her doll. She made her way towards the door, walking with slow deliberation and talking all the time deliberately and slowly:

"She says she gets enough of it at home—and there are only seven of them, and nine of us." She shut the door carefully on the last word.

John tried to remember how many of the nine he had seen, and was aware of Mrs. Thompson's restored attention.

"You were saying, Sir John?"

"I asked you if you knew Anne's address."

He watched her sharply, and he thought that her high, bright colour deepened.

"Her address? Well, I'm afraid—no, I don't really think—"

The door again. This time it opened with a jerk and displayed another biggish girl, an inch or two less in height than Delia. She wore a brown knitted dress, which had been oddly darned with blue. It bulged in such unexpected places as to suggest that it had been worn by some very stout person before it had descended to this angular young creature.

"Oh, Cilly, what is it? My second daughter, Celia, Sir John. Darling, what do you want?"

"Father says—"

"Darling, do say 'How d'you do?'"

"Father says, did you write for the sermon paper? Because if you didn't, he's just finished the last sheet." She cocked an impudent hazel eye at John. "Cheers if you didn't! We shall get out ten minutes earlier."

"*Cilly!*"

"Well, *did* you write?"

"Oh, Celia, darling, I'm so dreadfully afraid I didn't. It was the day the boiler burst—and Christabel had just come—and she said she wasn't going to stop—and Justin fell into the water-butt. I'm so dreadfully afraid I forgot all about it."

"Cheers!" said Celia.

The door closed abruptly behind her.

"Dreadfully careless of me!" murmured Mrs. Thompson, driving a hairpin distractedly into her hair. "Dreadfully careless! Yes, Sir John?"

Her resumption of the social manner was pathetic. John felt sorry for her, and very much in the way. But he wanted Anne Belinda's address, and he meant to get it. He got up.

"You're busy," he said. "If you'll give me my cousin's address, I won't keep you a moment—"

"But I don't think—I really don't know—I mean—surely, Sir John—"

"Haven't you got it?" said John.

"Lady Marr—" began Mrs. Thompson.

"Is she with Lady Marr?"

"I don't think—I really don't know."

"Mrs. Thompson, do you know where she is?"

"Lady Marr would surely—"

"I want to see her very particularly. *Do* you know where she is?"

"No," said Mrs. Thompson. "I don't."

Now that she was driven to a plain answer, there was a curious something in her voice. John wasn't sure what it was; it might have been resentment; it might have been anxiety. He characterized it in his own mind as "rum."

"Is she in England?"

"I don't know. I can't tell you anything, Sir John—I don't know."

"She doesn't write?"

Mrs. Thompson shook her head. There was no doubt that she was in some agitation.

"Since when?"

"Oh, for more than a year. I haven't seen her since the wedding, and I really don't know where she is."

"She wasn't at the wedding," said John quickly.

Mrs. Thompson looked distinctly frightened. She pressed her lips together and shook her head.

"Or at her father's funeral?"

She shook her head again. Someone came at a stumbling run along the passage and banged violently into the door. It burst open, and there rushed in a small, square, tear-stained boy whose breath came in gusty sobs.

"He's bashing C'ractacus! He's bashing him!"

"Oh, Justin!" said Mrs. Thompson in the same helpless, protesting voice with which she had said "Oh, Cyril!"

Justin stamped.

"He's bashing him now!" He flung himself at John and tugged him by the sleeve.

"*Come* at once! He's bashing him!"

"Oh, Justin!" said Mrs. Thompson again.

John found himself half-way across the floor with that hot, tugging hand at his wrist. Then he found himself running.

"Who's Caractacus?" he asked.

"He's my toad," panted Justin; a sob caught his breath. "Tin's bashing him!"

"All right, old man, we'll bash Tin," said John cheerfully.

They emerged from a side-door upon a rough lawn surrounded by a bank. The red-haired Cyril and another boy were engaged in throwing stones at the bank. Justin let go of John's wrist and hurled himself upon the stooping Cyril, who promptly lost his balance and fell sprawling and spluttering. Augustine, stone in hand, wheeled about, disclosing a rough, ugly face, and hands that had certainly not made the acquaintance of the new nail-brush.

"Where's C'ractacus?" panted Justin.

"Bashed!" snorted the indignant Cyril. He heaved himself up, and felt a heavy hand upon his shoulder.

"Hullo!" said John. "What are you up to?"

"We're bashing his old toad."

"Ever been bashed yourself?"

Cyril wriggled. Augustine looked sulky.

"He's gone into a hole—he isn't hurt. We were only getting a rise out of the kid. He blubs for nothing."

Delia drifted up to the group.

"I thought you two were going out to tea. Why on earth can't you leave Justin alone?"

"It's only that beastly toad of his."

Delia frowned.

"I don't care what it is. You're to leave him alone. And you're to leave his creatures alone. And if you want to go out to tea, it's time you went." She spoke in very lofty and elder-sisterly tones.

Cyril twisted his shoulder out of John's hand and ran away, making faces and calling back over his shoulder, "Dilly-dally, shilly-shally, goody-goody Delia!" To which Augustine added gruffly, "Go and boil your head and be a parson!"

John watched them disappear into the house. It would have given him a good deal of pleasure to knock their heads together.

When they were out of sight, he turned round. The small, square Justin was squatting down by the bank, obviously engaged in an attempt to coax the offended Caractacus from his dug-out. Delia stood with her long neck craned forward over a book. He remembered that Anne Belinda had lent her books; it occurred to him that a conversation with Delia might be profitable. He addressed her, and she came out of her book with a frown.

"I must say good-bye to your mother. I'm afraid I came when she was busy."

"She's always busy." Delia's tone was calmly indifferent.

"Well, I'll just say good-bye to her. And then I thought perhaps you'd show me the short cut to the Hall. There is one, isn't there?"

"But you've got your car."

"Er—yes. But perhaps you'd show me the short cut just the same. I could come back for the car."

Chapter Five

JOHN MADE his farewells, and walked down the untidy garden with a sufficiently reluctant Delia. She had tucked her book under her arm, and it was obvious that her one desire was to get away from him and read it. John, on his part, had no intention of letting her go. He plunged straight into what he had to say:

"I want to talk about my cousin Anne. You knew her, didn't you?"

Delia looked up, startled. She had dark lashes and beautiful grey eyes. She said "Oh," and then stopped. The boredom which had enveloped her like a fog was gone. She said "Oh," and looked at him with all her eyes.

John congratulated himself.

"Well?" he said. "Tell me about her. I can't get anyone to talk about her—and I want to talk about her pretty badly."

"Yes," said Delia with her eyes still on his face.

"Nobody will tell me anything about her. I saw her once, and I want to see her again. I want to know where she is."

A sort of mist came over Delia's eyes. She said with a gasp:

"I don't know—they won't tell me."

"Have you asked?" said John quickly.

"It's no use. You've asked yourself, haven't you? Was it any use asking?"

"Not much."

They had come to the bottom of the garden. A stone wall divided it from the churchyard; a yard or two to their right was a gate. John leaned against the wall.

"Look here," he said, "I've got to find her. If you'll tell me everything you know, there might be something that would help. For instance, when did you see her last?"

She stood in front of him hugging her book.

"It was the fifteenth of April—a year ago. She was going to meet Jenny in London, and she came to say good-bye. And we walked down this path together, and I said good-bye to her here." She jerked her head back and stared over his shoulder. "I don't like Jenny." Then she laughed, not at all mirthfully. "I expect I had better call her Lady Marr now—she's that sort."

John received an impression which he did not quite understand. He put it away in the back of his mind, to be analyzed later on.

"You said good-bye to Anne here on the fifteenth of April, a year ago. Did you think you were saying good-bye for a long time?"

Delia pushed back the hair that would straggle into her eyes.

"No, I didn't. I thought she was coming back in two days. She meant to come; but she didn't come. Jenny came back; but Anne never came at all. And they said she was ill, and that was why she couldn't go to the wedding. But I don't believe it."

"Why don't you believe it?"

Delia laughed again.

"If she was ill, why didn't Jenny go to her? I don't like Jenny, but I shouldn't think anyone would leave their own twin all alone in London if they were ill. Or if Jenny didn't go, why didn't Mrs. Jones go? She was their nurse, and she stayed on and did maid to them both. And she was devoted to Anne. She wouldn't *ever* have left Anne to be ill all alone. I don't believe for a single moment that Anne was ever ill at all."

This was better than Mrs. Thompson's hesitancies.

"If she wasn't ill, where was she?"

The eager look passed from Delia's face. She walked to the gate, opened it, and passed into the churchyard. Then she looked over her shoulder, hesitated, and came back to lean upon the gate.

"Why do you want to know about Anne?" she said slowly.

John found it hard to answer. The strength of his own determination was something which he did not attempt to account for; he only knew that it was there. After a silence that seemed to last a long time he said:

"I don't know—I've got to find her."

Delia looked at him across the gate.

"If I tell you something—" she began. Then the dark colour came into her face, and she stopped and shook her head. "I'd better not."

"Nonsense!"

"I'd better not. I—sometimes I think something dreadful must have happened."

"Look here," said John, "you tell me just what you know. I've got to find her."

"Oh!" said Delia. It was a sharply in-drawn breath that was very nearly a sob. Her face twitched. "You *can* go and look for her—I can't. You've all the luck, and I think I hate you for it!" She spoke with an extraordinary restrained passion.

"What does it matter who finds her?" said John reasonably. "If you're fond of her—" He broke off. "Don't you see, my dear girl, you and I don't matter a brass farthing? We don't matter, and our feelings don't matter. What matters is—Anne Belinda." His voice changed ever so little on the name. "Now, don't you think you'd better tell me what you know?"

Delia rubbed fiercely at the bony ridge of her nose. She believed firmly in this exercise as a specific against inconvenient tears; but in spite of it her eyes brimmed over.

"I don't know anything. But I'll tell you all the same. I came down to get a book. I thought everyone had gone to bed; but when I got to the study, there was a light under the door, so I listened, just to see if there was anyone there. I've got frightfully quick hearing, and I thought if Father was sitting up I should hear him move, or breathe, or fidget or something. You see, there was a chance that he'd just gone to bed and left the light on—he does sometimes. That's why I listened to start with. But just when I thought there wasn't anyone there, I heard Mother say, 'Poor Anne!' and then I simply had to listen. I don't care how dreadful it was—I simply had to. You know what it is when you care for someone so that it hurts all the time." Her voice went lower and lower. When she said, "it hurts all the time," it was just a tragic whisper and her great eyes shone.

John forgot the queer angles and the haphazard features dominated by the high, red, bony nose. He felt an extraordinary response to this wave of tragic emotion.

She went on speaking just above her breath:

"I listened. Mother said, 'It frightens me.' She said, 'I daren't think what may have become of her.' Then she said, 'Oh, Cyril!'— that's my father—and she began to cry."

"What did your father say?"

"He didn't say anything for a bit, except 'Now, Mary!' and things like that; but when she'd stopped crying, he said, 'Why don't you ask Jenny point-blank?' And Mother said, 'Oh, I couldn't!' And when he said, 'Why on earth not?' she said, 'What's the use? She'd only look sweet and tell me all over again that Anne was abroad and enjoying herself so much. And I couldn't bear it. No, Cyril, I really couldn't.'"

"And then?" said John.

"Then Father said, 'We've nothing to go on—nothing at all.' And Mother began to cry dreadfully, and she said—" Delia stopped and put her hand to her mouth.

"Go on."

"I can't."

"Why can't you?"

She stared at him almost accusingly. There was black misery in her eyes.

"I can't."

John came up close and put his hand on her arm. "Delia, you've got to tell me. I've got to know—I've got to find her."

"She said—she was crying all the time—she said, 'Oh, Cyril, why did Sir Anthony tell you never to say her name again?'" Delia choked, pulled her arm away, and spoke harshly: "That's what she said. What did she mean by it? Why wouldn't Sir Anthony let Father speak about Anne?"

"What did your father say?"

"He said, 'My dear, I don't know.' That's what they all say, till I'm sick of hearing it. Somebody ought to know."

John nodded.

"I'm going to. Did they say any more?"

"No. Mother cried a lot."

There was a pause. The spring sunshine made everything about them look very bright and clear; the church tower stood up black against a turquoise sky. John tried to sort out the very little he had learned from the vague, misty confusion of what he could only guess at.

"Delia," he said, "you say Jenny and Anne went to London, and Jenny came back alone. Something must have been said about Anne not coming back."

"They said she'd missed her train. I saw Jenny, because I'd gone up to the Hall to change a book—Anne used to lend me books. And when I asked where Anne was, Jenny said, 'Oh, she missed the train. She'll be down to-morrow.' But she wasn't—she never came at all."

"What did they say then?"

"They said she was ill—they went on saying she was ill. And then they said she'd gone abroad to get strong. But I don't believe a word of it."

"She might have been ill." John looked down meditatively at the topmost bar of the gate. A rough splinter stood up on it. He pulled it off carefully, and then broke it into little bits and dropped them one by one upon a clump of primroses at his feet.

"She wasn't. She wasn't ill—I'm sure she wasn't—I know when Jenny's telling lies." She gave her jerky laugh. "Jenny doesn't take me in a bit. When her voice goes sweet and she looks down under her eyelashes, I know she's telling lies every time." She paused. "I'll tell you something though—Sir Anthony really did think she was ill—*at first*." She laid a heavy emphasis on the words.

"How do you know that?"

"I met him just before the wedding, and he talked about it a lot; and he kept on saying how upset Jenny was about Anne not being bridesmaid, and what an awkward time it was for Anne to be ill, but he hoped she'd be better soon, and then I must come and see her. I asked him if he'd seen her, and how she was. And he said, No—he couldn't get about much—it was all he could do to manage the wedding—and Anne wasn't allowed to see anyone; but Jenny or Mrs. Jones rang up every day and got the news, and he hoped she'd be better soon."

John was recalling what Lewis Smith had said—Sir Anthony had altered his will within a month of the wedding; just before the wedding he was talking kindly and naturally of Anne; and then within a week or two her name was not to be mentioned, and he had altered his will. He frowned at the primroses and let fall the last tiny splinter of wood.

Delia had come closer.

"He said they rang up every day. He wasn't telling lies, poor old man; he really thought they did. But they didn't."

"How do you know?" said John sharply.

"You won't tell anyone? I should hate to get Mrs. Mellow into trouble. She's at the post-office. And she's a friend of mine, and I was having tea with her, and I said I expected that all those calls to London must give her a lot extra to do. And she said, 'What calls?' So I said, 'Isn't Miss Jenifer having a lot of London calls just now?' And she just laughed and said, 'Well, there was one about her wedding dress Tuesday, and one about a lot of business Thursday. But that's not going to worry me, my dear!' So I said, 'Doesn't she ring up a lot about Miss Anne?' And Mrs. Mellow said, 'No, my dear, she don't— and that's a fact. She don't ring up at all—not anything to do with Miss Anne, she don't. So I take it there isn't much amiss.'" Delia looked at him anxiously. "Look here, you'll be sure not to repeat that, because she's not supposed to talk about anything like that, and she might get into trouble."

John nodded impatiently.

"She told me one thing more," said Delia. "She told me there'd been a letter from Anne that morning—a proper letter, addressed in ink."

"How did she know?"

"Why, of course she knows Anne's writing. She's been postmistress for twenty years; she knows everybody's writing. She said there was a letter from Anne. And she said it wasn't the first. But she said they weren't any of them addressed to Jenny."

"Who were they addressed to?"

"They were all addressed to Mrs. Jones," said Delia.

Chapter Six

JOHN CAME AWAY from Waveney with Mrs. Jones' address in his pocket. He wasn't quite sure what to do about Mrs. Jones. It was obvious that she knew something—probable, in fact, that she could tell him everything that he wanted to know. But the more he thought about it, the less likely did it seem that he, a total stranger, would be able to induce her to say a single word. The thing wanted thinking over, and he made up his mind to sleep on it.

When he got to his hotel, he was informed that he had been twice called on the telephone. The second time a message had been left—Would he call up Horsham 000 as soon as he came in?

He went straight to the telephone box and gave the number. Whilst he waited to get through, he wondered idly who had been calling him. He had never been to Horsham in his life, and could think of nobody there with whom he had the slightest acquaintance. When the bell rang, it was a man's voice that said "Hullo!"

John said, "I was asked to ring up this number. My name's Waveney." And when the voice answered him it was all at once familiar.

"Oh, Maurice—Lulu Smith speaking. I'm down here to see my uncle, and he's very anxious to speak to you. Just hold on a minute."

John held on. After a short interval someone else spoke:

"Are you there, Sir John? Mr. Carruthers speaking. I am sorry to have troubled you, but I am anxious to have a few words with you."

"It's no trouble."

"Thank you. The fact is—" He broke off. "My nephew Lewis tells me that you had a conversation with him this morning. By the way, I am much interested to learn that you are old friends."

"Yes, I was most awfully pleased to see him again."

John began to feel a sense of anticipation; the conversation was the conversation he had had about Anne Belinda.

"Well, Sir John, Lewis' account of that conversation has given me a good deal of concern. You were, I gather, anxious to know the whereabouts of a certain person, and—er—well, I want to ask you to let the matter alone."

John was silent for a moment. A quick, hot anger prompted him to speech, and he would not speak until he had got the better of it.

"Can you tell me why?"

"Well—not in detail. I can merely assure you that your inquiries are unnecessary."

"When you say unnecessary, Mr. Carruthers, what exactly do you mean? I am making inquiries because I feel uneasy. The person we are speaking of was, to the best of my belief, left entirely unprovided for. When you say that my inquiries are unnecessary, do you mean that there is any provision which I don't know about?"

"No, not exactly."

"Then, will you tell me what you do mean?"

He tried, rather unsuccessfully, to keep an aggressive note out of his voice. He thought he detected a shade of reproof in the lawyer's reply:

"It's a little difficult to explain a very delicate matter in a conversation of this kind. May I, however, remind you that the lady has nearer relations than yourself?"

"Possibly," said John. "The question is, are they doing anything? Are they, for instance, making her an allowance? Can you assure me, of your own knowledge, that she is receiving an allowance from them?"

"Sir John, this is very difficult."

John took a pull on himself. He was putting the old man's back up, and that was a fool's trick. He spoke with a complete change of tone.

"I don't want to seem intrusive, or anything of that sort. I thought, if there was no provision, that a charge might be made on the estate."

"I see. It's very generous of you. I don't know quite what to say. I could make the offer on your behalf; but I don't think it is at all likely that it would be accepted. Perhaps you will come and see me when I get back."

John set his jaw. A month's delay! He said, in a voice full of protest:

"Why can't I meet my cousin? Where is she?"

He heard Mr. Carruthers cough.

"I'm afraid"—more coughing—"I'm afraid that's impossible. But there is another lady who is most anxious to make your acquaintance, Lewis tells me—Mrs. Courtney. She has a flat in Queen's Gate—I'm afraid I forget the number. Lewis met her this afternoon, and she expressed a very strong desire to see you—told him, in fact, that he was to send you to call on her. She's rather an imperious lady, but extremely charming, and a connection of the family."

"Thanks, I'll go and see her—Yes, another three minutes, please—Mr. Carruthers, is my cousin ill?"

"Not that I know of."

"Is she abroad?"

"I really can't say."

"Do you know where she is?"

There was rather a long pause. Then Mr. Carruthers said slowly: "Yes—I know."

"You *do* know?"

"Yes." And with that the line went dead.

John stood for a moment with the receiver in his hand. Then he hung it up and left the box.

At the other end of the line Mr. Carruthers had already rung off. He turned in his chair and showed a disturbed face to his nephew.

"Rather a difficult young man, Sir John Waveney," he said.

Lewis looked up from *The Times*.

"What's he being difficult about?"

"He wants Anne Waveney's address."

"Yes, I told you he wanted it. Is there any real reason why he shouldn't have it?"

"Yes, Lewis, there is."

Lewis Smith whistled.

"Well, I should say he was about the most obstinate devil I've ever come across. So the odds are he'll go on until he gets it."

Mr. Carruthers gave a short, annoyed cough.

"I've advised him very strongly to let the whole matter drop. You heard me. He seems to have some idea of offering her an allowance from the estate, and, of course, I shall be bound to pass the offer on. That's all very well, but as far as any personal advances go, I've the strongest possible reasons for discouraging them. And I rely on you, Lewis, to do the same."

"You can't tell me why?"

"No, I'm afraid I can't. You'll just have to take my word for it that young Waveney had better give up any idea of meeting his cousin."

"If he's got the idea—and he seems to me to have got it pretty strongly—he won't give it up."

"Surely the young man can take a hint!" Mr. Carruthers' tone was indignant.

Lewis said, "'M—I shouldn't say he could—not unless he's changed a good deal. He's one of those strong, persevering fellows that take a notion into their heads and stick to it through thick and thin. I ought to be the last person to complain of it, because I shouldn't be here now if he wasn't that sort. No one else would have thought it was possible to get me in that time I was wounded at Loos. As a matter of fact, it wasn't possible; but he did it somehow. He's an obstinate fellow, as I told you."

Chapter Seven

JOHN HAD a dinner engagement that evening. His host was the publisher who was producing Peterson's book in England, and the other guests were all men. He had not met any of them before. The talk was of Peterson, of books, and of the wild places of the earth.

After dinner a little man with a beard and a bald head moved up beside John.

"My name," he said, "is Fossick-Yates—Frederick Fossick-Yates. Does that recall anything to you?"

John wasn't sure. He temporized. There was something distantly familiar about the name, but for the life of him he couldn't pick up the connection.

The little man put his head on one side and regarded him with expectancy; behind his glasses his round, bright, prominent eyes were a good deal like the eyes of a bird that is watching a worm. Before John's hesitation became an embarrassment Mr. Fossick-Yates put an end to it.

"I wrote to Peterson—yes, several letters. It was about three years ago."

John began to remember a very persistent correspondent who had written a number of letters full of meticulous details about variations from type in European snakes.

"Yes, I remember," he said.

"Ah! Now, may I ask whether Peterson found my contributions useful?"

"He certainly used some of them—in the sixth chapter, I think. Oh yes, and there was a footnote later on."

Mr. Fossick-Yates fairly beamed. He shot a cuff and scribbled upon it with a small, neat gold pencil.

"Ah! The sixth chapter? *And* a footnote? I feel very much gratified, Sir John. I suppose you can't remember which of my data—"

"As it happens, I believe I can. The footnote refers to the case, which I think you cited, where the stripe down the viper's back was almost white instead of black."

Mr. Fossick-Yates snatched off his glasses and began to polish them furiously with his table napkin.

"Splendid!" he said. "Most gratifying—er—most gratifying! I assure you I feel quite overwhelmed. A footnote citing my viper. Can you remember in which chapter it occurs?"

"Fifteen," said John—"the one on albinism."

Mr. Fossick-Yates crammed his glasses back upon his nose. The angle they assumed gave his appearance an incongruous touch of abandon. He scribbled once more, and jerked his chair a little nearer.

"Sir John, I must persuade you! I have that very specimen at my house, not two miles away. You will come and see it! Of course, I have other specimens too—albinism has always enthralled me—er—yes, enthralled me. You will give me the pleasure of dining with me. My wife will be charmed to make your acquaintance. You may have heard of her. She was a prominent suffragist—she writes on social subjects. She is *the* Mrs. Fossick-Yates."

As John walked home, he wondered why on earth he had allowed himself to become entangled with the Fossick-Yates. They would give him an appallingly bad dinner, and he would have to look at all Fossick-Yates' specimens and listen through hours of protracted boredom to Mrs. Fossick-Yates on social subjects. He groaned aloud at the prospect, and cursed his folly. If Frederick Fossick-Yates had been a shade less innocently delighted over his mention in chapter six and the footnote about his viper in chapter fifteen, he would have gone on saying no or having previous engagements till all was blue. As it was, the beaming eyes behind the crooked glasses had betrayed him into this ghastly engagement.

He stopped thinking about Mr. Fossick-Yates, and let his thoughts go back to Anne Belinda. He began very methodically to sort out and file away all the different scraps of information which he had collected. He had not the very slightest intention of taking Mr. Carruthers' advice and letting the matter drop. That he had been advised to let it drop was, in fact, one of his most urgent reasons for not dropping it; at every hint of opposition his determination hardened.

It was years since anything except acute physical discomfort had kept John awake at night. As a rule, when his head touched the pillow, sleep came and remained, deep, peaceful, and dreamless until forcibly disturbed next morning. To-night he lay awake for a long time, trying to fit his scraps together. He held imaginary conversations with Mrs. Jones and with Mr. Carruthers—frightfully leery conversations, in which he extracted information from them which they were quite determined not to give up. The extraordinary ingenuity which he displayed was very encouraging to him; but a dreadful fear that it might evaporate in the daylight kept him from being unduly puffed up.

He must have passed directly from one of these conversations into an uneasy sleep, for quite suddenly he not only heard Mrs. Jones speaking, but he could see her—only she wasn't Mrs. Jones at all, but little Fossick-Yates in petticoats, with his beard, and his glasses all askew, and a wreath of primroses round his bald head. He said, speaking very earnestly, "If you really want to know, I'll tell you—but it's most frightfully confidential. The fact is, it's a yellow streak—not a white one, you understand, but yellow, yellow all through." When he said yellow the second time he began to throw primroses at John, and they turned into snakes as they touched the ground.

In his dream John began to run like the wind. He ran all up one side of the Amazon, and all down the other. And then all at once quite suddenly he was running down the Valley of the Waveney by a little crystal stream that lost itself in moss. Suddenly he stopped running, because there was nothing to run away from any more. He stood quite still and looked across the stream; and from the other side of it Anne Belinda looked at him and smiled. She wore her old brown holland overall, and her hair fell in two long dark plaits. She smiled at him, and an intense, joyful expectancy stabbed deep, deep into his dream. He didn't know in the least what he expected.

He woke, and found himself sittting straight up in bed, which was very odd indeed. The whole thing was very odd. He lay down in the dark and puzzled over it. It was strange to feel in a dream what he had never felt by day. He had had good times and bad times, but never before had he felt this utter poignancy of joy. It was quite beyond his experience; there was nothing easy or soft about it; it had a keenness that was only just not pain; it was something he did not know. It was a strange thing to find it in a dream.

Chapter Eight

JOHN WENT TO CALL on Mrs. Courtney next day. He was shown into the drawing-room and left there whilst the maid went to find her mistress.

He looked about him with interest. The room was not at all like any room he had seen before. Walls, floor and ceiling, curtains, woodwork, and chair-covers were all of one even shade of grey—and that not the bluish grey which is called French, but the real pure grey which comes from the equal mixture of black and white. Against this neutral background the few contrasting objects took on an added value. There were cushions of half a dozen shades of purple, from violet to cyclamen; there was a bright green clock on the mantelpiece, flanked by tall green candlesticks; on one long, bare wall there hung an etching of a black pine tree bending in the wind.

It was odd to find a break in so rigid a scheme. Yet a break there was; the room contained no nick-nacks, but there were three framed photographs on the piano, and they were all photographs of the same person. John had no difficulty in recognizing Jenny Marr—Jenny in her wedding-dress, with an exquisite lace veil on her fair hair—Jenny in Court dress, with feathers and a gleaming train—and, prettiest of the three, Jenny in soft, thin drapery bending over a tiny sleeping baby.

He wondered what Mrs. Courtney would be like; and as he wondered, she came in. Like her room, she was dressed in grey—he was to discover that she never wore anything else. Her masses of white hair were arranged in such elaborate waves and curls as to remind him of an eighteenth-century peruke. It was hair that would have suited well enough with delicate arched brows and a long oval face; but Mrs. Courtney's face was square, her features harsh, and her brown prominent eyes surmounted by broad, tufted eyebrows.

She shook hands with John, giving him a firm, rather hard clasp. Then she settled herself in a chair, observed him keenly for a moment, and said:

"I'm glad you came. You mustn't mind if I have a good look at you. I knew your father and mother." Her voice was deep and, like her features, rather harsh.

John was sharply surprised.

"You knew them? I didn't, you know."

"Yes, I know. It's a pity. Your father was the best-looking man I ever saw. You don't take after him."

John could not help laughing; she shot the sentence at him so suddenly and with more than a tinge of grievance in her tone. It was rather as if someone had been trying to foist an imitation upon her.

"No, I'm afraid I can't compete," he said.

Mrs. Courtney frowned.

"And you needn't imagine an old romance either. Your father was already besottedly in love with your mother when I knew him. He used to come and confide in me—they both did. Probably you can't imagine why." Her face softened in an extraordinary manner; the rather large mouth turned up at the corners in a wide, enchanting smile. "Your mother was the sweetest child in the world. She was seventeen then, and Tom was three-and-twenty. I was as old as the hills. Well, well, they were lovely and pleasant in their lives, and in their death they were not divided. But it's your loss."

"My great loss," said John simply.

She nodded.

"You can understand why I wanted to see you. I'm sorry you're not like them, but I dare say I shall get used to that. Now, let's come down to present day. There's something depressing about the past—don't you think so? People of my age generally live with their heads screwed round backwards, looking at things that have been over and done with for years. Thank the Lord, I don't do that! I'm interested in to-day. I'm interested in you. You're going to stop at home and live at Waveney, I hope."

"I don't know yet."

"Nonsense! What's the good of having a place if you don't live in it? You've got money to keep it up—and that's more than most people have nowadays. So you'd better look round you for a wife and do the old place up a bit. It was looking shocking the last time I was down there—just before Jenny's wedding that was. Have you seen Jenny yet?" A warm tone had come into her voice at the mention of Jenny's name.

"No," said John. His heart beat a little faster. "I want to meet her. And I want particularly to meet Anne."

"Anne?" The warmth was gone. "Jenny's my girl—my god-daughter, you know. She gets her Jenifer from me."

"Yes, I want to meet Anne," said John.

"'M—she's not a patch on Jenny. It always makes me quite angry when people pretend they don't know one from the other."

"Aren't they very much alike?"

"Oh, there's a *likeness*—I'm not saying there isn't. But they're as different as they can be. Jenny's the sweetest thing—like a sunny day."

"And Anne?"

"Oh, I've nothing against her. But she's not Jenny. Anyhow, you can't meet her, because she's been ill, and I believe she's still abroad. And look here, just let me give you a hint—when you do meet Jenny, don't go and worry her by talking about Anne."

"Why should it worry her?"

Mrs. Courtney's thick eyebrows rose.

"Because she's ridiculously devoted to her. I never can see why twins should be specially devoted to each other. But there it is, Jenny has taken this illness quite absurdly to heart. There she is, with an adoring husband, and a nice fat baby, and everything in the world to make her happy; and yet one only has to mention Anne's name to see her cloud over and look wretched, positively wretched. So I thought I'd just give you a word of warning."

John leaned forward.

"Mrs. Courtney, where is Anne Waveney? Can you give me her address?"

She looked at him with an effect of surprise.

"I don't know her address. I believe she's abroad somewhere. To tell you the honest truth, I've never taken very much interest in Anne. Jenny's my girl, as I told you."

"I want very particularly to know where she is. If she's ill, she can't be alone—someone must be looking after her."

"Oh, I expect she's all right again by now. She was ill at the time of Jenny's wedding. And then, I believe, she went abroad with Aurora Fairlie. She's a cousin on the Courtney side—you must have heard her name. She wanders about Europe and writes the sort of books I never read myself: *Platitudes from the Pyrenees*, *Meanderings in Morocco*, *Balkan Balderdash*, and so on."

"And Anne Waveney is with this Miss—er—Fairlie?"

Mrs. Courtney looked vague.

"Jenny said something about it. But, as I told you, I don't talk to her about Anne. It only upsets her; and I wouldn't have Jenny upset for a dozen Annes." She paused, smiled beautifully, and added: "I'm a fool about Jenny. But wait till you meet her."

It was as she said the last word that the door opened and Jenny came in. John would have known her from Amory's picture, and from the photographs, even without Mrs. Courtney's cry of "My darling!" and her close embrace. She turned, with one hand still on the girl's shoulder.

"I haven't got any manners—I always forget introductions. And, besides, you ought to have known each other for years."

Jenny turned her head, in its close black cap, and smiled a puzzled, deprecating smile. The movement and the smile were full of a natural grace and charm. She did not speak, but stood there smiling with a delicate lift of the eyebrows.

"It's your cousin, John Waveney," said Mrs. Courtney in her deep voice.

John shook hands, and became properly sensible of the fact that he was certainly lucky to have so charming a cousin. An old woman in Waveney village once said of Jenny Marr that everything she did became her. "If she talks to you, the time just passes like a flash. And if she don't talk, one can always look at her."

She was much prettier than John had expected. The thin black which she wore showed off a very graceful figure and a dazzling complexion.

John stayed ten minutes, and then made his farewells. From the moment of Jenny's entrance Mrs. Courtney's interest centred on her so obviously as to make him feel himself in the way. Jenny gave him three fingers and a pretty, friendly glance.

"You must come and see us. You will—won't you? I'm only up for the day, but you must come down to us for a week-end. I suppose this week's no good?"

"Well, as a matter of fact—"

"Could you come? Then do. As Aunt Jen says, we ought to have known each other years ago, and I want you to meet Nicholas."

He went out into the street, warmed with a pleasant sense of kinship. Jenny turned to Mrs. Courtney.

"He's rather nice. I like the quiet, straight way he looks at you. Thank goodness he's presentable. He might have been anything, really, what with going out to the colonies at eighteen, and the war, and knocking about all over the place ever since. You'd better start match-making for him."

"I told him he ought to marry and settle down. Jenny, he's frightfully interested in Anne. When's she coming home?"

"In Anne!" Jenny's pretty colour faded slowly. "How can he be interested in Anne?"

"I don't know. But he is."

Jenny's eyes filled with tears.

"Aunt Jen, *don't*! I can't bear it."

"Isn't she any better? Oh, my darling, don't cry! What a fool I was to ask!"

Jenny dabbed her eyes.

"It's silly of me. I won't. I do miss her so, Aunt Jen. And when you said that about John Waveney being interested, I couldn't help thinking how lovely it would be if—" Her voice broke into a sob.

"Well, perhaps it will be." Mrs. Courtney would have said anything to bring the sunshine back.

Jenny pressed her handkerchief to her eyes. Mrs. Courtney could feel her trembling. She said, "No—no," in a muffled, broken voice. Then she got up, went quickly to the window, and stood there fighting for composure. When she turned round she was still pale, but her smile had come back.

"Look what Nicko gave me yesterday!" she said.

She dropped back into her chair and held out a long chain of square-cut crystals held together by platinum links. The links were set with emeralds. The crystals were exquisitely carved.

"How lovely! But, Jen, it must have cost a fortune. Why not pearls? I do so love you in pearls."

Something flickered for an instant in Jenny's eyes. They were brown eyes—brown, sunny eyes; but just for that instant they looked dark and cold.

"I don't care frightfully for pearls," she said. Then, with a complete change of voice, "Aunt Jen, baby laughed at me yesterday—he did really. He saw me come in at the nursery door, and he turned his head and laughed. Nurse says he's most awfully young to laugh. She says babies of three months old often don't—and he was only two months yesterday. She says—"

She talked ecstatically for an hour about little Tony Marr. Mrs. Courtney did not mention Anne again.

Chapter Nine

JOHN ENJOYED his week-end at Waterdene—the small, well-chosen party, the gay ease, the informal friendliness which he found there. Jenny was a perfectly delightful hostess, and Nicholas Marr an equally delightful host.

The other guests were all young; Nicholas himself older than any of them by some years. John liked him, but wondered occasionally what lay behind a manner of so much charm. Sometimes he thought there might be a stiff, black pride behind it. He could imagine that Nicholas Marr would continue to be perfectly charming to a man whom he hated and meant to kill; he could imagine him absolutely implacable behind a smile. He had the dark good looks, the tinge of pride, which made the right complement to Jenny's sunny beauty.

Jenny, for her part, was very much pleased with her new cousin. He actually noticed that the baby had a dimple, a fact which she had insisted on from the first in the face of a good deal of scepticism from Nicholas. Also he admired her in a very proper and cousinly manner—and above all things in the world, Jenny loved the warm, sweet atmosphere of admiration and liking. She had had it all her life; father, brothers, Aunt Jen, had provided it without stint until she met Nicholas and received its distilled essence. And the more she received, the more she gave back. Small wonder that so warmly responsive a creature should be surrounded by a devoted court in the midst of which she moved with a singular grace.

After the first twenty-four hours John found that he could no longer see any likeness to Anne; there was a similarity of feature, but no more. Jenny was Jenny, and there was an end of it. She was a radiant creature in the full sunshine of youth, beauty, and happiness. In what shadowed place, under what sombre cloud was Anne? A curious resentment sprang up in him at the thought; he was filled with jealousy for Anne. Jenny had everything—friends and home, face and fortune, husband and child. What was Anne's portion? Where was she? Everything came back to that. He had meant to wait, but a strong impulse carried him away. He turned to Jenny with a question which he could not keep back any longer:

"Jenny, where's your sister Anne?"

They had been dancing together, and were sitting in one of the low window-seats of the long panelled room. At the far end of it a gramophone discoursed jazz. Three couples were still dancing. Nicholas Marr passed them with Pamela Austin. Her sleek, smooth black head was higher than his. It might very well have been a boy's head, and close cropped even for a boy. The brilliant scarlet dress, cut daringly low and ending at the knee, gave a shock of incongruity. Nicholas laughed as they passed, and Pamela waved her hand.

Jenny put her head back against the polished wood. She loved the dark background, which threw up her shining hair and the freshness of her tints. She was wearing a little white frock that made her look seventeen again; her soft, fair neck was innocent of even a school-girl's row of pearls. She looked at John and caught her breath.

What did you say? Shall we go on dancing?"

"No, I want to talk. I want to talk about your sister Anne. Do you mind?"

Jenny nodded.

"I—I can't—I can't really."

"That's just it. Why can't you?"

Jenny's heart fluttered dreadfully. If only she could get over minding about Anne. She was being a perfect idiot. If she could only control this stupid shaking and just say something, anything, quite casually and as if it didn't matter.

"Why can't you?" said John. He made his voice very gentle and persuasive. "Look here, Jenny, I can't help knowing there's something wrong. You see, I met Anne once—"

"When?" Jenny looked startled.

"Years ago—nine years. She was only a kid. She didn't know who I was. And I didn't know who she was until I saw Amory's portrait of you both."

Jenny's colour flickered. She said, "That hateful picture!" in a voice just above her breath.

John went on:

"I want to know where she is—I want to see her."

"You can't." It was a whisper.

John smiled. The smile frightened Jenny; it frightened her very much. She said:

"John, you can't—really."

"Why can't I? Don't you think you had better tell me?"

She shook her head. There ought to be something that she could tell him. If she didn't tell him something, he would go on trying to find out. She tried very hard indeed to keep steady and to find words.

"John, you can't, because—"

"Well?"

Why on earth had she asked him down here? If only the gramophone didn't make such a noise, she might be able to think. Pamela and Derek Austin were singing too—ridiculous words that buzzed in the general din like flies buzzing in a train. She sat up straight and pushed her wedding ring down hard until it cut into her hand.

"She's been ill—she's abroad."

"Yes, Mrs. Courtney told me that. She's with a Miss Fairlie, isn't she?"

Jenny nodded. She kept her eyes on John's face. If he made her go on, it would be his fault, not hers. She hoped with all her heart that he would be satisfied and not ask anything more. The hope failed as it rose.

"Then will you give me her address? I'm at a loose end, and I should rather like an excuse for a prowl abroad."

It was no use. Anything she said would be his fault. She didn't want to say it. She had tried her very best not to tell him anything. Her eyes were hot with the rush of tears. She turned her shoulder on the bright, noisy room and pushed open the casement window behind them. A breath of lilac-scented air came in. She spoke in a little sad voice, very low:

"John, you can't see her. She can't see people—she can't even see me."

"Why can't she, Jenny?"

Jenny's voice trembled lower still.

"Can't you guess?"

"I'm afraid not. I'm afraid you'll have to tell me."

Jenny jumped up.

"Not here," she said in a stifled voice. "They're all looking at us—I saw Pamela look."

She slipped out of the window on to the flagged walk outside. The drop was not more than a couple of feet. John followed her, and saw her move away in the dusk like a white moth. The sound of the gramophone died to a blurr.

The house stood half-way up a gently sloping hill. From where they stood the ground dropped by successive terraces to the open water-meadows through which there flowed a broad and shallow stream. A fitful moonlight brightened the water-flow and the white lilac blooms on the lower terrace.

Jenny stopped where a grey stone vase lifted a sheaf of scented tulips to the darkness. The colour was lost, but they smelt like violets.

"Well, Jenny?" he said.

Jenny faced him. The dusk gave her confidence. Why had she not come out before? Now that he could not see her, she could tell him.

"John, you must think me very foolish," she began. "I ought to be more used to it. But I can't get used to it. We always did everything together; and now I haven't seen her for a year, and she hasn't even seen baby." Tears came into her voice.

"Yes. But why?"

Jenny stamped her foot.

"I suppose you like hurting me like this! I suppose you like hurting people!"

"I only want to know where Anne is."

"She's where you can't go to her. Why don't you believe me? She got ill just before I was married, and they shut her up. They—they won't let anyone see her."

John had known that it was coming; it was as if he had watched it coming from a long way off. Yet, now that it was here and the vague unformulated dread had taken form in the spoken word, everything in his nature rose up against it in a violence of denial that was purely instinctive. He heard the wind stir the tulip leaves; he heard Jenny take a sobbing breath; he heard Pamela Austin's clear, high, boyish voice in a snatch of syncopated tune. He waited until he could speak quietly:

"Do you mean that Anne is mad?"

Jenny cried out at that.

"I'm sorry—but I've got to know—is that what you mean?"

"Oh!" said Jenny. It was a very piteous little cry. She put both hands over her face as if the darkness were not shield enough. "Oh, John, it breaks my heart! My darling Anne!" she said, and broke into convulsive sobbing.

Chapter Ten

ANNE WAVENEY CAME OUT into the spring sunshine and looked about her. She was carrying a small suitcase. A woman who was passing stared. Anne turned to the right and walked away, with her head held high and her heart beating rather quickly. After a minute or two she forgot all about the woman. She looked at a blue sky full of light, at the puddle in the road which showed that it had rained last night, at a child with a riot of copper-coloured hair, at a slinking sandy cat; and for the moment all these things were equally beautiful and equally dear. A real cat, prowling in a real London street; real people, going on errands, meeting each other, talking to each other; a real baby in a perambulator. As she passed the baby, Anne made dancing eyes at it, and the baby said "Goo," and waggled a much sucked rattle.

Anne turned the corner and hailed a passing taxi. She had planned all this many times over, had thought of it day and night until sometimes she wondered whether she had not drawn all the thrill from it in anticipation. But no anticipation had given her quite this sense of having wings; she was so full of happiness that it seemed to lift her and carry her without her own volition.

She sat in the taxi and looked eagerly out of the window. How awfully short everybody's skirts were! She was wearing a pretty grey tweed coat and skirt and a close black felt hat turned up in front. The coat and skirt and the hat had been quite new a year ago. They were quite new now; but they were out of date. People were wearing brims again—little brims, and higher crowns—awfully becoming. And her skirt was inches too long, though she and Jenny had felt rather daring when they wore these twin coats and skirts last year. She wondered what Jenny had done with hers. "I can ask her—I can ask her to-day—I can see Jenny to-day—I can ask her anything I like!"

She drew a long trembling breath of happiness. The thought of seeing Jenny so soon brought the colour to her cheeks and a dancing sparkle to her dark blue eyes. Her thoughts danced too. Then she set herself to plan. Dancing thoughts were all very well, but she had got to be practical; there was a lot to be done before she went down to see Jenny.

She had given the address of the hotel at which she and Mrs. Jones had stayed more than a year ago. But now, as they turned into the familiar street, a sort of cold horror swept over her. She had not known that she would feel like that. It was unreasonable, it was foolish—but there it was.

Suddenly there came into her mind the name of another hotel. On the impulse she leaned out of the window and gave the address to the driver. As she drew back again, the cold horror receded, leaving her trembling with relief.

The place would probably be just what she wanted—frightfully respectable and not too expensive, since Aurora Fairlie always stayed there when she was in town. She wondered, with a little laugh, where Aurora was and what she was doing.

A few minutes later she was explaining to a blasé booking clerk that she wanted a room just for the day. A key was put into her hand, and a register pushed forward for her to sign, without the girl so much as raising her eyes. Anne felt a little chilled. She was in the mood in which one likes to assure total strangers that it is a lovely day. Her real need was a fellow creature to whom she could say, "I'm so *dreadfully* happy!"

She signed the register, and, just as she was pushing it back, she saw Aurora Fairlie's broomstick signature at the top of the left-hand page. There it was, large, black, awkward, and quite unmistakable.

Anne fled to the refuge of the room that had been allotted her. Of all people in the world, she least wished to meet Aurora Fairlie. She was breathing a little quickly as she locked the door and set her suitcase down on the bed.

Aurora! What an odd bit of luck that she should be here! Now, what exactly did Aurora know? That was the question; and no one but Jenny could answer it. Everything came back to Jenny in the end.

Anne turned from the bed and went across to the dressing-table. She tilted the glass and looked long and earnestly at her own reflection. After a moment she took off her hat. She couldn't go and see Jenny, looking like this. Her hair was too awful. She must have it properly cut and waved. For the rest, there was something a little unfamiliar in what she saw. Her skin had the even pallor that comes from an indoor life. She rubbed her cheeks, and as the quick blood stained them, she felt that she knew herself a little better. There were dark marks under her dark eyes, and her face was thin—a good deal thinner than it had been a year ago. This thinner oval of her face made her eyes look startlingly large. The likeness to Jenny was very much in abeyance.

With a sudden movement she pushed the glass so that she could no longer see herself and went back to the bed. Sitting sideways on it, she opened the suitcase and, burrowing, produced three old letters. They were addressed to Miss Annie Jones. Anne removed the envelopes, tearing them into very tiny scraps and throwing the scraps out of the window. Then she took up the letters and read them through. They were all from Mr. Carruthers, and were written throughout in his own hand.

The first, dated just over a year ago, began:

"Dear Miss Jones,
    "It is with great regret that I have to inform you of the sudden death of your father ..."

Anne read it through to the end, and then tore it up.

The second letter also began with a regret. This time Mr. Carruthers regretted having to inform her that her name did not appear in her father's will, everything having been left to her sister. Anne turned rather white as she laid the fragments of this letter beside the others.

She took longer over the third letter. It ran:

"DEAR MISS JONES,

"Your sister wishes you to be informed that she has a son, now a month old. She wishes you to know that she is very well. Your other sister has been travelling all this year with Miss Dawn. Your sister wished you to know this. Will you ring me up before communicating with your sister?

"Yours truly,

"L. AUSTIN CARRUTHERS."

Anne caught the corner of her mouth between her teeth as she read. Not only Jenny to see, but Jenny's baby. Lovely! Lovely! Lovely! Lovely and strange—Jenny with a baby! She shut her eyes for a minute and tried for a picture of it. Nothing would come but Jenny's face. Not Jenny's face as she wanted to see it, but as she had seen it last, white to the very lips, the eyes wild with terror.

She jumped up with a quick little cry. Why did she always see Jenny like that? It was the thing that hurt most of all; and, more than anything else in the world, she wanted to blot it out with the picture of the real, happy Jenny, all love and smiles, with her little son in her arms. That was what she was going to see to-day.

She glanced at the letter again. The pen was the pen of Mr. Carruthers; but the words were certainly Jenny's words. Jenny was letting her know where Anne Waveney was supposed to have been all this year—"Your other sister has been travelling with Miss Dawn." It hadn't taken her a moment, of course, to recognize Aurora. So she had been travelling with Aurora Fairlie. Just for a moment her upper lip lifted in a smile; she wondered whether Aurora knew. Then the smile faded, and she frowned. The letter was clever: Jenny was clever. Anne hated the cleverness as much as she loved Jenny. She hated it with a quick, rebellious hatred.

She tore up the third letter. Then she put all the bits into the waste-paper basket and went along the corridor to telephone to Mr. Carruthers.

It took her some time to get on, and as she waited, she began to feel a little frightened. She didn't really want to talk to Mr. Carruthers. She couldn't imagine why he should want to talk to her. No, that wasn't quite true; it wasn't a bit difficult to imagine the sort of things that her father's lawyer might feel it his duty to say to her. "Wouldn't" was the word, not "couldn't." She *wouldn't* imagine those things.

"Hullo!" said a voice very loudly.

Anne said "Hullo!"

The voice said "Hullo!" again in a faint, dying whisper.

Anne went on saying "Hullo."

When the voice had come a little nearer, she asked for Mr. Carruthers.

The voice said, "Who?"

Anne said, "Mr. Carruthers."

The voice became very loud again. It said, "This is City oooB. There is no one of the name of Jones here."

Anne giggled. She had forgotten how mad telephones could be.

"I said Carruthers—I didn't say Jones—I don't want Jones."

She didn't really want Carruthers either. This helped her to bear up when the voice said reprovingly, "Mr. Carruthers is away. He has been ill. Would you like to speak to Mr. Smith?"

Anne repressed a warm feeling of relief. She wished Mr. Carruthers a speedy return to health; but the reprieve certainly raised her spirits. She said hastily:

"No, I don't want to speak to Mr. Smith. I only wanted to ask whether Lady Marr is at Waterdene."

"Oh yes—I believe so. As a matter of fact, we addressed some papers there this morning. Who is it speaking?"

"Thank you," said Anne, and rang off.

She went back to her room and put on her hat and gloves. Then she went downstairs, where she looked up an afternoon train and despatched a telegram: "Arriving three-thirteen. Anne." She glanced at the little wrist-watch which had been Sir Anthony's present on her twenty-first birthday. She had just time to have her hair cut, but no time to dawdle. She was almost at the outer door, when she turned sharply aside and bent to the fastening of a shoe.

Aurora Fairlie, in a monstrous hurry, passed within a yard of her. Her heavy shoes creaked as much as ever—Aurora's shoes always did creak. Anne looked back and saw the broad tweed-clad shoulders and rough deer-stalker hat disappear in the crowd. She slipped into the street half laughing, and once again she wondered whether Aurora knew that Anne Waveney had been travelling with her for a year.

At Aristide's she found an assistant who remembered her and mourned over the neglected condition of her hair.

"I've been right out of civilization," said Anne. "It *is* awful—isn't it?"

The young lady threw a complacent glance at her own immaculate golden waves.

"Well—" she said, and left it at that, adding: "Of course, I'll do my best."

Her best was a very talented best. As the clever fingers did their work, Annie Jones receded, and Anne Belinda Waveney emerged upon the world. At the same time the world displayed itself to Anne Belinda. The young lady had a fluent tongue as well as clever fingers. She talked all the time, and while she talked, Anne gathered up the news of twelve lost months: There had been a strike—a general strike, and a coal strike. The coal strike was still going on, but the general strike had been brought to an end, largely, she gathered, owing to the unparalleled courage, resource, and ingenuity of the young lady's gentleman friend—"Drove a lorry right down to the docks for food—and we quite in a way about him. And, as far as I could see, he seemed to be enjoying himself, though I'm sure I don't know why. At it from morning till night he was—and very hard work, and no regular meals. And all he did was to laugh and say it was just like old times when he drove a lorry in the war. And what I said to him was what I think any young lady might feel—That's not too hot for you, miss? Just say if you feel it—what I said was—well, I said, 'You may say what you like, and how anyone can enjoy working overtime, let alone not getting paid anything extra'—I'm giving you a nice loose wave in front, same as you always had—'Well,' I said, 'whether it's like old times or not, we don't want any of your nasty foreign wars over here.' Now, miss, there's one side done, and if you take the glass, you can see how you like it."

Chapter Eleven

THE NEAREST STATION was five miles from Waterdene. Anne took a taxi, and tried to recover the golden moment of anticipation whose glory had passed when she stepped out upon an empty platform— empty, that is, to her. Other people were being met. The fat young woman who had travelled down with her had been met by a stout young man, who kissed her very heartily, to their mutual satisfaction. The old lady in the next carriage had been met by a thin daughter in spectacles and a surprisingly bright green motor veil. The little boy in an elder brother's cut-down suit had been embraced by a stout, placid grandmother. Yet for Anne the platform was empty. She sat, smiling tremulously and trying to think of all the reasons which might have kept Jenny from meeting her.

When they came in sight of the gates, Anne's heart began to beat so fast that she stopped trying to think at all. Two minutes more, perhaps three, and she would have Jenny again. There was only the length of the drive between them.

The taxi swung in at the open gate. About thirty yards farther on the drive took a sudden turn. The over-arching trees cast a pleasant flickering shade. Anne, leaning from the window, saw the river gleam beyond the trees. And then she saw Jenny.

The taxi stopped. Afterwards she knew that Jenny must have signed to it to stop; at the time, she thought of nothing but Jenny herself. She had the door open and, forgetting the suitcase, she ran across the gravel to the sunlit patch of grass where Jenny stood.

It was Jenny who remembered all that Anne had forgotten. Her hand went out, but it kept Anne safely at arm's length. She said,

"Wait." And then she left Anne and spoke to the driver, repeating the word.

"Will you wait down there by the lodge?" That was what she said.

Anne heard the words, but they did not seem to mean anything, because she was still thinking only of Jenny. She looked at her now as she came hurrying back.

Her first sight of Jenny's face was to have blotted out all the bad dreams of Jenny frightened; the straining eyes, the agonized pallor were to be blotted out. Yet somehow they were not blotted out. As Jenny came up to her and put her hand on her arm, Anne had the most terrible feeling that this pretty, smiling composure was just an illusion, and that behind it there was the terrified Jenny who had haunted all her dreams. The hand on her arm was stiff.

"Come through here—this way. Anne, *why* did you come?"

They were in a narrow walk that wound its way into the shrubbery on the right of the drive. Tall bushes of holly, berberis and yew rose high above their heads; a little farther and the path was almost a tunnel. Jenny hurried on until it opened into a curious square clearing. A hedge of clipped holly gave it high, impenetrable walls. In one of the walls a window had been cut. It framed a brilliant, exquisite picture of blue sky, sunny water, and green meadow. The place itself was dark and cold.

As they came into it, Anne flung her free arm about Jenny.

"Oh, Jen!" she said.

Just for a moment there was a response. Then Jenny stood away, her hand dropping to her side.

"Why did you come?" she said. "Oh, *Anne*, why did you come?"

A sense of confusion came over Anne. The whole of her consciousness was so full of the joy of being with Jenny again that there was literally no room in it for anything else. But something else was pushing against the door of her thought, pressing to come in. The darkness of this overshadowed place added to her bewilderment. She put out her hands and said, speaking slowly and doubtfully:

"Why, Jen, where—I mean—didn't you want me to come?"

"I told you not to come. I told you not to do anything till you'd seen Mr. Carruthers."

"He's been ill. He's away." Then after a pause, "I wired."

"What's the good of wiring? You didn't wait for an answer—and I only got the wire ten minutes before you arrived. We'd been out to lunch at Greystones. It was *all* I could do to get away from the rest of them and catch you at the gate."

Anne's eyebrows drew together; her eyes dwelt on Jenny with a puzzled look.

"Have you got a party?"

"People for the week-end. But, *anyhow*—Anne, you *must* see that you can't possibly come here like this."

Anne went on looking. Part of her mind was thinking how well Jenny looked, and how pretty—white suited her. Part of it was not thinking at all, but trying, with an awful sense of strain, to keep out that pressing, pushing something which sought to force a way for itself.

"Why, Jen?"

Jenny came nearer.

"Why on earth didn't you wait until you heard from me? You *ought* to have waited."

"No—I don't think so. I had to see you—I had to know what you'd been saying to people. As it was, I nearly ran into Aurora. And I thought—" She gave a little laugh.

"Aurora!" Jenny's tone was quite horrified.

"Yes, my child, Aurora. If I hadn't been frightfully quick, she'd have seen me. And before she sees me, I think I should just like to know how much Aurora knows."

"She doesn't know anything."

"How do you mean she doesn't know anything? I'm supposed to have been travelling with her. Doesn't she know that?"

"No, she doesn't. I wrote to her, and the letter came back. And I didn't think she'd be coming home for months, because Leonard Fairlie said that Mabel told him that Aurora was just off to

Kurdistan. So I made sure that she wouldn't be back for ages. Are you *certain* it was Aurora?"

Anne laughed again. Jenny never believed anything she didn't want to believe. If it suited her to feel sure that Aurora was in Kurdistan, she would continue to feel sure in the face of the most daunting evidence.

"Of course I'm certain. I saw her. She's staying at Haydon's Hotel—I saw her signature in the register."

"I must see her," said Jenny. "Or—or—you can see her for me. We really oughtn't to lose any time, and the very earliest day I could possibly go to town would be Wednesday. Yes, you'd better see her. Look here, you'll catch the four-forty-five if you hurry. I told the taxi to wait."

A stab of pain pierced the confusion of Anne's thoughts. Jenny had told the taxi to wait. She was not to stay at Waterdene; she was to go back to town, and she was to go back at once. Jenny's hand was on her arm, pushing her a little.

"Anne, do wake up! You must hurry if you want to catch the four-forty-five."

A stab of anger followed the stab of pain.

"Why should I catch it?"

"Oh, you *must*!"

"Why, Jenny?"

Jenny slipped her hand into the crook of Anne's elbow.

"Anne—please go—oh, please!"

But Anne stood her ground.

"Why, Jenny?" she repeated.

Jenny snatched her hand away.

"Why do you make it so hard for me? You must know that you oughtn't to have come here. I can't possibly have you, and you're just making it as dreadful for me as you can."

"I can't possibly have you." When Jenny said that, Anne's guard came down. All the joy and the light and the brightness that had filled her thoughts went dead, and cold, and dark. She did not move or show any sign. But she lost count of time for a little. She did not

know how long it was before her mind was clear again—cold and dark, but clear.

"*Oh*, you're making it so hard for me!" said Jenny.

"I'm sorry." Anne spoke quite simply and without sarcasm. "There are things I want to ask you. There's plenty of time. You say that Aurora doesn't know anything. Who does know?"

"Mr. Carruthers—"

Anne moved her hand impatiently.

"Naturally—since he wrote to me. And, from what he wrote, I—I suppose—" She stopped, then forced herself to go on: "I suppose Father knew."

Jenny was crying a little.

"Anne, I couldn't help it."

"Who told him?"

"He guessed."

"How could he?"

"He guessed there was something—he got it out of Nanna. You don't suppose I wanted to tell him?"

"No, I suppose you didn't. Anyone else, Jenny?" Anne's voice was so quiet that Jenny took heart.

"Only Nicholas," she said, and began to dry her eyes.

Anne took a quick breath.

"What does Nicholas know?"

"Anne—don't! I couldn't help it—I didn't mean to tell him."

"What did you tell him?"

"It was an accident—I didn't mean it. Father made a most frightful scene, and Nicko heard something he said, and then I couldn't get out of it. I *had* to tell him."

Anne took a step forward.

"What did you tell him, Jenny?"

"Anne—don't look at me like that!"

"Did you tell him—*everything?*"

Jenny burst into tears.

"You don't know Nicko—you don't—no one does. He's so frightfully proud. You don't know him."

"Did you tell him what you told Mr. Carruthers—and Father?"

"I had to."

"I see." The two words took the last of Anne's breath for the moment.

The tears were running down Jenny's face, but Anne's eyes were quite dry. When she said "I see," she did see quite clearly. She saw where she stood, and where Jenny stood, and that there was a great gulf between them. On the far side of that impassable gulf there was not only Jenny, but all the world that Anne had known and loved. In that world there was no place for Anne any more; she was cut off from it, utterly, completely, and irrevocably. A horror of isolation, a horror of outer darkness, began to move stealthily towards her. She felt their approach, and could do no more than stand to meet it. There was no place for her. There was no refuge.

"Oh, Anne!" said Jenny. "Why did you come? I could have come up and met you quietly and explained *everything*. What's the good of looking like that? You're making it so hard." Her voice broke in a sob. "And it's not my fault if Nicko simply *won't* have you here. But he won't—he won't hear of it. He says I can give you half the money—he's awfully generous; but he says you must promise not to come here or even to write. Look here, I'll meet you in town and tell you all about it. But you must go now—you really must."

"Yes, I'm going," said Anne. She spoke in a colourless, gentle voice. She was looking in Jenny's direction, but she did not really see her. She seemed to herself to be looking into a mist. Jenny was somewhere in the mist, but she couldn't see her or reach her. She knew that she must go. Someone—yes, Jenny—had told her that she must go. And there was something about a train—she had to catch a train and go away into that outer darkness. She turned and began to grope her way slowly and stiffly along the wall of holly until she came to the opening through which she and Jenny had come.

Chapter Twelve

JOHN WAVENEY HAD SPENT a very pleasant morning. He found himself liking his cousin Jenny a good deal. She certainly had a most charming gift for making each of her guests feel that he or she was an integral part of a delightful whole.

John was sorry that the pleasant week-end was over and that the evening would see him back in town. But both Jenny and Nicholas had bidden him come again and come often. "You mustn't forget you're a cousin, John—and I haven't a lot of cousins like some people have." This was Jenny. And Nicholas Marr had nodded and said, "No, we're rather poor in relations, both of us— pretty nearly destitute, in fact." And there he stopped suddenly, and as suddenly frowned.

John did not accompany the Marrs to Greystones. He went for a tramp after lunch and walked round Tenstone Hill. He came back very cheerful, and turned in at the lodge gate whistling. A taxi was waiting in the road outside, the driver immersed in a newspaper. He was just past the turn of the drive when he heard footsteps on his right. Someone was coming through the bushes at a sort of stumbling run. He turned, went back a yard or two, and looked up the path that left the drive to wander amongst dark yews and hollies. It was down this path that someone was running; and in a moment he saw that it was a woman. She came down the path with hurrying, halting feet, her hands stretched out before her as if she were pushing something away.

John stood where he was and waited for her to come to him. And as she came, he recognized her. It was Anne Belinda. The likeness to the child of nine years ago was dead; only the ghost of it lived in Anne Belinda's wide, blind eyes. The likeness to Jenny was gone as if it had never been. And yet John recognized her beyond any doubt. It was Anne.

She stumbled against him and stopped dead, her groping hands clenched on his arm, her face quite close to his, her eyes drowned in anguish, not in tears. The sight of her moved John to the depths. It was as if she were walking in her sleep, separated from him by some horrible dream; for though she was touching him, holding him with desperate fingers, it was plain that she neither recognized him nor knew what she was doing. For the moment she was deaf and blind to outward things. What image was before her eyes, or what voice in her ears, he could not tell. It was not his image, or his voice.

She held his arm with the force of agony, and he laid a warm, steady hand on her shoulder and let it rest there, waiting. A long, full moment passed, and then, as they stood there on the edge of the drive, there came to them from the direction of the lodge the sound of voices—Pamela Austin's high ringing laugh.

Anne gave a quick gasp, and he felt her quiver. The shoulder upon which his hand weighed had been rigid; now it shook. She gasped again, and this time there were words in the sobbing breath: "Don't I—let—" She pushed him from her and gave back a pace.

The voices were very near, just round the turn of the drive. John went to meet them, and found Derek and Pamela in their usual high spirits. Pamela greeted him with a scream of joy:

"Come and do the Charleston up the avenue! Derek's rotten on gravel. I say it gives it snap. Come along and show him." As she spoke, she burst into song at the top of a piercing soprano.

Derek instantly began an imitation of fighting cats, and the three of them danced past the danger-point and up the drive until John professed himself out of breath.

"You must be in rotten training! I don't get blown like that." Pamela's voice was full of scorn. "Hi, Jenny, where are you off to? Come and dance!"

Jenny's white figure had appeared with almost startling suddenness. She came out between two pyramids of yew and stood there looking back over her shoulder.

Pamela and Derek began to run, but John turned and went down the drive again. He heard a chatter of voices receding. As soon as he was out of sight, he quickened his steps. But when he came to where the path turned off, it was empty. He walked up it, following its windings until he came to the dark clearing with the holly walls and the window which looked to the river.

There was no one there. The place oppressed him. The shadow of Anne's grief lay upon it. It was here that she had been hurt—how deeply, grievously hurt—and by whom?

A second winding path led from the clearing on the farther side. John thought of Jenny coming out between the pyramids of yew. If Jenny and Anne had met and parted in this place, what had happened between them to send Anne stumbling down that nearer path blind with misery?

John walked down the path that Anne had followed, and hurried to the gate. The taxi was gone. A furious anger because Anne had been so near and he had let her go blazed up in him. Why hadn't he gone back along the path with her? Why had he let her go out of his sight?

The lodge-keeper's bicycle leaned against the wall beside the gate. John helped himself to it without scruple. He had no idea of when the next train left Dene Vale, but he meant to catch Anne if it was humanly possible to do so. He made record time over the five miles of roughish road, only to hear the engine whistle when he was still a hundred yards from the gate of the station yard. When he dropped the lodge-keeper's bicycle and pushed past the porter, who demanded a platform ticket, the train was well under way. It afforded him a very good view of the back of the guard's van.

He rode slowly back to Waterdene. Anne had come and gone. He had seen her, touched her, and lost her within so small a space of time that it seemed like one of those flashing dreams that break the monotony of sleep. He was left with no reasoned thought, but with two or three very vivid impressions—Anne's grip on his arm, her cold rigid grip; the pain that blinded her eyes; the little heart-shaped mole between the thumb and forefinger of her right hand. He remembered that little mole; he remembered seeing it on the brown childish hand nine years ago. He was aware of having been very deeply moved. He was also aware of a steadily rising anger.

His determination to find Anne Waveney had from the first been whetted by the opposition which he encountered. Why could no one give him a straight answer? Why could no one tell him the truth? Fear, tact, evasion, lies—he was sick to death of them and in a mood to speak his mind roughly. Last night, now—Jenny must have been lying to him then. He tried to remember exactly what she had said, and discovered how little it amounted to. She had tried, as they had all tried, to put him off. She had hinted—oh, more than hinted—that Anne was out of her mind. And she had cried. Strangely enough, it never for one moment occurred to John that what Jenny had hinted might be true. He was quite sure that Jenny had lied to him, though he didn't know why. As he walked up the drive, he hummed tonelessly:

"Cassidy was a gentleman,
Cassidy did me brown.
Cassidy's wife wears a diamond hat
And pearls all over her gown."

He came up to the house with his mind very strongly made up. He would be fenced with no longer. When he told Jenny, as he meant to tell her, that he had actually seen Anne, she could hardly refuse to give him Anne's address.

He walked into the middle of the group that was having tea on the lawn under the biggest cedar and took a cup from Jenny without speaking. Derek and Pamela were throwing buns at each other with the maximum amount of noise and laughter. The sun shone warm and soft on the bright green of the grass. Pamela's scarlet frock dazzled in it. John looked at Jenny as he took his cup from her steady hand. She had very pretty hands, smaller than Anne's and whiter, much whiter. Her brown eyes smiled up at him.

"You've walked too far—you look quite fagged, she said.

"Oh, I didn't walk very far."

He took the vacant chair beside her and began to drink his tea in an abstracted silence. That Anne and Jenny had met he felt sure. If he had had any doubt before, it was gone now. Jenny had been crying; there were faint marks under her eyes, and the dark lashes through which she had looked up at him were not quite dry. Jenny cried rather easily. She had cried last night when he talked to her about Anne. Anything might have made her cry. But all the same he was sure, quite sure, that she and Anne had met. He drained his cup and set it down.

"Can you let me have Miss Fairlie's address?" he said quite casually as he turned.

"But she's in Spain!" Jenny flushed a little as she answered him, and her eyes widened.

"Yes—her address in Spain."

"I don't know—she's always travelling about. You don't take sugar, do you?"

"Yes, please. But when you write to your sister, how do you address the letters?"

"Poste restante, Madrid," said Jenny, and gave him his cup so full that the tea slopped over into the saucer.

John emptied the saucer upon the grass. As the last drop fell, he said:

"Anne's still with her—with Miss Fairlie, I mean?"

Jenny said, "Of course," and said it a shade too quickly; the words were no sooner across her lips than she felt cold with fright. If by any chance John had seen Anne. He couldn't have seen her. He might have passed her in the drive; he couldn't possibly have recognized her.

Pamela's voice broke in, calling to John:

"Where on earth did you go to after our dance? You ought to have sat out with me and told me how well I did it."

"I had something to see about." John's tone as non-committal as it well could be.

"Well, you've missed the great bun contest. I'm three up on Derek. And I'm thinking of going in for the world's championship. I'll back myself to catch buns and dance the Charleston against anyone. Oh, I say, that's an idea! Me doing the Charleston whilst

Derek throws buns at me and I catch them in my teeth. It would make a perfectly ripping stunt. Come on, Derek! Let's show them!"

Everyone looked round laughing at the long, undulating scarlet figure. She swayed this way and that, opened her wide mouth to its widest extent, and actually caught Derek's first bun with a dexterous snap. The next one hit her in the eye, but she caught it as it fell and hurled it back amid shouts of "Rotten shot! Play the game!"

There was so much noise going on that the sound of Miss Aurora Fairlie's massive tread and the inevitable creak of her stout shoes passed unnoticed.

It was John who saw her first. He looked round at Jenny and saw the big, square-built figure standing a couple of yards away, feet well apart, hat tilted back from the large brick-coloured face, and hands clasped upon a very manly looking stick.

Before he could speak, Miss Fairlie said, "Hul*lo*, Jenny!" And Jenny sprang up with a little scream:

"Aurora!"

"My good child, don't look so scared!"

"I thought you were in Spain," said Nicholas Marr.

"Crossed yesterday. Beastly tossing. Why does one travel? I shall stay at home and knit."

"How did you come?"

"Car, of course. You don't catch me going in a train in a blessed country like this, where the roads are like billiard tables. Oh, Lord, I'm dry! Give me some tea."

Jenny linked an affectionate arm in Aurora's.

"Come up to the house, and I'll give you some there. This isn't fit to drink."

"I'm not particular. It's wet—and I'm dry."

She laughed loudly, poured herself a cup of tea, and drank it off standing, regardless of Jenny's protestations:

"Oh, Aurora, *don't*! Come in. Please come in!"

"Don't!" said Miss Fairlie loudly. "You're pinching me! It's ripping out here. I don't want to come in a bit."

Jenny's "Aurora—please" reached no one's ears but Miss Fairlie's, but Nicholas came to his wife's assistance.

"Come along in and see the boy. No one's allowed food or rest in this house until they've told Jenny he's the finest baby they've ever seen. We'll feed you when you've perjured yourself sufficiently, but not before."

With his hand on one arm and Jenny's on the other, Miss Fairlie submitted to being walked off.

John stood looking after her. First Anne; and then Aurora. What on earth did it all mean? He would have given something for ten minutes' conversation with Miss Fairlie now, before Jenny had her innings. As they neared the house, he saw Nicholas leave the two women and hurry on, presumably to order fresh tea.

Aurora turned upon her cousin at once.

"What's all this to-do?" The small slaty eyes, set unbecomingly amongst sandy lashes, were shrewd and a little annoyed. "You pinched me black and blue down there. What on earth for?"

"I had to see you alone."

"Oh, did you? And why?"

"I'm going to tell you. Aurora, *please* not here."

"What on earth have you been up to?"

"Nothing! Nothing!"

"H'm!"—Aurora's grunt sounded very cross—"the sort of nothing which means something too bad to talk about, eh?"

"No, no! Come in here. This is my room. No one will come in, and you can have tea comfortably. They'll bring it in a minute."

"Jenifer Marr, you didn't lug me away from a perfectly good tea on the lawn to babble about buns in a boudoir."

"Aurora—*please*."

The admired Lady Marr felt uncommonly like a school-girl in a scrape.

"Oh, come off it, Jenny! Lord—I'm hot!" She pulled out a silk handkerchief of Spanish colouring and mopped a frankly perspiring brow. "My good girl, if you've anything to say, say it, and don't gawp at me; for I can't stand it. Get it off your chest!"

"Aurora, did you get my letter? No, I know you didn't."

"Then why ask me if I did?"

Jenny's colour rose sharply.

"Aurora, you're making it so difficult!"

Aurora laughed.

"My good girl, that's what people always say when they're boggling over something that isn't going to sound very pretty. Better let me have it plain. If it's anything ugly, it won't look any the better for being dressed up."

"I *did* write to you," said Jenny with tears in her eyes. "I *did* write—but the letter came back."

"What did you write about?"

"I wrote about Anne."

"The deuce you did!" said Miss Fairlie. "And what has Anne been doing?"

An indescribable look of painful hesitation crossed Jenny's face. Something in the look startled Miss Fairlie.

"Why, Jenny," she said, "you don't mean to tell me that Anne—"

Jenny burst into tears.

Oh, *yes*!" she said. "And I've told everyone that she's been travelling *with you* in Spain."

Chapter Thirteen

MISS FAIRLIE REFUSED to stay to dinner. She admired the infant Tony in a brisk and rather perfunctory manner, and then insisted on returning to the garden and sitting where she could see the river.

"An English spring smells better than the foreign sorts," she said as she creaked into the largest chair. "Wallflower"—she sniffed loudly—"lilac, syringa. Don't care frightfully for syringa myself; it always reminds me a little of white rats."

"Aurora!"

"Can't help it—it does. My brothers used to make me clean the cages, and I've never really cottoned to syringa since. But the other things are A 1. That what-you-may-call-'em over there is topping. What is it?"

"I don't know," said Jenny vaguely.

Miss Fairlie changed the subject with her usual uncompromising abruptness.

"I want to talk to John Waveney. Bring him over here and tell him who I am. What's he in such a rage about? Is he stopping here? Haven't you been treating him nicely?"

"Is he in a rage?"

"My good Jenny!"

"Well, I don't see why he should be. He's been here for the week-end. I thought—"

"What did you think?"

"I thought he was going directly after tea. He said he had to get back to town."

"Oh, then I can give him a lift."

Jenny was appalled. The last thing she desired was an intimacy between John and Aurora. To be sure, Aurora had promised; but all the promises in the world would never make her tactful. Before she had time to recover, John had joined them.

"I mustn't miss my train," he said; and instantly Aurora must needs push in and offer to drive him back to town.

"I was just telling Jenny to call you. I'm Aurora Fairlie. Jenny, where are your manners? You used to have quite nice ones. I don't mind introducing myself; but it's really your job, and I object on principle to doing other people's jobs for them. Well, John Waveney, I'm a cousin of Jenny's, and Jenny's a cousin of yours, so I don't propose to be very ceremonious. Is a lift back to town any good to you?"

John accepted the lift with alacrity. A little later, when Aurora was talking to Nicholas, he addressed Jenny in a quiet but unmistakably purposeful tone:

"There's something I want to say to you. Shall we walk to the end of the lawn?"

Jenny sprang up at once. Aurora's words had frightened her. If John were really in a rage, she had better see him alone and find out why he was angry. She had unlimited faith in her own ability to manage him, or any other young man.

"We'll get you some lilac to take back to town, Aurora," she called back over her shoulder as she went; and John frowned involuntarily. How quickly and smoothly she had found a reason for leaving the others! Something in the perfect ease of voice and manner jarred him sharply.

They came to a standstill by the largest lilac bush, and Jenny picked a spray.

"Well?" she said.

John was past pretence. He looked at her with a hard, angry look, and seemed entirely unaware of what a pretty picture she made, with the evening sun on her fair hair and her white dress, and the lilac in her hand.

"Look here, Jenny, I'd better tell you straight out. I saw Anne this afternoon."

"You saw Anne." She repeated his words as if she hardly understood them.

"Yes, I saw her. So it's no use your trying to put me off any more."

"How did you see her? How *could* you see her?" Jenny's voice was low and frightened.

"I saw her. That's all that matters."

"But you don't know her."

"I knew her at once. I want her address."

"Why didn't you ask her for it?" said Jenny with an angry lift of the head.

"There wasn't time. She—the Austins were coming up the drive—she didn't want them to see her. I went on with them. They were playing the fool—you saw them. When I got back, she was gone—her taxi was gone. I missed her at the station by about half a minute. Her address, please, Jenny."

Jenny shook her head.

"Is she with Miss Fairlie? Or was that a lie?"

"Oh!" said Jenny. Her brown eyes were furious.

"I want the truth, and I'm going to get it. I want Anne's address."

Jenny's manner changed.

"I thought we were friends. You're being—"

"Outrageous. Yes, I know. But I've got to have that address, Jenny."

Jenny broke a branch of lilac before she answered. If she gave him the address, he would go, and she would have time to ring Anne up and warn her that he was coming. Anne wouldn't want to see him. She could easily change her hotel. Or, better still, she could go to the rooms that Nanna had suggested. Rooms would be quieter than an hotel; there was always the risk of meeting someone one knew. She broke two more sprays, and then she said:

"She's at Haydon's Hotel, Bayswater."

"With Miss Fairlie?"

"Yes, Aurora's there too."

"Why didn't they come down together?"

"Anne wanted to see me."

Anne wanted to see Jenny. And Jenny had sent her away looking like that!

"What did you say to her? What did you do to her?" said John in a low, rough voice. "She looked—"

Jenny gave a little cry that was almost a sob.

"I can't explain—Anne wouldn't like me to explain. It's—it's breaking my heart!"

John displayed a good deal of indifference to Jenny Marr's breaking heart.

Later on, when he was driving up to town with Miss Aurora Fairlie, he received some outspoken advice:

"My dear boy, it's not the slightest use your asking me any questions about Anne Waveney, because I can't answer them. I'm not going to tell lies to please Jenny or anyone else. I'm uncommon bad at them for one thing, and I don't approve of them for another. But I *can* hold my tongue about Anne and her affairs, and I advise you to do the same. Least said, soonest mended."

Jenny's forebodings were certainly being realized. John said nothing, and Miss Fairlie continued to give him advice:

"You leave Anne alone. She won't thank you for butting in, and that's a fact."

"I shall stop butting in," said John deliberately, "when Anne tells me to stop butting in."

Aurora Fairlie was one of the most inquisitive women alive. A desire to probe the situation to the bottom very easily got the better of her discretion.

"I thought you didn't know Anne. Why, you've never even seen her."

"Once." His tone was very dry. "She wasn't a family secret then, but just an awfully nice kid."

"Good Lord!" said Aurora. "Are you in love with her?"

John boiled over. "What a rotten thing to ask! I tell you she was a kid. There isn't a soul in the family that seems to care a damn where she is, or what she's doing, or whether she's got tuppence to live on. All they care about is some rotten convention and what people will say."

"I see," said Aurora. She took her left hand off the wheel and clapped him on the shoulder. "All right, go ahead. I don't care a brass boddle myself; but it's only fair to warn you that you're looking for trouble. The family'll curse you. Jenny and Nicholas'll hate you like the worst sort of poison. And Anne'll probably say 'Thank you for nothing.' As I said, *I* don't care."

John's face of stiff rage relaxed in a sudden grin.

"No more do I," said he.

In her heart of hearts Aurora approved him. Obstinacy appealed to her, and she read obstinacy written large all over John Maurice Waveney. She wondered how much of his search for Anne was dictated by just that obstinate determination to be neither said nor bid.

They arrived at Haydon's Hotel, only to be told that Miss Waveney had left directly after lunch. Pressed by Aurora, the girl at the desk managed to remember Anne's arrival.

"Yes, Miss Fairlie, it was this morning. No, Miss Fairlie, she particularly said she wanted a room for the day. I quite understood she wasn't staying." Aurora was turning away, when the girl bent forward. "There was a telephone message for her just now—a country call."

John's mind leapt to Jenny; Jenny telephoning from Waterdene; Jenny telling Anne he was coming—warning Anne to keep out of his way.

"Thank you. Just let me know if she comes in." Aurora turned to John. "Must have been Jenny calling up. I don't suppose anyone else knew Anne was here. I expect she'll blow in presently."

"She won't."

"What makes you say that?"

John shook his head.

"She won't come here again," he said.

Chapter Fourteen

As soon as Miss Fairlie had left Waterdene, Jenny made her way to the library, rang up the exchange, and asked to be put on to Haydon's Hotel. As she waited for the call to come through, she moved restlessly to and fro about the room. It was still quite light out of doors; but the library windows looked to the east, and all the corners of the room were full of soft dusk shadows; the book-lined walls helped to darken it.

Jenny switched on the green-shaded lamp which stood on Nicholas Marr's writing-table beside the telephone. She stayed there fidgeting with the inkstand, the pens, the piled-up papers. Nicholas was the neatest of men. Even as she moved the sticks of red and blue sealing-wax, Jenny knew how much it would vex Nicko to find them anywhere but in their own allotted place.

She turned her back on the table and crossed to where the windows stood open to the light, soft breeze. She left them open, but drew the heavy brown curtains close. It was as she was coming back from the windows that Nicholas Marr came in with a "Hullo, Jen! I wondered where on earth you'd got to."

"Ssh!" said Jenny. "Nicko, shut the door. I'm telephoning to Anne."

"What!" His astonishment was unmistakable.

"Yes. Nicko, do shut it. I haven't seen you for a minute. I thought Aurora would never go. She's perfectly awful, the way she says she can't stay, and won't stay, and nothing will induce her to stay; and then she just sticks and sticks and sticks, and doesn't go and doesn't go and doesn't go, until you're ready to scream. I very nearly *did* tonight."

"*What's* this about Anne?" Nicholas Marr's thin dark face fell into frowning lines.

"Oh, Nicko!" said Jenny. She came and leaned against his arm. "Nicko, it was dreadful! She came here."

"Who came here?" said Nicholas sharply.

"Anne did."

"When?"

"This afternoon. We'd just got back from Grey-stones, when the telephone bell rang. And, fortunately, I heard it and went myself. And it was a telegram from Anne to say she was arriving at three-thirteen. Wasn't it awful?"

"She didn't *come*!"

"She did. I simply rushed, and I just caught her in the drive and made the taxi wait outside whilst I dragged her off into the Holly Room. No one ever comes there—hateful place!"

"Well? What did she want? Good heavens, Jenny! What possessed her to come here? It's indecent!"

"Don't!" said Jenny. "Don't! Nicko, please, *please* don't!"

He shook off her hand impatiently.

"It's unforgivable! She should have gone to Carruthers as she was told. Why didn't she?"

"He's been ill—he's away."

"What nonsense! He's got a partner. Well, go on. What happened? How did you get rid of her?"

Jenny looked at him with wide, distressed eyes.

"Nicko, don't look like that! I said everything you told me to say. I said—" She choked and held his arm in a trembling clasp. "Oh, don't! Oh, Nicko, are you angry? I did say everything."

"I'm not angry *with* you—now, Jen, don't be a little fool—I'm angry for you. Don't you know the difference? I won't have Anne here, and the sooner she knows it the better. I won't have her here, and I won't have you bothered. She can write two or three times a year if she likes. If she attempts anything more—well, the money'll stop, and she can just see how she likes getting along without it." He gave a short laugh and flung an impatient arm about Jenny. "Look here, I forbid you to cry. There's nothing to cry about. I'll take good care she doesn't bother you. Just tell me what you said."

Jenny struggled for composure. Nicholas hated real tears most dreadfully. He liked to tease her until her eyes were wet, and then kiss the long wet lashes; but real tears, the tears that came from an aching, frightened heart—these were another matter.

"I told her"—Jenny dropped her voice till she could keep it fairly steady—"I told her about the money. I said—she could have half—if she didn't come."

"Well? What did she say to that? Jen, you little idiot, don't shake so!"

"She didn't say anything."

"Did she understand?"

"I don't know—I really don't know. I was so dreadfully afraid she'd miss her train. I kept begging her to go. She told me she was at Haydon's Hotel, and I kept begging her to go back there, and I'd write, or come and see her. And at last she went. But—oh, Nicko!"

"What?"

"John saw her."

"John?"

"John Waveney."

"How d'you know?"

"He told me. He said he must have her address."

"You didn't give it!"

"I had to." Then, at his exclamation, "No, wait! It was really better than having a fuss. That's why I'm ringing up Anne now. She won't want to see him; and if I tell her he's coming, she can just go off quietly to those rooms Nanna told me about. You know—we thought how suitable they were."

The telephone bell rang. Jenny gave a great start, and then ran round the table and took up the receiver.

"Yes!" she said breathlessly. "Yes. Is that Haydon's Hotel? Is Miss Anne Waveney there? Can I speak to her?"

There was a pause. Jenny put her hand behind her, pulled up the writing chair, and sank down upon it. She felt quite suddenly as if she could not stand any longer. She wanted to hear Anne's voice— wanted it so much that the longing made her feel giddy. But what was she going to say to Anne, with Nicko listening?

Nicholas Marr sat on the edge of the table, his eyebrows drawn together in a black frown, his lips set hard and thin.

"What?" said Jenny suddenly. "Oh, she must be! Are you *sure*?" There was a pause. "And she didn't say where she was going? Are you quite sure she didn't say?... Oh! Thank you!"

She hung up the receiver and looked with bewildered eyes at Nicholas.

"Nicko, she's not there!"

"Dining out?" There was more than the suspicion of a sneer in the words.

"They say she didn't mean to stay—she hadn't engaged a room. They say she left directly after lunch. That would be to come down here." Her voice trailed away into a frightened whisper. "Nicko, she brought a suitcase—I saw it in the taxi."

Jenny had a sudden picture of Anne expecting a welcome. The picture made her shiver with pain.

"What infernal cheek!" said Nicholas. Then he came round to Jenny and patted her shoulder. "Look here, Jen, I won't have you upsetting yourself like this. Anne's made her bed, and she's got to lie on it. Haven't you got me and Tony?"

She looked at him without speaking for a moment. When Nicko's eyes softened to her like that, Jenny cared for nothing else in all the world. The picture of Anne grew dim. After a moment she looked down.

"Nicko"—she spoke in a low, hurried voice—"Nicko, if no one knows—after a time—don't you think—I mean couldn't we— couldn't we all be friends again? No, don't say anything, Nicko— please don't say anything yet. Don't you think if we waited—Oh, Nicko, she *is* my sister!"

"No!" said Nicholas Marr very harshly. "I won't have her in my house—I won't introduce her to my friends—I won't have her with you and Tony."

Jenny gave a little shiver. She had known it would be no good. Nicko never altered his mind about anything. She made one last effort; but she made it without any hope:

"Nicko, sometimes I've thought—John—John Waveney—he takes such an—*extraordinary* interest in her—if they met—if he—"

Nicholas stared in incredulous disgust.

"What are you thinking of?"

Jenny got up. It wasn't any good. There was nothing she could do for Anne.

Chapter Fifteen

ANNE WAVENEY HAD only just caught her train. She stumbled into a crowded third-class carriage and sat down on the edge of the seat next to a billowy woman in a black coat and skirt and a bright pink jumper, very low in the neck. On her other side there was a thin little girl who tried to make room for her. The billowy woman did not try at all.

Anne sat up very straight and did not really notice them. To a sense of shock and agony there had succeeded the sort of blank which is like a fog. In this fog impressions came and went, half realized, featureless, and dull. The train stopped at every station. Sometimes people got out, and sometimes people got in. The carriage was rather hot. The baby in the corner cried fretfully. A strong smell of bananas and peppermints hung on the air.

Anne sat quite still on the very edge of the seat with her suitcase pressing against her knees. She was actually on the verge of sleep when the train ran into the terminus. As she stepped out on to the platform, it seemed to tilt beneath her feet, and a porter put his hand under her elbow and said, "Steady, miss." Anne thanked him, and her giddiness passed.

She walked towards the barrier, and set the suitcase down whilst she looked in her purse for her ticket. It was when she was standing there with the open purse in her hand that the fog suddenly lifted. She was very tired, very bruised, very cold at the heart; but the fog was gone. She looked into her purse for a moment, and then she presented her ticket, passed through the barrier, and made her way to the waiting-room.

She walked easily and without hurry, and when she reached the waiting-room she put down her suitcase and leaned back in the corner of a brown leather-covered settee. Then she took out her purse again.

There was exactly one shilling left in it.

Anne looked at the shilling. It was all she had. It was tea, and supper, and bed, and bath, and breakfast. Twelve pence— one shilling.

"What a perfect, absolute fool I've been!" said Anne to Anne. The hotel, the hairdresser, the taxi, underwent a startling metamorphosis. From being ordinary everyday items of expenditure, they became with dreadful suddenness Extravagance—sheer flaunting Extravagance and Vice.

Strangely enough, it was as she looked at the shilling that Anne's courage rose. Here was something to meet, something that challenged every scrap of pluck she possessed, something that drew a blank cheque on resource and ingenuity, *something to think about that wasn't Jenny.*

Leaning back there with her eyes shut, she began to think clearly and vigorously. She had been offered help to get a job. Anne winced away from the recollection of her own answer: "Thank you very much, but I have friends to go to." That hurt too much. The measure of her confidence then was the measure of how much it hurt to remember that confidence now.

"Don't be such a fool!" she told herself. "No, you *are* a fool, and you've got to stop it—you've got to stop it at once. It's your own fault you got hurt. Get hold of that—it's your own fault. You're always like that, and it always gets you into trouble. The *idea* of rushing off like that—taking Jenny by surprise! It was absolutely idiotic—*idiotic!*"

The conviction that it was she who was to blame had an astonishingly healing effect. She had frightened Jenny—descended on her without warning, when she had a house-party too. It was really unforgivable. Resolutely, Anne began to blot out of her memory what Jenny had said and how Jenny had looked. Resolutely, she blamed herself, and no one but herself, for the pain at her heart: "You asked for it—you just asked for it. Don't sit there pitying yourself. You've got to go somewhere—you've got to get a job." For so irrational a thing is human nature that not all Anne's resolution would bring her to the point of taking the one thing Jenny had offered her—money. She would have taken love, and shelter, and a home, and with them the half of Jenny's inheritance; and she would never have had a thought of obligation. But neither now, nor at any other time, could she bring herself to take the money without the love. She must forget, deeply and utterly. For Jenny's sake she must forget that Jenny had ever offered her her lost share of their inheritance—upon terms. She pushed the thought away with all her might.

"Learn and labour truly to get my own living." She and Jenny had said their catechism together. Jenny always would say, "*Earn* and labour."

"Oh, *do* stop thinking of Jenny! You've got to get a job. *You've got—to—get—a—job.*" She opened her purse again and looked at the shilling. "That's all you've got till you get a job. *Now* will you stop thinking about Jenny? Where are you going to sleep? That's what you ought to be thinking about—supper, bed, breakfast—and a job."

She could get a glass of hot milk for twopence, and a penny bun. No, she couldn't afford the bun. She couldn't afford the milk either for the matter of that. On the other hand, if they would let her stay here all night, she could afford bread and milk for supper and bread and milk for breakfast.

She left her suitcase where it was, and went and asked the attendant how long the waiting-room remained open. She came back to her place feeling rather shaky; the idea of being turned out into dark streets at one a.m. really frightened her. The woman had looked at her too with a nasty sideways look—a prying, accusing look, which became more pronounced when Anne had forced herself to ask whether she knew of any respectable place where she could get a bed for the night.

She sat down again. It was now half-past seven—fifteen hours at least before she could take the first step towards getting a job. It was still light, even in the gloomy waiting-room; but in the open it would not be dark, not really dark, much before half-past ten.

Anne made up her mind. She couldn't face being turned out in the middle of the night. Outer darkness—*horrid!* She would stay here till half-past ten, and then she would have some milk—and a bun if she was frightfully hungry. And then she would walk across the bridge and get down to the Embankment. There were places there where you could sit. She had read in books of people spending the night on the Embankment, and it wouldn't be so dreadful if she got there before it was quite dark. Meanwhile she was going to sleep.

Having made her decision, she felt all at once incapable of anything more. She had stopped feeling sad, or shocked, or frightened, or cold, or hungry; her mind was just an empty place like a stage when the theatre is shut and the players gone. She put her head against the padded leather back of the waiting-room bench and passed into a deep and dreamless sleep.

Jenny Marr lay awake that night, and pitied herself a good deal for doing so. She tried counting sheep, and she tried saying the multiplication table; but neither of these exercises produced even a slight drowsiness. There was a little electric lamp on the table by the broad, low bed, but she did not dare to turn it on, lest she should wake Nicholas. Nicholas would know why she couldn't sleep; he would know that it was because of Anne; and Jenny simply didn't feel as if she *could* talk to Nicko any more about Anne.

She edged herself up on her pillows and looked across the room to the windows, which were open and uncurtained. There was moonlight outside, a level wash of moonlight, flooding the still air. It was so still that Jenny could hear the faint flowing sound of the river. Inside the room there was a sort of clear dusk, which showed shape and outline, light and shade, but no colour. The delphinium-blue carpet, the silver rail at the bed-foot, the blue and rose and lilac pattern in the chintz curtains, were all one deep, even grey.

Jenny looked into the dusk, and pleased herself by calling up the vanished colours. It was such a pretty room, with its wide windows looking out over the green spaces where the river ran. Jenny had chosen all the furniture herself. She had chosen some of it with Anne. She remembered the day they found just the one chintz in all the world—a chintz to dream of, with lovelier flowers than real ones, in colours too beautiful to be true.

Something stabbed Jenny sharply. She had said that to Anne, "Oh, Anne, it's too good to be true!" And Anne had said, "How silly! Why on earth should *anything* be too good to be true?"

Jenny pulled the fine linen sheet higher; her crêpe-de-chine nightdress was thin; there was a faint chill upon the moonlight. She snuggled down a little. Her thoughts slipped back again to Anne. Why on earth hadn't she gone back to Haydon's Hotel? Perhaps she had gone back. It would be so awkward not to know where she was—awkward and tiresome; because, of course, someone must see her and arrange about the money. They *must* know where she was. Nicko said she would write—"You'll hear from her fast enough." Of course, she'd be bound to write. But suppose she didn't—"Suppose she never writes—suppose we never know!"

A frightful sense of isolation came upon Jenny. Everyone asleep; everything so still; the faint, faint sound of distant running water. Jenny was alone, as one is sometimes alone in a dream. She was alone, and she was afraid—dreadfully, shiveringly afraid. She said, "Anne, where are you? Anne! Oh, Anne!"

And Anne was leaning on the dark parapet of the Embankment. She was cold, she was hungry, and she was very tired; but she watched the moonlight on the water with eyes that were quiet and serene.

Chapter Sixteen

ON THE FOLLOWING MORNING John dug his car out of the garage where he had left it over the week-end to have a radiator leak repaired, and proceeded to Waterdene at a fancy speed. He was, as a matter of fact, in the state of temper which demands an outlet. He wanted to break the law, to defy policemen, and to quarrel with Nicholas Marr—more especially he wanted to quarrel with Nicholas Marr. Since Anne had now completely disappeared, it was quite obvious that he had to quarrel with someone.

He found Nicholas in the library and opened fire at once:

"Look here, Marr, I've had about enough of this! Do you know where Anne Waveney is, or do you not?"

"Why do you want to know?"

"Not your business why I want to know. I do want to know; and what's more, I mean to know."

Nicholas appeared to withdraw a little. His manner remained pleasant, but it was a sort of hundred-yards-away pleasantness; it gave John the feeling that he was regarded as a rough and mannerless backwoodsman.

"All right," said Nicholas. "I don't know."

"You don't?"

"You asked me if I knew where she was. Well, I don't know. Anything else?"

John's anger deepened. It ceased to be the sort of anger which would find satisfaction in violence, and became colder, deeper, and more controlled.

"Does anyone know where she is?"

"Not that I know of. She—as a matter of fact, she came down here yesterday."

"I know she did."

"She came down here, and she forced an interview with Jenny. She upset Jenny very much. To be quite candid, I've forbidden her the house. I won't have her here. And I won't have Jenny upset.

"Now we're getting down to it," said John. "You can't say a thing like that and leave it there. You'll have to explain."

"Better not." Nicholas paused. "I said more than I meant to. Every family has its quarrels and its black sheep. They're really best left alone."

"By outsiders—that's what you're getting at, isn't it? I'm to mind my own business. Now, this is what I've got to say—I consider that this is my business, and I don't admit that I'm an outsider. If Anne had a father or a brother, it would be his business all right. Well, she hasn't—but she's got me. I'm a damned poor substitute, but I regard myself as a substitute. That's what I want you to tumble to—I'm the nearest male relation she's got—I'm in Tom Waveney's place. I didn't know Courtney, the elder one, but I knew Tom— served in his company when I joined up. He was a thundering good chap. If he were here, I shouldn't have to butt in. But he isn't here, and the way I look at it, I've got to do what he'd do."

"You're the head of the family, in fact," said Nicholas with the faintest possible inflection of sarcasm.

"Yes, I am. I didn't want to be; but as it happens, I am. Now will you explain?"

"You'd better let it alone, John. You can take it from me that you won't do any good—"

"I won't take it from anyone. You've got to explain."

Nicholas looked at him with curiosity. Was it just obstinacy that made him so insistent?

"Well," he said, "I'll explain. But you won't much like the explanation. As I said, every family's got its black sheep. One doesn't exactly enjoy talking about them. Anne's a bad lot—a rotten bad lot. I dare say you've guessed as much."

John did not know whether he spoke or not. He was one raging protest. He did not know whether he spoke, or whether the sound that broke from his lips was wholly inarticulate."

"You must have guessed there was something."

"Go on," said John. His lips felt stiff.

"It's a damned unpleasant thing to have to say," said Nicholas, frowning; there was a note of sharp distaste in his voice. "It's damned unpleasant. But there's no getting away from it. Anne's a wrong 'un right through—a thief, if you want to know."

The word was like a blow. It wasn't what he had expected. He did not know quite what he had expected—but not this, certainly not this. A thief! The word left a cold, sick feeling. He had not been looking at Nicholas; but he looked at him now, and found something of his own repugnance in the dark, withdrawn look which met his own, only to elude it.

"Inconceivable, isn't it?" said Nicholas. "You can't believe it any more than any of us could believe it—at first. You'd better hear the whole thing whilst we're at it. It's not the sort of thing one wants to talk about very often."

"No."

"It happened just before Jenny and I were married. It nearly killed Jenny. It did kill Sir Anthony."

"What happened?"

"Jenny was in town staying with her godmother, Mrs. Courtney. At the end of her visit Anne came up for a couple of days. Mrs. Courtney couldn't put her up—as a matter of fact, she never cottoned much to Anne. She's a dashed clever woman—she never liked Anne."

"Well?"

"Anne stayed at an hotel with her old nurse, Mrs. Jones. She and Jenny were to meet and go down to Waveney together. Well, Jenny started, picked Anne up, and took her off for a final fitting of her bridesmaid's dress, whilst the nurse took the luggage to the station. They were driving along, when Anne suddenly called out. Jenny couldn't make out what was the matter. Anne said she must stop the taxi and let her get out. She said, 'Go on down to Waveney. I'll come by the next train. And if I can't come, I'll write.' She got out of the taxi and legged it. Jenny was most awfully frightened—she didn't know what had happened, and she didn't know what to do. In the end she went to the station and met Mrs. Jones, and they went down to Waveney together. Anne didn't come by the next train, or by any other train. Jenny didn't dare tell her father. She said Anne was staying with friends. Two days afterwards there was a letter from Anne, addressed to Mrs. Jones at her married daughter's address in Clapham. Anne said she'd been arrested—for stealing."

"Stealing what?"

John found his mind extraordinarily clear. All the time Nicholas was talking he was picking out one detail here and another there, and filing these details—they must all be gone over very carefully later on. He said, "Stealing what?" and watched Nicholas with a hard, steady gaze.

"A string of pearls. You may have noticed that Jenny doesn't wear pearls. That's why. Anne went into a shop belonging to a little Jew man called Levinski, and she took a string of pearls worth about eight hundred pounds and left a sham lot in their place. This was in the morning, and she got clear away. When she was driving with Jenny, they passed the shop, and Levinski saw her. He'd come out to have a look at his window. He jumped into a taxi just as he was and gave chase. She'd just enough decency not to drag Jenny into the business—or she may have thought she'd more chance of getting away on foot. Anyhow, Levinski came up with her and gave her in charge. The pearls were in her bag. She gave her name as Annie Jones, thank the Lord."

"Go on," said John.

Nicholas raised his eyebrows.

"Jenny tried to keep the whole thing from her father. He was pretty shaky—never really held his head up after the sons were killed. Mrs. Jones helped. They told the old man that Anne was ill—in a nursing home in town—not allowed to see anyone. Poor Jen! It must have been the most awful strain. They used to pretend to telephone for news every day. It was pretty ghastly. We were married in the middle of it all. Jenny told me about it when we'd been married a week, and the next thing was a wire from Mrs. Jones, calling us back. Sir Anthony'd found out, and it just smashed him. It nearly smashed Jenny too. It's a pleasant bit of family history, isn't it?"

John's gaze did not shift.

"Damnable!" he said. "Go on."

"That's about the end. She pleaded guilty, and she got a year. She's just out, and she had the audacity to come down here and force herself on Jenny."

There was a pause.

"Who knows?" said John.

"Jenny and I, the nurse, Carruthers, and yourself."

"And Miss Fairlie?"

"Jenny told her yesterday—she had to, because when people press her too hard, she's been telling them that Anne was abroad with Aurora."

"I see." John looked away.

There was a long pause. Then, as Nicholas began to find the silence awkward, John jerked his head up and shot a question at him:

"Sir Anthony altered his will before he died?"

"Yes—fortunately; it gives us the whip hand. Apparently Anne expected to be received as if nothing had happened. I'm prepared to let Jenny go halves with her, provided she takes herself out of England and stays there for good."

Another silence. This time John didn't look away; instead, he studied Nicholas Marr's face critically—a hint of sarcasm in the eyes; a hint of fastidious disgust; something set and implacable about the line of mouth and chin.

"Have you made this offer?" he asked.

"Jenny made it yesterday."

John put that away with other things.

And what did she say?"

Nicholas shrugged his shoulders.

"She went off to catch her train. She didn't give any answer, and Jenny was naturally too much upset to press for one."

Just for an instant John felt again the cold agony of Anne's grip, and saw again her blind and anguished eyes. Then he said:

"You think she didn't answer. I think you're wrong." His tone was rather abstracted.

"What on earth—"

"You say Jenny offered her money to stay away. You say she didn't answer. I think she did. She never went back to the hotel. Do you know where she is now?"

"Not at the moment. But I don't flatter myself we're quit of her." John nodded.

"You don't know where she is; and you won't know where she is—that's what I think. I think you've had your answer—I think you had it when she didn't go back to the hotel."

"Oh, you think that. I wish I did!"

John's jaw set rather grim.

"I want to know how much money she's got."

"I haven't the least idea."

"She hasn't any of her own?"

"No."

"But she'd have had some on her, I suppose?"

"I suppose so." Nicholas did not seem to be greatly interested.

"The few shillings a girl would have in her purse—perhaps a pound or two. And she'd been to an hotel, and she'd paid her way down here, and had a taxi and kept it waiting. There wouldn't have been very much left when she'd taken her ticket back to town." John got up. "Thanks. I'll be getting along."

"Where on earth are you going?" said Nicholas staring.

John looked back over his shoulder as he moved towards the door.

"I'm going to find Anne," he said.

Chapter Seventeen

ANNE WAS IN the middle of an interview with Miss Pettigrew. Miss Pettigrew sat at a table on which there was a typewriter, a cyclostyle, a telephone, and a large ledger. She had greyish-brown hair, done in the fashion of the later nineties, and a round and rosy face, out of which there looked two kind but searching eyes. The eyes were of the brightest possible shade of blue.

"You came out yesterday?" Her voice was exceedingly clear and brisk.

"Yes."

"Now, I wish you'd just looked in. It was a pity you didn't—yes, really a pity. Why didn't you?"

"I was going to friends."

"Yes?"

Anne said nothing. Miss Pettigrew allowed about thirty seconds to pass; then she said:

"Well, the trouble is that we've nothing for you to-day. Are you staying with your friends?"

"No."

The very bright blue eyes were not blind to Anne's change of colour. A brisk voice inquired:

"And where did you sleep last night?"

Anne looked up with a hint of humour.

"I didn't sleep very much. I sat on the Embankment."

"No money?" asked Miss Pettigrew.

"Eightpence," said Anne with a little smile.

"They didn't send you out with only eightpence?"

"Oh no. I thought I had plenty—and I'm afraid I squandered it."

Miss Pettigrew gave a sharp little nod. "Thought her friends were going to take her in, and then found they wouldn't," was her summing up of the situation.

"Well, that won't do," was what she said aloud. "I'll try and get you in somewhere for to-night. It's not so difficult at this time of year. It's the winter that's the bother. Now, let me see—what can you do?"

"I don't mind what I do—to start with."

"Any experience?"

"I'm afraid not."

The telephone bell rang, and Miss Pettigrew picked up the receiver.

"Yes—that's right. Yes, Miss Pettigrew speaking. What name did you say? Oh, good morning."

A buzzing murmur began, and went on for some time, Miss Pettigrew punctuating it with such remarks as "I see," "Yes, yes," and "Well, I'm very sorry." Presently she threw a quick glance at Anne and said, speaking into the telephone:

"If you will wait for a few moments, I'll ring you." Whereupon she hung up the receiver. "That," she said, "was Mrs. Yates. She always comes to us. She wants a house-parlourmaid."

Anne looked hopeful.

"I could do that," she said.

"Without experience?" said Miss Pettigrew, and saw Anne's colour rise.

"Yes, I'm sure I could."

"I'll send you to see her. She's desperate for someone, because the last girl I sent her walked out yesterday without notice. She's very much annoyed—naturally. It's not an easy place." The last sentence was as dry as you please.

Again a spark of humour kindled in Anne's eyes.

"How long do they usually stay?" she asked.

Miss Pettigrew's own sense of humour was a quality which she was at some pains to keep under sound control. Her rosy face was quite grave as she replied:

"From three days to three months."

"Why?" asked Anne.

"That, I think, you'll have to discover for yourself. They don't complain—"

"But they don't stay." Anne paused. "I can't very well afford to pick and choose," was her conclusion.

Miss Pettigrew nodded approval.

"That's sensible. I don't give advice; but if I did—"

Anne gave the encouraging smile which belonged to Anne Belinda Waveney, and not to Annie Jones. It startled Miss Pettigrew a little.

"I should be very grateful for the advice."

"Well, it doesn't amount to much. I don't advise, as I said; but if I did, I should say, 'Just cultivate being a little deaf.' People who talk a lot don't always mean everything they say. Don't be too thin-skinned, and remember that six months' good character will make it a lot easier for me to get you something better."

Anne said "Thank you" out of a really grateful heart.

Chapter Eighteen

JOHN DROVE HIS CAR slowly back to town. He drove slowly because he wanted to think. He wanted to stand away from his interview with Nicholas and get it in focus. At present it was so much out of focus as to appear monstrous. The one horrible word "thief" stood out like a deformity thrust right into the lens of the camera; he could see nothing clearly for it, and whenever he looked at it he felt the same old sickness. "Thief"; "prison"—words like these had no reasonable connection with oneself, with one's family, with the women of one's family. That they should be brought into relation with them was monstrous.

He drove in clear, pale sunlight between hedges where the hawthorn blossom hung like a heavy fall of snow. The sky overhead was the pale, pure blue that speaks of clean air and a freshening breeze. There were clouds coming up out of the north-east—clouds like blown feathers, as white as the thorn blossom.

When he had run ten miles, John had himself in hand. He went over all that Nicholas had said to him, and all that he had said to Nicholas. Then, when he had fixed the detail firmly in his memory, he did what he had set out to do—he stood away and looked at the interview as a whole. The thing that struck him at the end was the thing that had struck him at the beginning—not Anne's part, but Jenny's—the amazing number of lies which Jenny had told, and the apparent ease with which she had told them.

Right away at the beginning Anne gets out of the taxi, and doesn't turn up in time for the train. Jenny doesn't wait for her. Jenny and Mrs. Jones go by the train which Anne has missed. And Jenny tells her father that Anne is staying with friends in town. Why? Why on earth didn't she just say that Anne had missed the train? If she started to tell lies like that on Anne's behalf, it meant that she knew jolly well that Anne wasn't coming back, and that she'd got to be accounted for. After that floods of lies—and she must have told them well, or someone would have found out. Nobody did find out until Jenny went away on her honeymoon and left the lying to Mrs. Jones. Mrs. Jones was obviously nothing like such a good liar as Jenny, and Sir Anthony found out.

Jenny told Nicholas about Anne a week after their wedding. That was one of the things which had hit John between the eyes. Jenny told Nicholas when they'd been married a week. That meant she'd been feeding Nicholas with lies just the same as she'd been feeding everyone else. She'd been telling him about the nursing home, and Anne not being allowed to see anyone, and the daily bulletin—"Darling Anne's better to-day. Isn't it lovely?" or, "Oh, Nicko, Anne's not so well." She'd been telling him this—this bunkum—and wailing because Anne couldn't be her bridesmaid. And then, when they'd been married a week, she had the nerve to tell him she'd been making a fool of him along with the rest of the general public.

John gave a short angry laugh. He wondered how Nicholas Marr had taken it. And then, quite suddenly, he realized that Nicholas had never looked at the thing at all from this particular angle. Nicholas Marr from his point of view could see only Anne and her impossible offence against her family and against society. Jenny fell into her place as one of those whom Anne had wronged. "Why, he wouldn't even notice that she'd been lying—he didn't notice when he was telling me."

John, on the other hand, saw Anne and Jenny, and Jenny's story about Anne as one sees things in a fog. The fog was a fog of lies. The lies were Jenny's lies, and they plunged the whole story and the whole situation into obscurity. Amongst so many lies, why should anything be true? Why, for instance, should Jenny's account of what happened before Anne got out of the taxi be any truer than the story Jenny told to Sir Anthony to account for Anne's non-arrival? *Had* Anne written to Mrs. Jones, and if so, what did she really say?

John thought that he would go and see Mrs. Jones. He took the address which Delia had given him from his pocket-book and refreshed his memory. Mrs. Jones was living with a married daughter at 21, Edwin Road, Clapham; and to Edwin Road, Clapham, he accordingly took his way.

Hedges of flowering thorn are pleasanter to drive between than rows of yellow brick houses all exactly alike. Dirt soon mitigates the offence of the yellow brick, and one house varies from another in possessing, or lacking, an aspidistra; but the general effect is one of a yellowish-grey monotony. Edwin Road may, or may not, have been named in compliment to a great architect. It is quite certain that he can have been very little flattered.

John found number twenty-one, and knocked on a door whose blistered paint bore witness that this was the sunny side of the street. The window on his left had Nottingham lace curtains, as clean as it is humanly possible for Nottingham lace curtains to be in Clapham. The curtains were drawn across the window, and between them stood an aspidistra in a bright pink china pot. Between the pink china pot and the tightly closed glass of the window was a long, rather debilitated strip of cardboard upon which the word "Apartments" had been printed by hand.

The door opened and disclosed a plump, pasty-faced woman in a bright blue overall. John inquired for Mrs. Jones, and was ushered into the parlour, where white shavings blocked the fireplace and a funereal black marble clock ticked heavily at the aspidistra.

The married daughter's pride in the gentility of this room was evident. She threw a complacent glance at the two armchairs upholstered in crimson plush, which had figured in an auction ten years ago as "Gent's, plush, easy," and "Lady's ditto." Her eyes also dwelt fondly on the three-legged table—"real mahogany"— upon which there reposed in state a large picture Bible, a bound copy of *Good Words*, and two photograph albums. Then she turned her head.

"What name shall I say?"

"Sir John Waveney."

Twenty years before, Mary Jones would have dropped him a curtsey. Mrs. Porter ducked her head and—almost—gave at the knees. "My! If I wasn't took aback!" she said afterwards over an excellent supper of tinned salmon and fresh cucumber. "'Im standing there and saying, 'Sir John Waveney,' and I'm sure no one 'ud 've took 'im for a baronet."

At the time she said nothing, only ducked her head and got awkwardly out of the room. John heard her, heavy-footed on the stairs, and was left with nothing to do but observe his surroundings.

There was a dark green paper on the walls. Mrs. Porter considered it a good wearing colour. There were striped pink and white antimacassars on the backs of the crimson armchairs. A lustre cup and saucer of a lovely bronze colour sat on the mantelpiece next to the horrible clock and was balanced on the other side by a peculiarly atrocious blue vase with cheap gilt handles.

John liked the cup and saucer, though he did not know that it was old and good. He was touching it when Mrs. Jones came in with a measured dignity of step. She was rosy, where her daughter was pallid, and she had the firmly buxom figure of a generation whose stays were really stays, and tightly laced at that. Over the stays she wore a black stuff dress, also heavily boned, and a high black stuff collar with buckram in it, and a little turned-over collar of Swiss embroidery. The collar was fastened by a large old-fashioned brooch with a border of plaited gold and a centre of plaited hair. She also wore a thick gold watch-chain and little gold earrings like buttons.

John turned with a friendly smile, and was fairly startled by her air of respectful hostility. She shook hands with him, and her hand was cold, plump, and limp. He didn't know quite what to say or where to begin, and found himself stumbling into some inanity about the weather—something to the effect that it was a fine day.

Mrs. Jones said, "Yes, sir."

"Lovely, driving up—not too hot, you know."

Mrs. Jones said, "No, sir." She had small grey eyes. Her grey hair was very neatly parted in the middle and plaited into a tight, flat bun at the back of her head. Not a single hair was out of place.

"I've just been staying with Lady Marr for the week-end."

Mrs. Jones said nothing, and after a desperate pause John plunged on:

"I expect you're wondering why I've come to see you. (Oh, Lord! That's not tactful!) I mean I wanted to see you awfully, because I want to have a talk with you."

Mrs. Jones said "Yes, sir" again.

Then, to John's relief, she offered him a chair and sat down herself. But when they were both seated there ensued a perfectly awful pause. Mrs. Jones did not seem to mind. She gazed politely and resentfully at the wall about six inches to John's left and she kept her hands folded upon her knee.

John broke the silence with a manful effort.

"I wanted to see you because I wanted to talk to you about my cousins—you nursed them all, didn't you?"

"I took Mr. Courtney from the month," said Mrs. Jones austerely.

"I never met Courtney. I wish I'd met him. I served under Tom."

Mrs. Jones pressed her lips together, then opened them to say, "Mr. Courtney was the handsomest young gentleman in the county, and Mr. Tom was that clever at his studies there wasn't no one to come near him." Her lips shut tight again; her little grey eyes dealt faithfully with any pretensions which this new Waveney might have to either looks or brains.

"Lord! What a refrigerator!" groaned John. But he went on:

"I said I wanted to talk to you about my cousins. I really want to talk about my Cousin Anne."

"Yes, sir." ("Never batted an eyelash!" was John's comment.)

"I want to see her very particularly."

"Yes, sir."

"And I thought perhaps you could give me her address. Can you?"

Mrs. Jones became a little more frigid; there was a note of definite hostility in her "No, sir."

"Mrs. Jones," said John, sitting forward, "I want to find my cousin very badly. Do you know where she is?"

"Miss Jenny—I should say her ladyship—would be the right person to tell you that."

"Would she? And supposing she doesn't know?"

"Her ladyship would be sure to know."

"She doesn't. (That ought to break the ice with a crash.) I don't mean just that she says she doesn't know. She *really* doesn't—this time."

Mrs. Jones gave no sign of anything having broken. She merely repeated her last words: "Her ladyship would be quite sure to know."

"She doesn't know. She's said she didn't know, when she really did; but this time she doesn't know."

"That's for her ladyship to say."

("That's the lie direct.") Then aloud, "You're not making it very easy to talk to you. Look here, I'd better tell you. I know the whole story. (I wonder if I do—and I wonder how much this old image knows.)"

Mrs. Jones didn't speak. She looked politely at the wall.

John sprang up.

"I tell you I know the whole story. Lady Marr's been telling everyone that her sister was in Spain recovering from an illness. I didn't believe the story, and this morning Sir Nicholas told me the truth. He told me that my cousin had been in prison for a year."

Mrs. Jones took a moment. Then she said:

"It's not for me to say one thing or the other." Her voice was quite steady, but the plump folded hands shook.

"Yes, it is. I say, do stop being like this! I've come here because I wanted you to help me. I can't do anything unless you come off this awful frozen-up stunt. After all, you nursed Anne, you looked after her when she was a jolly little kid; and it's not in reason that you shouldn't have some human feeling about her. I'll be bound to say the family doesn't seem to have any. They don't seem to care a damn where she is, or whether she's got any money, or what she's doing."

"Nobody," said Mrs. Jones with trembling dignity—"nobody can never cast it up at me that I didn't do my duty."

John struggled with this for a moment, and then decided to ignore it. At any rate, the ice was gone.

"I don't believe she's got any money. I don't see how she can have much, anyhow. She came out of prison yesterday, and she went to an hotel for the day, and in the afternoon she went down to see Jenny. And Jenny sent her away broken-hearted. I saw her. She looked as if Jenny had killed her. Then I missed her at the station. And she went off in the London train, and no one's seen her since. She didn't go back to the hotel. Jenny doesn't know where she is. She isn't lying this time—she really doesn't know. I thought there was just a chance she might have come to you. Did she?"

Mrs. Jones stopped looking at the wall. She looked at John and shook her head.

"Do you know where she is? Do you know anything?"

A very large, round tear rolled suddenly down Mrs. Jones's smooth red cheek.

"Are you telling me true?" she said. And then, with a little hard sob, "Lord ha' mercy, sir!"

"Of course I'm telling you the truth. Why should I tell you anything else? I only wish to goodness I could get the truth out of some of you for a change. I'm pretty well sick of lies—I can tell you that. First she's ill; and then she's abroad; and then she's mad; and now she's lost!" He gave a short angry laugh. "Lost, and, for all I know, without a penny; and, for all any of you care, starving."

Mrs. Jones was much impressed; she liked to see a man angry—real gentlemen were often angry. Sir Anthony had had a most notable temper. Her nursery reminiscences included horrific tales of battle between Mr. Courtney and Mr. Tom. John ceased suddenly to be an outsider. "Looks a proper Waveney, he does, when he's angry—and, Lord knows, I've seen enough of them angry to tell."

Having reached this point, she also reached the meaning of John's words, and at once suffered an access of distress and confusion.

"I'm sure no one could ever bring it up against me that I didn't do my duty by them all," she said. "And twins is day and night work, as everyone knows, and if one of them was quiet, the other 'ud begin, till it was more than flesh and blood could stand."

John made an impatient movement.

"I'm asking you if you know where Anne is. Do you?"

"Her ladyship—"

Mrs. Jones broke off at the look on John's face. "The very moral of Sir Anthony in one of his *worst*," she said to herself. And if she quaked, she also admired.

Do you know where she is?"

"No, sir, I don't."

"You're sure?"

"Gospel sure."

"Then no one knows." He did not shout as Sir Anthony would have shouted; but the passion was plain in his voice.

He went to the window in a couple of strides, pushed aside the lace curtains, and stood looking out into the dull, drab street, the smoky blue sky—just a dull strip of it was over the greenish slate of ugly roofs—and the smoky yellow brick of ugly houses. There were miles and miles and miles of streets like this—poorer, uglier streets; poorer, fouler, uglier streets than this; slum streets, congested with foul and ugly people, full of hideous sights and hideous sounds. Where did a penniless woman drift to in a great city like this? Where in all this city was Anne Belinda? He turned, his anger gone away, his heart sick and sinking.

Mrs. Jones was standing beside the table, leaning on it. Some of the rosy colour had left her face. John put a hand on her shoulder.

"Can you think of anyone she might go to?"

"No, sir, I can't. Her ladyship—"

"I tell you she sent her away—Anne went to her and she sent her away." His brow darkened and a heavy flush rose to it. "She sent her away. She offered her money to stay away."

His hand dropped heavily, and Mrs. Jones cried out:

"She wouldn't do that! Miss Jenny'd never do that!"

"I tell you she did. She offered to give her money if she'd go away and promise never to come back. She's gone away penniless. And Jenny needn't trouble about her coming back. I should think she'd die before she'd come—I should think she'd starve."

"No, no, sir—it wouldn't never come to that!"

"Why wouldn't it? You're all the same—you don't really care what happens to her. But it's unpleasant to think of anyone starving, so you don't think about it. It's quite simple and easy. You say, 'Oh no, it could never come to that;' and you just don't think about it."

Mrs. Jones began to weep.

"No one's never brought it up against me that I didn't do my duty," she said in a weak, confused voice." No one's never said it, nor no one's never thought it, nor had any call to—and I've been in the nursery since I was thirteen—and only a year married when Jones was taken, and me with Mary Ann six weeks old, and her ladyship expecting Mr. Tom—and glad and proud I was to go back to her and take the baby."

"Look here—" said John.

"Her ladyship never looked to a thing, she'd that confidence in me. And there's no one can ever say she thought different, or had any call to think different. Mr. Courtney, and Mr. Tom, and Miss Jenny, and Miss Anne—I took them all from the month. And I left my own child to strangers, and never grudged it. And there's no one can say I didn't love them all as well as if they'd been my own, and better—Mary Anne, she casts it up at me to this day that I loved them better."

John put up his hand and stopped her.

"There, that's enough. Sit down!"

Mrs. Jones drew a long, surprised breath. Then she sat down.

Chapter Nineteen

IF ANYONE HAD TOLD Mrs. Jones that within half an hour of entering her daughter's parlour she would be meekly taking orders from "that there Sir John" and gazing at him with a submission hitherto reserved for Sir Anthony, she would certainly not have believed him. Nevertheless when John said "Sit down!" she hastened to obey, and, having obeyed, sat looking at him in reverential awe.

John did not speak for a moment; he glowered. Then he said:

"That's enough about all that. I want you to go back to the time before Lady Marr was married. She went to town to stay with Mrs. Courtney, and you and Miss Anne came up for a couple of days. Is that so?"

Mrs. Jones nodded. Then she sniffed, and nodded again.

"Everything was so 'appy," she said. "Who'd ha' thought it?"

John had pulled his chair up to the table. He tapped impatiently upon it now.

"I want to hear just what happened."

"It was all so *'appy*. Oh, deary me! Who'd ha' thought the way things was going to turn?"

"Just tell me from the beginning and go right on You came up to town with Anne—"

"We came up on the Tuesday, and we went with Miss Jenny to see 'er wedding-dress tried on. Miss Jenny, she knew as I was dying to see it, and she fixed it so as I could come to the fitting. And there she was, looking as beautiful as a queen, and me and Miss Anne and the dressmaker—a foolish French piece with the shamelessest red lips as ever I saw in all my days—all with our breath fair taken away at how lovely she looked. The dress wasn't nothing to the lovely way she looked, though it was a very 'andsome dress and made beautiful."

John tapped again, and Mrs. Jones went on hurriedly:

"There we was, and Miss Jenny the loveliest thing I ever saw, and all of a sudden something come to me, and I said, 'Why, Miss Jenny, my dear, where's your pearls?' And Miss Jenny she colours up quick, and she says, 'I don't want any pearls on my wedding day, Nanna. Pearls are tears, you know, and we're all going to be much too happy to cry.' I looked round at Miss Anne, and I saw she looked anxious like. And it's come over me many times since that that was the first time that trouble and pearls came into my mind together— but, dear knows, there were tears enough before we'd done!"

John sat in a frowning silence for what seemed a long time. Curiously irrelevant this story of Jenny, and her wedding-dress, and her "pearls are tears"—irrelevant and haunting.

"What were these pearls of Jenny's?" he said at last.

"Sir Nicholas give them to her when they were engaged, and I don't know that I ever saw her leave them off before."

"She doesn't wear them now," said John slowly.

"No, sir, I've noticed she don't."

"Has she still got them to wear?" John did not know that he was going to say this until he heard himself saying it.

"Oh yes, sir, she's *got* them," said Mrs. Jones in rather a surprised voice. "Last time I was down there she'd her jewel-case open, and I took 'em out and let 'em slip through my fingers—they've a wonderful smooth feeling—and I said, 'Don't you never wear 'em, my dear?' And she said, ever so sad, 'Oh no, Nanna, I *can't*.'"

"Why?" John shot the word at her rather sharply.

"Because of Miss Anne. Oh, sir, you don't know how cruel she took it to heart, or you wouldn't ask. Night after night there'd be her pillow soaking wet, and in the morning she'd put rooge on her cheeks so as no one should know as she'd been crying the best part of the night."

"All right—go on. Tell me what happened next day."

"We was going home, back to Waveney, Miss Jenny and all, and Miss Jenny came to fetch Miss Anne to have her bridesmaid's dress fitted."

"Wait a moment," said John. "Jenny came to the hotel? How did she come?"

"She came in a taxi, and she ran in all of a hurry, and she said, 'Come on, Anne, I've got a taxi waiting.' And she kissed me and said, 'We'll meet you at the station, Nanna,' and she went off with Miss Anne. And many's the time since I've wished Miss Anne 'ad kissed me. But there, it was always Miss Jenny that had the loving ways."

Jenny's loving ways left John singularly cold.

"And then?" he said.

"I went to the station, and I waited there. And just on the tick of the time Miss Jenny runs up and pulls me into a carriage and bangs the door. I put my head out and called to the porter as I'd engaged—a nice, curly-headed young man, he was, and put me in mind of my brother Joseph's youngest—and I caught his eye and saw the luggage safe. Then I turned round, and there was Miss Jenny, all of a tremble. 'You shouldn't run so 'ard,' I said; and with that she began to cry like a broken-'earted thing. 'Where's Miss Anne?' I said, and she went on crying till she frightened me, so presently I took her by the shoulder pretty 'ard, and I said, 'Where's Miss Anne?' And she sort of come to herself and stopped crying."

"What did she tell you about Anne?"

"First of all she told me that Miss Anne had met a friend and was coming down later. But I hadn't had her in the nursery for nothing, and I knew well enough it wasn't true. So I kept my hand pretty 'ard on her, and I said, 'You'll tell me the truth, Miss Jenny, or you don't stir from this seat.' So then she told me."

"What did she tell you?"

"She told me Miss Anne was in a scrape, and she didn't know how bad it was. She cried dreadful. She said Miss Anne might come out of it clear. And she squeezed my arm till it was black and blue, and she said, 'Oh, Nanna, pray hard, *pray hard*, that she'll come out of it all right.'"

"Is that all she told you?"

"She told me Miss Anne 'ud come down by the next train if so be as she got away. I don't mind saying that frightened me, and when Miss Anne didn't come, I went on dreadful. And at last Miss Jenny told me that it was trouble with the police, and that I must help her to keep it from Sir Anthony, because it would kill him. And I did my best; but it come out in spite of me, and it killed him sure enough."

"How did Jenny know what the trouble was? She was driving with Anne, and Anne stopped the taxi and got out. How did Jenny know—" He stopped, and Mrs. Jones broke in:

"Miss Anne must ha' told her."

"There wasn't much time."

"Miss Anne saw the man that accused her, and he saw her, and she told Miss Jenny quick what she'd done, and slipped out, thinking as he'd follow the taxi. And that's what I've found it 'ard to get over, for if he'd followed after Miss Jenny and she'd got mixed up in it, it might ha' come to her marriage being broke off."

John moved impatiently.

"How could she have got mixed up in it? You say the man recognized Anne. Well, Anne was gone. If he followed Jenny, he'd only have thought he'd made a mistake." He spoke harshly; it enraged him to think of Anne's nurse bearing Anne a grudge, a senseless grudge like this.

An obstinate look came over Mrs. Jones's face.

"It might ha' come to the breaking off of Miss Jenny's marriage, if that there man had a-followed her and thought as she was Miss Anne."

"Rubbish! How could he have thought she was Anne?"

The obstinate look deepened.

"Anyone might ha' took one for the other, let alone a man with a heathenish name that had never seen neither of them before."

"Nonsense!" said John. "They're not a bit alike—and everything else apart, Jenny's hair is fair, and Anne's is dark."

"And how much 'air has anyone got to see these days? Flying flat in the face of Scripture, I call it. And you mayn't think as how they're alike, but they used to be took for one another constant. And that day I might ha' had to look twice myself, for they was dressed alike, which they'd always done till Miss Jenny got engaged."

"They were dressed alike?"

"They'd their new spring coats and skirts on, both of them—grey—and little black hats, more like caps than hats, the way they was being worn just then, and as like as two peas."

John pushed his chair back suddenly. He went over to the window and stood there. He looked out, but he saw nothing; his heart was racing, and his thoughts raced too. When he turned at last, it was to meet Mrs. Jones's eyes fixed upon him in a stare of respectful curiosity. She looked away at once in some confusion.

John asked her two questions, and took the answers away with him.

Chapter Twenty

FROM A PUBLIC telephone-box John called up Mr. Lewis Smith:

"Look here, I want a private detective—inquiry agent—you know the sort of thing."

Mr. Lewis Smith sounded rather surprised.

"What on earth for?"

"I want one."

The surprise turned to mild amusement.

"All right—have one. But why ask me? We don't keep 'em on tap."

"Don't be an ass! Can't you put me on to one?"

"Well—let me see—you might try Messing. Here's the address. But, I say, if you're still on the same tack, for the Lord's sake go easy."

John rang off. He was sick to death of warnings and discretion. He meant to find Anne Belinda, whatever happened or whoever stood in the way. As a preliminary, he found Mr. Messing, and didn't very much like the look of him.

Mr. Messing sat at a writing-table with everything very businesslike about him, and a clerk in the outer office. John did not like Mr. Messing's fingernails, or his tie, or his beady eyes, or his sharply pointed nose; he did not like the way he did his hair. He frowned as he said:

"I—er—I want to trace someone. That's the sort of thing you undertake, isn't it?"

Mr. Messing opened a most impressive ledger and discreetly covered all the entries with blotting paper.

"You'd be surprised," he said affably, "if I were to tell you some of the people we have traced. But that's the drawback to confidential work like ours—one can't talk about it, can't advertise oneself. Of course one's work gets known. Now"—he poised a ready pen—"you want to trace someone, you said?"

Mr. Messing had no accent; he had only the sort of voice which is so associated with an accent that there is something startling about its absence.

"I want to trace a girl called Annie Jones," said John rather gruffly. ("Beastly place! Perfectly revolting sort of fellow! Absolutely damnable to have him ferreting about after Anne. But must find her. Tell him as little as possible. How little can one tell him?")

"Annie Jones—" Mr. Messing poised his pen.

"Yes. She came out of Holloway yesterday."

"Have you been to the police?"

"No—certainly not. She came out yesterday, and she went to see some friends in the country, and got back to Waterloo at about half-past six—and her friends are anxious because they don't know where she is, and they're afraid she hasn't got much money."

"'M—the friends' address?"

"I can't give you that. It doesn't matter in the least. All that matters is to find out where she went when she got back to London."

"Has she any friends in London?"

"She hasn't communicated with them—they don't know anything. They're anxious."

"'M—description?"

Beastly—unutterably beastly to have to describe Anne Belinda to a fellow like this. All the same she'd got to be found.

"Dark hair, cut short." (He remembered her long, dark plaits with a curious pang.) "Pale face." (She couldn't go on being so dreadfully pale as she was when she held his arm and looked at him with blind blue eyes.)

"Face pale—"

"Eyes dark blue. Dark lashes." (They wouldn't go on being drenched with tears.)

"Dress?"

"A grey coat and skirt, and a sort of black cap that hid her hair."

"Any marks?"

The little heart-shaped mole sprang sharply into John's remembrance; but for the life of him he couldn't give it to Mr. Messing as a clue. He shook his head, and concluded the interview as quickly as possible.

Anne's height—he knew where she came to against his shoulder; but that was another of the things that one couldn't come out with. He made a rapid calculation, and offered Mr. Messing five foot five.

"Very average," said Mr. Messing. "Very average. Well, Mr.—I don't know that I caught your name."

"Robinson," said John.

"Well, Mr. Robinson, we'll put the inquiry in hand without delay—hospitals, mortuaries, the police, and all the different charitable places; hostels, refuges, and so forth; likewise the prisoners' aid and similar societies. We'll go right through them all, and I don't doubt but what we'll have news for you in next to no time. Address, please?"

John gave the solicitor's address, and departed to ring up Lewis Smith once more and tell him to send on by express messenger any communication for Mr. John Robinson. At his hotel he found a fat bundle of proofs waiting for him, and was glad to take refuge in work.

It was next day that he remembered with a shock that he had engaged himself to dine that evening with Mrs. Fossick-Yates—*the* Mrs. Fossick-Yates. "And she'll talk about women's wrongs, and little Fossick-Yates'll talk about albinism in toads, and—oh Lord! What a jolly evening we shall have!"

As a prelude to the jolly evening he spent a very busy day. At intervals he rang up Lewis Smith to know whether Messing had communicated, and on the last occasion was rebuffed in highly unprofessional terms.

The Fossick-Yates had a flat in one of the least accessible backwaters of London. John, having elected to go there by tube, found that he had to change twice, take a bus, change into another bus, and then walk half a mile.

There was no lift, and he mounted fifty-five steps in a mood sufficiently far removed from jollity. He had no sooner pressed the electric bell than the door flew open and Mr. Fossick-Yates, eager and hospitable, welcomed him in.

"My dear fellow—my dear Sir John—this is very nice of you— very nice indeed! Ah, yes. Now, you'll take off your coat and—Ah, yes, there's a peg here. I'll move my cap. Now, let me see—your hat—your hat and scarf—Ah, yes. Come along in."

He dropped the scarf which he had taken from John as he spoke, bent to retrieve it, and dropped the hat. It was John who finally hung them up, and was then ushered into the drawing-room and presented to Mrs. Fossick-Yates, a tall and very handsome woman, with hair arranged after a pre-war fashion and a well-cut, rather massive black satin dress, which displayed magnificent shoulders. She shook hands very graciously, and introduced John to "My friend, Miss Webster," a tall, drooping young woman with bobbed flaxen hair and very large blue eyes which dwelt upon Mrs. Fossick-Yates in a permanent ecstasy of admiration.

Miss Webster wore an inordinate amount of greenish gauze, which appeared to be wound round and round her after a semi-oriental fashion, and she fairly clattered with bead chains. There was a mother-of-pearl one from Palestine, and another of rough turquoise lumps threaded on gold wire from Kashmir; there was a short necklace of Indian amethyst, and a long chain of Indian cornelian. She also wore a very large brooch of bright blue butterfly wing set in hammered silver, and two large marquise rings in the same startling kingfisher shade of blue. She rattled when she walked.

They passed into the minute dining-room of the flat, to find soup waiting for them in little earthern pots. A lamp, with a dark red shade, hung down low over the polished mahogany table. Though it was still daylight outside, the thick maroon curtains had been drawn, leaving the greater part of the room to a sort of crimson twilight. The light of the lamp was concentrated on the table; it made the folded napkins look very white and the silver very brilliant.

Mrs. Fossick-Yates and Miss Webster faced each other across the narrower part of the oval table. The light fell full upon their hands and arms. It caught the red and blue and pearl of Miss Webster's chains and dazzled upon the large diamond sun which adorned the front of Mrs. Fossick-Yates' black satin dress; it left their faces in shadow. John and Mr. Fossick-Yates, with the length of the table between them, found even their plates in a state of semi-eclipse. John slid his forward into the light, and was inwardly amused to see that his host instantly followed his example.

Whilst they drank their soup Mrs. Fossick-Yates talked to John about criminal law amendment, a subject upon which she discovered him to be completely ignorant. She was just warming to her explanations of some recent measures when she was obliged to interrupt herself by treading on the electric bell-push as a signal to her parlour-maid that soup was now disposed of.

John heard the door open behind him, and was aware of a shadowy figure removing plates.

"Shamefully inadequate though these measures have been, they have, in some degree, served to call public attention to a subject which is culpably neglected by a majority—a disgracefully large majority—of those who have the vote."

"Yes, *indeed*," said Miss Webster, swaying forward into the light.

"The condition of ignorance—By the way, we are teetotallers. Barley-water is so wholesome. Annie, the barley-water to Sir John—so rich in vitamins! Frederick, the fish is in front of you; will you help it? As I was saying, the dense and culpable ignorance—"

John was left with the sound of many rolling words. He ate some remarkably fishy fish, and washed it down with a glutinous substance flavoured with lemon. He had never tasted barley-water before, and concluded that he had no quarrel with water, but preferred barley in soup.

Mrs. Fossick-Yates went on talking. She talked about the Coal Strike, and Communism, and the terrible state of Russia, and prison reform, and temperance legislation, and the wrongs of women; and Miss Webster clanked ecstatically; and whenever he possibly could, Mr. Fossick-Yates talked across the table about reptiles. In its lighter moments the conversation recurred to food values, and John learned without interest that apples were now considered useless, and that oranges and lemons were the acme of good living. He found himself disliking Mrs. Fossick-Yates more than he had ever disliked a human being before. Without thinking very much about it he had always considered himself progressive; but as Mrs. Fossick-Yates went on talking, he began to feel ferociously reactionary.

"Isn't she *wonderful*?" said Miss Webster in an undertone.

"When I was in Cornwall in eighty-nine," said Mr. Fossick-Yates hurriedly, "I came across some very curious—"

The diamond sun surged into the light as Mrs. Fossick-Yates leaned forward.

"I will send you a card for both meetings, and I am sure you will find them very stimulating and informative."

"Oh *yes*!" said Miss Webster.

"Some very curious, almost, if I may say so, legendary—nay, perhaps wholly legendary—"

"The chief speaker on the earlier date will be my friend, Jane Caradoc. You are, of course, familiar with her writings."

"Wonderful!" said Miss Webster. The cornelian chain slipped into the sauce to which she had just helped herself, and she retrieved it with some confusion.

"There were distinct traces," said Mr. Fossick-Yates, bringing his bald head well into the circle of light, "distinct traces of—er—er—a belief in the survival up to a fairly recent date of the larger reptilian forms—"

"Barley-water, sir?" said a voice at John's elbow. A hand and a crystal jug emerged from the darkness behind him.

John tore himself from Jane Caradoc and the larger reptilia in order to repel a second jorum of what he considered the most repulsive drink he had ever swallowed since the day when Blake major had dared him to drink gum and ink. He saw the crystal jug, he saw the hand that held it. He began to say "No, thank you," and did not know whether he finished saying it or not, because the hand that was offering him barley-water was Anne Belinda's hand. The little heart-shaped mole midway between thumb and forefinger swam before his eyes. The light passing through the handle of the jug made a rainbow that slid to and fro over the smooth skin. For a moment the rainbow crossed the mole, then slipped away. The hand withdrew.

John sat dazed, and let the rolling periods of Mrs. Fossick-Yates' eloquence go by; the drumming of his own pulses was all that he really heard.

Chapter Twenty-One

THE DINNER seemed to be interminable. The food was all badly cooked, and, as Mrs. Fossick-Yates continually insisted, exceptionally rich in vitamins. Anne came and went, a slim shadow in the outer circle of twilight. John could just see her, not as Anne Belinda, but as a parlour-maid in a white apron with a bib to it and a mob-cap that covered all her hair.

He began to be thankful for Mrs. Fossick-Yates' conversation; it seemed incapable of flagging, and merged without effort into oratory. It would have been dreadful if he had had to talk.

When Mrs. Fossick-Yates at last rose to her feet, she was loth to leave so attentive a listener.

"We shall expect you in five minutes," she said. "Remember, Frederick, *five minutes!*"

Twenty minutes later Mr. Fossick-Yates had just got into his stride. He had displayed his specimens, quoted at length from an article he had sent to the *Revue des Deux Mondes*, and was in the thick of a somewhat involved account of a journey he had once undertaken to the Dolomites, when the door opened and Anne stood on the threshold, a silhouette against the lighted hall.

"Coffee is served, sir."

"Thank you, thank you; in a moment. Tell Mrs. Fossick-Yates we will join her directly. So there we were, my dear fellow, with the train gone and all our luggage in it, and not one of us knowing a word of German. Fortunately, I had some chocolate in my pocket. But there, I'm afraid that we ought to join the ladies. Perhaps"—he sighed and coughed—"perhaps I shall have the opportunity of telling you the rest of the story later on—yes, yes, later on."

They found Mrs. Fossick-Yates pouring out coffee in an aloof, offended manner, whilst Miss Webster polished her cornelians with an old-fashioned lace handkerchief.

"I hope the coffee is not cold," said Mrs. Fossick-Yates. She handed John a cup. "My husband has no sense of time."

"My dear!"

"None." She tasted her coffee, and set the cup down rather harder than was necessary. "It *is* cold," she said.

"But then, the evening is so delightfully warm," said Miss Webster brightly.

Mrs. Fossick-Yates made the sound which is usually written "Pshaw!" and reared her neck majestically.

"I would send it out to be heated, but that would scarcely be fair to the servants. I believe in consideration for those who serve us. Thoughtlessness is the key-note of the present age—thoughtlessness and a total lack of discipline. Don't you agree with me, Sir John?"

John drew up a chair beside her. He had to find out whether Anne was living here or whether she had just come in for the evening. Suppose she were to disappear again. Suppose she were to go away and hide from him. Did she know who he was? Would she know him if she saw him? He didn't think so; but he couldn't be sure.

He drew up his chair and said perhaps the most tactless thing that it was possible for him to say:

"Do you keep your servants a long time, Mrs. Fossick-Yates?"

There was a slight but frosty pause. Conversation with Mrs. Fossick-Yates did not as a rule admit of pauses. John had just began to realize that his question was not a happy one, when the lady said:

"I think I *ought* to. But one learns not to look for gratitude in this world, Sir John."

"How true that is!" said Miss Webster.

John racked his brains for something to say. He wanted to ask about Anne, and had just enough sense left to realize that it wouldn't do. Fortunately Mrs. Fossick-Yates had found the text for a new discourse.

"The servant problem—" she began, and was launched. She touched lightly on what might be called the historical aspect. "The good old days, Sir John, when mistresses and maids shared, in the stillroom and the kitchen, those domestic labours which have since so unfortunately fallen into disuse and disrepute." A survey of the years from 1914 to 1918 followed: munitions, high wages, fur coats, grand pianos, preposterous ideas, discontent—these words emerged like drops flung up by a torrent.

Slightly dazed, John continued to listen.

Leaving 1918 behind her, Mrs. Fossick-Yates had embarked upon a masterly analysis of post-war conditions of female labour in general, and domestic service in particular. As she approached her peroration, Anne came in, took the coffee-tray, and went out again.

John dared not look at her after the one glance which showed her very pale, with dark marks under her dark blue eyes. When the door shut, he said quickly:

"You seem to have solved the question very satisfactorily as far as your own household is concerned."

"Mrs. Fossick-Yates is so *wonderful*!" said Miss Webster.

"I hope she may turn out well," said Mrs. Fossick-Yates. "I hope so—but they very seldom do. Not that I allow myself to be deterred by ingratitude or lack of response. No matter how often I am disappointed, I shall continue to give a helping hand to those who need it."

"Did this one come from *The Second Chance*, dear Mrs. Fossick-Yates?" said Miss Webster.

John blessed her in his heart.

"Yes, I always go there. A most admirable society, Sir John, and very well described by its name."

"What does it do?" He hoped his voice sounded indifferent.

Mrs. Fossick-Yates condescended to male ignorance.

"They give prisoners a second chance—find them employment and so forth. The maid who waited on us at dinner has just come to me from them, and I must say I think she seems promising."

"You're so *wonderful* with them!" said Miss Webster.

"I always take a very firm line. I believe it is the only way. I do not believe in beating about the bush; I believe in absolute frankness. I said to this girl just what I say to them all.

"She's *marvellous* with them," murmured Miss Webster.

"I said to her, 'Annie Jones, I am giving you a *second* chance—I believe in giving everyone a second chance. But I can only *offer* it to you. It lies with you to take it and make good, or to neglect this opportunity and slip deeper into the mire.'" She paused, and John realized with horror that he was expected to say something.

He said, "Er—"

"Of course I am very firm—it is necessary to be very firm. I do not believe in locking things up; it only constitutes an additional temptation. I say quite frankly, 'Here is a list of the silver, and here is a list of my personal jewellery. The carpets and the bronzes are valuable—Mr. Fossick-Yates' specimens are *not*. And I always know to a penny how much money I have in my purse. If *anything* is missing I shall send for the police at once,'"

"Isn't she *wonderful*?" breathed Miss Webster.

John thought her so wonderful that the impulse to hit her over the head with the largest and heaviest of the valuable bronzes was almost more than he could control.

Chapter Twenty-Two

HE DID NOT SEE Anne again. Mr. Fossick-Yates went with him to the door, and after giving him three wrong hats in succession, followed him out on to the draughty stone landing, and completed at great length the thirty-year-old story of how he had missed his train.

John listened, and did not listen. How was he going to see Anne? Parlour-maids had afternoons out; he wondered when Anne would have an afternoon out.

"The road," said Mr. Fossick-Yates earnestly, "was very steep and very dusty, and we were all beginning to feel more than a little hungry. If it had not been for the chocolate in my pocket—"

Perhaps Mrs. Fossick-Yates was so wonderful that she didn't give her parlour-maid an afternoon out. What a woman! Oh, what a woman!

"But, of course, the worst of chocolate is that it makes one so very thirsty. And, as I said before—"

John wondered what little Fossick-Yates would say if he were to seize him by the lapel and say, "When does your parlour-maid go out?" He checked the impulse to experiment, and learned with what gratitude that long dispersed party had happened on a streamlet.

"Nectar, my dear fellow!" The little man's eye kindled at the memory. "Delicious! Unforgettably delicious! Er—I'll walk downstairs with you."

John shed him at last a quarter of a mile down the street. He walked back to the hotel in a turmoil of thought. He was profoundly disturbed without knowing why.

It was Anne Belinda who disturbed him. The effect that she had upon him was one that no one else had. You liked people, or you didn't like them. You made friends with some people, and not with others. You were fond of some; and a few you loved. None of them had this extraordinary disturbing effect. To hear a thing about Anne Belinda wasn't like hearing the same thing about anyone else.

Anne Belinda wasn't like anyone else. He had talked to her nine years ago for perhaps twenty minutes, and he had never forgotten it, never forgotten the least detail of how she looked and what she said. Then two days ago he had seen her again for less than a minute, and he could still feel her desperate grip upon his arm; the storm of her agony still shook him.

To-night—to-night had left him with the strangest feelings of all. It was as if Mrs. Fossick-Yates and her flat and her dinner-party, her subservient husband, and her adoring friend, were all part of an insubstantial dream into which he had strayed. He had moved in the dream and mixed with the creatures of the dream, and all the while he was aware of Anne, who was real, moving to and fro in a waking world just out of reach. Dreams go by contraries. In the dream, he and the other unreal people had sat in a lighted circle, with Anne beyond it in the twilight. Dreams go by contraries. It was Anne who was in the light; it was Anne who was real. And the most desperate need of his life was to get out of the dream and go to her.

He went back to Ossington Road next day. He had no definite plan of how to come to speech with Anne. He thought of telephoning, and was daunted at the prospect of Mrs. Fossick-Yates answering him, or listening whilst Anne answered. He thought of writing.

But suppose she got his letter and just ran away. Suppose she had recognized him last night; and suppose she had run away already!

The Fossick-Yates might have spoken of him as Sir John, or they might have said Sir John Waveney—anyone might have said Sir John Waveney. Even if Anne had only been there thirty-six hours she might have heard his name a dozen times. She might have heard it once, or she might not have heard it at all. If she had heard it, she might have run away. And if she had run away, how in heaven's name was he to find her? He had called off Messing that morning, and he simply could not stick the idea of letting him, or anyone like him, go prying and ferreting after Anne.

It was about three o'clock when he turned the corner of Malmesbury Terrace and walked slowly up Ossington Road. It was a long road, and at one end there were a few shops, whilst at the other the houses became steadily larger and more expensive. The big block in which the Fossick-Yates had their flat stood about half-way up the street, just where the ground began to rise.

John was still in the neighbourhood of the shops when he saw Mrs. Fossick-Yates, in a black corded silk coat and a crinoline hat with a large grey ostrich feather, come down the opposite pavement at a brisk yet stately pace. She carried a grey parasol, with a violet handle carved to represent a parrot's head.

The nearest shop was a greengrocer's. John was inside it before the lady had taken another step. He gazed at bananas, oranges, apples, French cherries, and early strawberries. What on earth could one buy in a greengrocer's shop? There were bottled plums on a shelf, and baskets of potatoes, and bunches of spring onions, and boxes of dates. He bought a box of dates, asked for change for a pound note, and then, after a glance over his shoulder, inquired if he could have six coppers for sixpence.

By the time a damsel with bobbed red hair had obliged him with twelve halfpennies, the coast was clear; Mrs. Fossick-Yates, her feather, and her parrot were off the map. John put the dates in his pocket and went away whistling. No one would go out at three o'clock in the afternoon dressed like that unless they meant to stay out for a good long time. His fancy dwelt fondly on Mrs. Fossick-Yates staying out for a good long time. But still he had no idea of how on earth he was going to get hold of Anne.

He walked on past the block of flats and began to mount the hill. It was a very fine afternoon; there was a blue sky and a light breeze. The houses on the hill had gardens, in which laburnum and crimson may were coming into bloom. There were guelder roses and lilacs, and neat, flat beds full of wallflower and forget-me-not. Some of the beds were edged with white arabis and some with the big, pink double daisies, which his nurse had always called bachelors' buttons. He remembered having a really frightful quarrel with a little girl who said that bachelors' buttons were blue, and that the red daisies were hen-and-chickens; it had come to loud screams and the pulling out of hair, and the two nurses had never really been friendly any more. He had forgotten the little girl's name, but he could remember putting out his tongue at her whenever they met. The little girl did not put her tongue out; she looked well brought-up and superior, and stuck her nose in the air, and she and her nurse always crossed over to the other side of the road.

John turned at the top of the hill and walked back. When he was about half-way down he saw someone come out of the block of flats and stand on the pavement. The sun dazzled on a white cap and a white apron. The girl who wore the cap and apron had a letter in her hand. She looked down towards the shops and up towards the hill. The pillar-box was on the left-hand side opposite the third house with a garden. She began to walk up the hill towards the letter-box.

It was Anne Belinda.

John felt as if someone was shouting to him. He would have liked to shout himself; he wanted to shout at the top of his voice and go pounding down the road to meet Anne Belinda. He subdued this impulse, and having arrived at the letter-box, began to absorb information as to the hours of clearance.

He leaned against the box so that Anne could not reach the slit. She had come up to the box, and he was aware of her standing there, only half a yard away, waiting for him to move.

He stood up suddenly and looked at her in an odd excitement. She was still very pale. It wasn't only the black and white that made her look pale; she looked as if she had been crying. He must say something quickly, or she would think he was a lunatic.

He kept his hand on the pillar-box, and he said:

"Anne Belinda."

Chapter Twenty-Three

ANNE HAD NOT TAKEN any particular notice of the man at the pillar-box until he straightened himself and looked at her. Then she recognized last night's guest, and wondered why he was behaving so oddly. He did not look in the least like the sort of man who speaks to you in the street.

Then suddenly she was cold with anger because he was speaking to her. She had time to be angry, to look past him as if he were not there, before she realized that he had called her Anne Belinda. The realization brought the bright colour to her face. She looked down at the letter in her hand, and said:

"Let me pass, please."

"Anne!"

"I don't know you."

"I must speak to you."

Anne turned in a whirl of anger and began to walk quickly down the hill. John came after her in a couple of great strides.

"I'm a perfect fool! Of course you don't know who I am. Do, please, listen for a moment. I'm John Waveney—John Maurice Waveney, your cousin."

Anne stood still. Then, without a word, she turned round and walked back to the letter-box. Her cousin, John Waveney—he had called her Anne Belinda—he was John Maurice Waveney. But she wasn't Anne Waveney any more; she was Annie Jones, who had been in prison for stealing, and who was being given a second chance as Mrs. Fossick-Yates' parlour-maid.

She posted her letter, and stood there for a moment looking down. She felt giddy; the sunlight was full of little bright specks.

"I really am a fool—I've frightened you—I'm most frightfully sorry. But I didn't know how to get hold of you. I was afraid, if I let you go—I say, are you all right?"

"In a minute," said Anne. The words were rather unsteady; the ground on which she stood seemed to wave up and down.

That passed. She had closed her eyes so as not to see the little dancing specks of light. She opened them now, and there was only clear, sunny air between herself and John Waveney. He was looking at her with so much concern that she smiled.

"I'm all right now. I must go back."

"I want to talk to you most awfully."

The smile just showed in her eyes.

"Here? I'm afraid—"

"No, not here, of course. But I must see you. Mrs. Fossick-Yates has gone out—I saw her go. Is the little man in?"

"Yes."

"Go back and ask him if you can go out for half an hour. I'll wait down at the bottom where the shops are."

Anne bent her head and walked away. Her thoughts were racing. John Maurice Waveney—what an extraordinary thing! She had heard them say "Sir John" last night. How had he found her—and why? And how many people in how many houses had seen her standing by the pillar-box in her cap and apron talking to a man?

John walked down to the bottom of the road, and kept an eye on his watch. If she didn't come in a quarter of an hour he would go to the post office and ring her up. He wasn't going to have any more nonsense. He had found her, and he was going to talk to her whilst the coast was clear. Half an hour ago he had felt comfortably certain that Mrs. Fossick-Yates had gone out to tea; he now had a horrible conviction that she might come back at any moment.

In the end it was Anne who came—Anne in a grey coat and skirt with a little black cap, just as he had described her to Messing.

You couldn't really describe Anne; you could only describe her clothes. There was the way the corners of her mouth lifted, and there was the way her eyelashes came down over her eyes; and there was the way she looked when she was angry, and the way she looked when she was sad. You couldn't describe any of these things—no one could. They were like things that he had known always, and they held a secret which he wanted most frightfully to guess. They were Anne Belinda.

She came up to him with a little colour in her cheeks.

"I didn't have to ask—he asked me. He said would I be so very good as to take a parcel to the post office; and he apologized three times, because he had only just sent me out with a letter."

"Where can we go?"

"Well, *I've* got to go to the post office."

He frowned.

"I can post the thing afterwards. Let's find a tea-shop or something, where we can talk."

"No," said Anne. "I've only got half an hour, and I must post the parcel myself."

"Nonsense!"

"I said I would. Why do you want to speak to me?"

"I've been looking for you ever since I got home." He hated the pain that clouded her eyes.

"Why?"

"Well, first of all I wanted to find you; and then—well, I suppose I'm obstinate. Everyone seemed so dead set on my not finding you—" He broke off, a little flushed. This was not in the least what he had meant to say.

Anne's clear regard dwelt on him for a moment. Then she said, sadly and clearly:

"They were quite right. I didn't want to be found. I want you to promise me not to tell anyone that you have found me. I want you to leave me alone."

They walked for a moment in silence. This end of Malmesbury Terrace was very quiet—a row of mid-Victorian houses with veiled windows and an air of decorum. Just beyond was the busy High Street, where the trams slid to and fro with a metallic screech, and cars and vans and a very hardy race of bicyclists competed for the remaining road space.

"I can't leave you alone," said John in a gruff, angry voice.

"Please," said Anne more sadly still.

"No—I can't."

"Why?" The word broke rather a long pause.

John didn't answer; he didn't know what to say, so he didn't say anything. This is the most exasperating thing that a man can do. Any woman would rather have anything said to her than have to watch her own words sink deeper and deeper into a bog of silence.

Anne coloured sharply and broke in.

"How did you find me? No one knew—and I've only been here two days."

"I've been looking for you ever since I came home. I—I've been anxious about you; I wanted to be sure you were all right."

"How did you find out where I was?" Her tone accused him.

To her surprise he grinned suddenly.

"I didn't find you. I'd been straining every nerve trying to, and making a nuisance of myself to everyone. And then, when I didn't know what to do next—there you were. Little Fossick-Yates had bothered me into saying I'd come and see his specimens, and I was most frightfully fed-up with the whole show. And then all of a sudden I found you there."

"But—how? I—don't understand. How did you, how could you, know it was me?"

"It was your hand."

"My hand?"

"When it came over my shoulder and you said 'Barley-water.'"

"But how could you recognize my hand? You've never seen it—you've never seen me."

"Oh yes, I have."

They had come to the end of Malmesbury Terrace. The traffic of the full High Street went by them like a river in flood. Anne stopped by the wall of the last grey house.

"When?" she said. "When did you see me? Tell me."

John felt a curious reluctance to tell her. His colour rose; then a sparkle came into his eyes.

"You promised to cry for me if I was killed."

"*I* did?"

"Nine years ago—at Waveney."

"But I never saw you before to-day."

"You're forgetting yesterday," said John, "—*and* another time—*and* nine years ago at Waveney, when you promised faithfully that you would cry."

"I—promised? Oh!" A very faint and far off memory stirred. "Were—you—wounded?"

He nodded.

"I had a crocked leg. It was in '17. I was due to go back in a week, and I thought I'd like to have a look at Waveney—I'd never seen it. And we talked. You asked me if I had any relations, and when I said 'No,' you seemed awfully bucked and said that was splendid, because then it wouldn't matter about my being killed."

"Oh, I *didn't*!"

"Yes, you did. You were frightfully serious about it. And then you were afraid you'd hurt my feelings, and you promised you'd be sorry."

Rather a charming remembering look came over Anne's face. She looked younger—a little shy, confused; but her eyes were arch.

"Was it you? How dreadful of me! But—" The archness died. "Courtney and Tom had gone. We'd been all smashed up. My father never really got over it. I suppose I was thinking how horrible it was for the people who didn't get killed."

"I suppose you were, poor kid."

"But still I don't see how you knew me."

"It was the little mole on your hand. I noticed it the first time I saw you; and somehow I remembered it. And when I saw you again—"

"Last night?"

"No, not last night."

"When?" She looked a little startled. A few minutes ago he had been just a name—an unknown kinsman who had stepped into her brothers' inheritance through the tragic fortune of war; yet suddenly there was a nine years' memory between them. She was talking to him on a deep, intimate note, and to both of them the intimacy was as natural as if they had shared the same nursery; it was the sense of kinship that was so strong.

"When did you see me again?"

"I don't think I can tell you that. You didn't see me."

Anne turned so pale that he was shocked. What did she think? What had he made her think? He said quickly:

"Don't! I saw you at Waterdene. You'd had a bit of a shock—you didn't see me."

Very dimly, Anne remembered that there had been someone. She had held on to someone. She had been faint, and giddy, and blind; and she had held on to someone and said: "Don't let them come!"

"Was that you?"

The roaring traffic went by as they stood on the edge of it. When everyone is busy and hurried, two people can be very much alone.

"Yes. There's nothing for you to worry about. You didn't see me. And I didn't mean to tell you, but you looked as if you thought—as if you thought—"

"Thank you," said Anne. "You—were—kind." She drew rather a fluttering breath. Her own thoughts were shaking her; it had come to her suddenly and horribly that he might have seen her in the dock. She moved forward with quickening steps. She hated the place where the thought had come to her.

They came out into the full roar of the High Street.

"Do you know the way?"

"No—I must ask."

She turned and spoke to a woman with a pram.

"She says we have to cross over. The post office is just where that tram is stopping. I do hate crossings."

A year inside high walls leaves one sensitive to noise and rush. Anne stepped off the pavement, and had to struggle with a desire to run. Trams were so dreadfully sudden, and the noise they made— the sort of mingled whirr and clang—was like the sound of some relentless, uncontrollable machinery. Anne hated machinery. She had once been taken over a large factory, and she had come out white and shaking.

She had not taken two steps before she felt John's hand under her elbow. He took her across in such a cheerful, businesslike manner that she was unable to be angry. He must have seen that she was a fool about crossings. If she had an ounce of spirit she would be angry with him.

She decided that her spirit was broken, and looked up at him with laughing eyes.

"Noble preserver!" she said, and slipped into the post office with the parcel.

She came back looking rather alarmed.

"It's frightfully late. We must hurry. I mean I must hurry. You'd better not come."

He piloted her across the road before he answered. It was frightfully nice to be taken over crossings. It was like old times, when the boys used to take her about with them.

On the far pavement she turned to him and said good-bye.

"I'm coming to the bottom of the road."

"You'd better not."

"I haven't nearly finished all the things I've got to say. As a matter of fact I haven't begun. Look here, when do you get out? I mean really out, not just a rush round to the post."

"We have rushed awfully—haven't we?"

"Absolutely flown! Look here, when *do* you go out?"

"Thursdays, I believe."

"To-day is Thursday."

"Yes, but you don't get out when you've just come. It'll be next Thursday."

"How absolutely rotten! What about Sunday? I'm sure parlour-maids go out on Sunday, because I used to go to Sunday supper with my cousin, Letitia Ramsbotham, and she always used to say 'I've no maids on Sunday, so we'll wait on ourselves.' And I know she had two, and one of them was a parlour-maid."

Anne burst out laughing.

"What a frightful lot you know! I'm to get every other Sunday afternoon and evening, and it doesn't begin till Sunday week."

"Well, when does Thursday afternoon begin? I mean what time do you get out?"

"Oh, after lunch, when I've cleared away and washed up."

"Two o'clock?"

"Goodness no! Nearer three!"

"I'll be at the bottom of the road at half-past two. Look here, you're walking most frightfully fast—I can't keep up."

Anne took no notice of this. She said: "You'll probably have to wait," and then coloured. "You oughtn't to meet me."

"I'm going to."

"It would be much better if you didn't—much better for both of us. I'm not Anne Waveney any more; I'm Annie Jones."

"Then I'll meet Annie Jones."

Anne had spoken without looking at him. Now she turned her head a little, and the ghost of a smile lifted the corners of her mouth.

"Annie Jones will lose her place if she is seen walking out with a wicked baronet."

"If you're Annie Jones, I'm Annie Jones' cousin. Anyone can walk out with their cousin. Anyhow I've got to see you. There's a whole lot of business to talk over."

They had come to the lower end of Ossington Road.

"I must go," said Anne quickly. "But there's one thing—"

"What is it?"

"You—won't—"

"Of course I won't. What is it?"

"You won't tell anyone I'm here? *Promise* you won't tell anyone."

John looked at her clear and hard.

"You'll have to give me a promise in exchange. I won't tell anyone you're here if you'll give me your word that you won't run away again."

"I don't want to run away."

"Promise you won't then."

"I won't—till after Thursday."

John took her hand in his. It was too thin. It was much too thin.

"I promise not to tell anyone where you are till after Thursday," he said.

Chapter Twenty-Four

ANNE HURRIED BACK to the flat. When she had changed into her uniform she went into the tiny kitchen. A rich smell of curry rather more than filled it. There was a newspaper on the floor. The dishes which had been used for lunch were piled higgledy-piggledy in the sink, and the curry saucepan, clogged with congealed sauce, stood on the drip board.

Mrs. Brownling was sitting at the kitchen table playing patience. She was a middle-aged woman with a plump, pale face, vague, shifty eyes, and a fuzz of oddly coloured light hair, which she wore after the fashion of the nineties, in a deep curled fringe with a net over it.

She had served a short sentence for shop-lifting some years before, and now drifted incompetently in and out of the households of the very charitably minded or those who could get no other cook.

"Am I late?" said Anne.

"Black on red—seven—eight—nine—there aren't any tens in this pack. Late? Back in a flash I should have said. And why not stay out whilst you are out?"

"It's tea-time," said Anne, filling the kettle.

"Ten of clubs—now what in the world's the use of the ten of clubs? Tea-time? Well, there's only him in if it is. You go easy, my dear, and don't flurry yourself. He wouldn't notice if he didn't get his tea this side of midnight. Or if he did notice he wouldn't say anything—not if he was starving."

Anne laughed.

"I think he's kind."

"Jack," said Mrs. Brownling—"jack of spades." She paused with the card in her hand. "I knew a gentleman once, a friend of my poor husband's, that used to call it the jack of diggers. He was a very amusing gentleman, but not—not *quite*, you know. My marriage was a bit of a comedown altogether, my father being a clergyman and all. Queen of hearts—king of clubs—that finishes that."

Anne was glad to hear it, for she was wondering where on the littered table she was going to cut bread and butter for tea.

"Sweetly pretty vicarage I was brought up in, too." Mrs. Brownling began to gather up the cards, which were very dirty, broken-backed, and dog's-eared. "I'm sure I never thought in those days that I'd come down to this." She began to shuffle the cards in a slow, meditative way. "My husband was in business—did I tell you? Nothing low. But a shop's a shop, and I was brought up a perfect lady. I'm sure I couldn't make a bed, or mend a stocking, or cook a potato when I was twenty."

Anne arranged the bread and butter which she had cut. She might have remarked that Mrs. Brownling could not cook a potato now. She smiled instead, and began to make the tea.

"Oh, deary me!" said Mrs. Brownling. "You never know your luck—do you? Some go up, and some go down. You take my advice and look out for a comfortable, easy-going widower that's tired of being run by his mother-in-law. That's where a girl can get her chance. And the children needn't be anything of a bother if you know how to manage. Get 'em off to school, and get your house and your husband to yourself. There! That's real good advice." She shot the cards across the table as she spoke, and laughed a foolish, rather unsteady laugh.

Anne went out of the room with the tray. Mrs. Brownling was a trial. The kitchen table was always littered with her dirty, greasy cards. She could not so much as boil an egg without producing a complete state of disorder; and she never washed up a plate, dish, or saucepan until she had run through the whole stock. Anne had to share a bedroom with her—a bedroom in which most of Mrs. Brownling's personal possessions lay about on the floor. She took an interminable time to dress and undress, and she talked continually, pouring out muzzy, variable tales of former greatness. Sometimes she was the daughter of a clergyman, sometimes of a doctor, or a solicitor. Towards midnight she would occasionally hint at an aristocratic descent crossed by the bar sinister. This flight of fancy invariably ended in tears.

Anne found it all extremely trying. She never had any privacy; she had to live in the closest possible association with a dirty, foolish person; and nothing would induce Mrs. Brownling to sleep with the window open. There were moments when she regretted Holloway.

On Friday morning she took in a type-written envelope addressed to Miss Annie Jones. It was from John. He wrote:

"Dear Anne,

"I didn't give you my address. I meant to—it was awfully stupid of me to forget. Mind you let me know if you want anything. And don't forget about your promise, or about Thursday. I shall be just round the corner *at a quarter past two.*

"Yours,

"J. M. W."

Anne locked the letter up in her suitcase. It was the first nice letter she had had for more than a year.

"No one writes to me," said Mrs. Brownling with an injured sniff. "But it was different when I was a girl. Girls don't seem to attract young men now like they used to. Did I tell you, dear, how I used to drive my father on his rounds in a nice, high-stepping dogcart with the wheels picked out in red? He was a doctor, you know, in a very good practice up in the north. And I'm sure you wouldn't *believe* the letters I used to get from young men. Did you say your letter was from your young man?"

"No, I didn't," said Anne.

"Now I thought it was a man's writing."

Anne laughed outright.

"Why, it was typed!"

"I always had a good eye for a young man," said Mrs. Brownling complacently.

On Saturday there was another letter:

"DEAR ANNE,

"I don't think I gave you my telephone number. It might be useful for you to have it in case there was anything you wanted me for in a hurry. I hope you would ring up if there was.

"Yours

"J. M. W.

"P.S.—The best time to ring me up would be at breakfast-time, because I'm always in at breakfast."

It was Mrs. Fossick-Yates who gave Anne the third letter on Monday. She looked at it first, and read the post-mark. Then she said, "Typewritten," in the sort of voice in which counsel for the prosecution might present a particularly damning piece of evidence.

Anne didn't say anything. She took the letter and turned away; her finger-tips tingled a little. How foolish of him to write again—how terribly foolish! It must be confessed that she did not find the folly altogether unpleasant.

This time John wrote:

"DEAR ANNE,

"I hope you haven't forgotten about Thursday. I think I'll be there at two o'clock; because if they lunch at one, that would give you loads of time to get cleared up.

"Yours,

"J. M. W."

Half an hour later, when Anne was polishing the dining-room table, Mrs. Fossick-Yates sailed into the room and assumed a majestic pose on the hearthrug.

"One moment, Jones."

Anne straightened herself. The rubbing had brought a little colour to her cheeks. She wore a blue print dress, the value of which was to be deducted from her wages.

"Er—Jones," said Mrs. Fossick-Yates.

"Yes, madam?"

"I think you should realize the—er—importance of dissociating yourself once and for all from any—er—connections you may have formed in earlier and less desirable surroundings."

Anne said nothing.

"Correspondence with former associates is not a thing which I should expect you to encourage."

Anne looked at her across the shining table. Why was she so horrid? Why couldn't she be decent? The first sharp stab of anger was gone. It just seemed silly, and a pity.

"Answer me, please!" said Mrs. Fossick-Yates.

"I don't know what to say."

"I should like an undertaking that you will not correspond with your old associates whilst you are under my roof. I cannot help knowing that you receive letters daily, and I think it only kind to caution you. I will say no more."

Mrs. Brownling said a good deal more:

"What coloured eyes has he got, my dear? Tell me that, and I'll tell you whether he's got a constant disposition. The first gentleman I was engaged to had the most lovely hazel eyes you ever saw; and he threw me over to marry a titled lady. I never saw a man so put about as my poor father was. He'd had losses, and bad ones, that week—I told you he was on the Stock Exchange—and I thought there would have been murder done, which isn't a thing that any young lady would like to have her name mixed up in, and so I told him."

Chapter Twenty-Five

THERE WAS NO letter from John on Tuesday. Mrs. Brownling appeared to be aware of the fact. She sighed heavily every time Anne came into the kitchen.

"I wouldn't take it to heart if I were you, dear. There's better fish in the sea than ever came out of it."

"I'm not taking anything to heart," said Anne laughing.

"There's many a broken heart that's hid by a smiling face," said Mrs. Brownling, letting all the potato peel fall upon the kitchen floor. She peeled potatoes so badly that it was all that Anne could do not to take the knife out of her hand and do them herself. A potato that had passed through the hands of Mrs. Brownling was a gashed and mutilated object of about a third its original size.

"Not but what a broken heart's a hard thing to put up with," she continued, dropping the potato. "I remember when I was engaged the second time, I thought I'd never get over it—after it was broken off I mean. He wasn't handsome; but he had a way with him. And when he stopped writing, which he did quite sudden, I'm sure if ever a girl had a broken heart, I did. So I can feel for you, dear."

"There's nothing to feel about. Do you want this potato?"

"Put it in with the others. Well, dear, I won't say you're not right to be proud. Talk about pride, I'd an uncle, an army officer, that was almost too proud to live—military manners and a moustache, and all the girls after him. My poor mother worshipped him, but my father didn't hold with the army. He said lawyers saw too much of what came of it—He'd a very good law business that he came into from an uncle."

"I thought he was a doctor," said Anne.

Mrs. Brownling sighed heavily.

"He was, and he wasn't. I'm sure he might have been anything, he was so much thought of. But there, we all have our troubles, and least said's soonest mended—isn't it, dear?"

On Wednesday John wrote, apparently for the purpose of reminding Anne that the following day would be Thursday. He added that he was quite sure she could get out by a quarter to two at least, and that he would be waiting just round the corner at half-past one.

He had been waiting for an hour and a quarter when Anne came into view. He took her hand and said reproachfully:

"You *didn't* hurry."

"Why should I?" said Anne. And then she smiled at him. "I always told you it would be nearly three before I should get out. You didn't really come at half-past one, did you?"

"Of course I did. Look here, it's a topping afternoon, and I've got the car. I thought we could run right out into the country."

Anne had meant to be aloof and repressive, but she could not keep the blood from her cheeks or the sparkle from her eyes. To be carried smoothly and swiftly through miles and miles and miles of scented summer air; to see the sun on endless fields—after the flat and Mrs. Brownling's kitchen it was heaven.

John touched her sleeve as she got in.

"You haven't got a coat."

"I don't want one on a day like this."

"Sure?"

"Quite sure."

The car began to move; the grey streets along which she had walked wearily began to slip away like old, grey dreams. John sat by her side frowning.

She ought to have a coat. She ought to have her own clothes. They must be somewhere. She must have had clothes. He made a note to go and see Mrs. Jones again and find out about Anne's clothes. She ought to have a coat. It was all very well to-day, but he was going to take her for a lot more drives, and it wouldn't always be warm.

Anne's voice broke in upon his thoughts.

"Tell me about Jenny's baby," she said.

"Jenny's baby?"

"You said you were at Waterdene. You must have seen the baby. Didn't you?"

"Of course I saw it. Jenny's frightfully proud of it. She shows it to everyone."

"What is he like? Who is he like?" said Anne eagerly.

"Like? Oh, I don't know."

"Is he like Jenny?"

"I don't think so."

"Is he like Nicholas? Can't you tell me? I—I haven't seen him."

The little quiver in her voice filled John with rage against Jenny and Nicholas Marr. Some of it got into his voice as he said:

"It's just a baby."

Anne thought, "I've made him cross." She wanted so dreadfully badly to hear all about the baby and all about Jenny; and now she had made him cross. And suddenly she felt tired and weak, and she was sorry that she had come. She shut her eyes on two hot tears.

John looked sideways at her and cursed the Marrs again. What did she look like that for? She hadn't any colour at all, and there was a little line of pain on either side of her mouth. He did not know that he loved Anne, but he wanted to kiss those lines away. He said, very angrily indeed:

"Does she give you enough to eat?"

Anne's eyes opened very wide. He saw that her lashes were wet. She said:

"Who?"

"That beastly Fossick-Yates woman."

"Oh—why?"

"You don't look as if you were eating anything."

"I am really."

"What did you have for lunch?" And, as she hesitated: "I don't believe you had anything."

"Yes, I did."

"What did you have?"

Anne began to laugh because she suddenly remembered Mrs. Brownling's uncle with the military manners. She said: "Bread and butter." And John fairly snorted with rage.

"I bet it was margarine! Was it—or wasn't it?"

"It was."

"All right," said John. "We can't talk about it here, because I've got to steer, and if I really let myself go we shall probably run into a tram. When we do get out into the country there are quite a lot of things I'm going to say."

"You *are* like Mrs. Brownling's uncle!" said Anne.

They left the tram-lines behind, and presently there were no buses and fewer and fewer cars. The road was edged with trees instead of houses, and the blue sky looked down on a green world. They turned off on to a narrow road that climbed through a pine wood to an open moor.

John stopped the car, and they got out.

"First you're going to eat; and then we're going to talk. I brought a picnic basket because I thought it would be jollier to get right away like this."

They sat down on the young green heather, with the sun-filled, pine-scented air all round them. The moor rose up behind to the bluest sky in the world. In front of them it fell away to woods and fields. On the far horizon a line of blue hills merged into a blue haze.

Anne did not know that she was hungry until the basket stood open and displayed its extravagant contents—a sort of combined lunch and tea. She did not eat enough to satisfy John, but she certainly ate more than she would have believed possible. After a year of prison fare and ten days of Mrs. Brownling's cooking, to eat civilized food again created the illusion of having stepped back into the old life.

She stopped being Annie Jones, and was Anne Waveney, with the clock put back a year. The scent of the pines, the warmth of the sun, the sound of the light fresh breeze that went softly by—all these things were outside the life of Annie Jones. Anne Waveney let herself savour them to the full, just for half an hour.

When they had finished their meal, John packed everything away with the neatness of a man who has lived much in camp and can put his hand to any domestic job as well as a woman, or better. John himself would certainly have said better. He shut the lid of the basket down, came over to Anne, and sat down on the green heather beside her.

"Now let's talk."

They had been talking all the time lightly and pleasantly, but the moment he said "Now let's talk," there was a constraint between them.

"The bother is I don't a bit know how to begin."

"Don't begin."

Anne's eyes were on the blue horizon mists. Anne Waveney's life was as far away from her as those far hills. She could not go back into the past and live it again. She had been dreaming of it for half an hour, and now she must come back. She would have liked to dream a little longer.

She looked into her dream and said:

"Don't begin."

"I must."

She turned with a sigh to meet his frowningly intent look.

"I haven't an idea how to begin, so I shall probably make a mess of it. You see, you've really only seen me once. I can't count the times you've forgotten, because, if you've forgotten them, as far as you're concerned they don't exist. Oh, Lord! I'm getting tied up! But this is what I mean: I expect I feel like a stranger to you. But I'm not a stranger; I can't feel like one, and I can't behave like one. And I can't give you time to get used to me, because something's got to be done at once."

"I don't see that."

"You would if you were me. Good Lord, Anne, just put yourself in my place for a moment. I come home; I step into your brothers' shoes; I take everything—I take the house you were brought up in, the place that was your home; and I can't even find anyone who'll tell me where you are, or what you're doing, or whether you've got anything to live on. And when I do find you, you're working your fingers to the bone for that perfectly awful Fossick-Yates woman. For Heaven's sake put yourself in my place and think what I feel like!"

Anne looked down into the heather. It was a deep forest. Far away down in it there were tiny busy creatures going to and fro upon their business, or upon each other's business.

She said, "I see," in a low gentle voice.

"You see, I'm not a stranger—I can't be. If I've got your brothers' place, I've got to do what they would do for you. You must see that."

"How do you know that they would do anything?" Anne's voice died away. Courtney and Tom had nothing to do with Annie Jones who had been in prison.

"You're talking nonsense! Now, look here, this is what I want to do. Your father altered his will." He did not look at her as he spoke. "He left eight hundred a year to Jenny, instead of four hundred to each of you. People do odd things when they're ill, and I don't want to say anything about what he did. But you ought to have that four hundred a year out of the estate; and I'm going to see that you do have it."

"You can't."

"Of course I can. It's absolutely simple."

Anne looked at him for the first time, straight and steady.

"You mean that you would give it to me?"

"I mean that it would come from the estate."

"From you."

There was a pause.

"That's just the way you put it."

"It's the way it is."

"Look here, Anne, are you so beastly proud that you won't take a provision out of your own father's estate?"

All the colour went out of her face.

"I won't take what my father didn't leave me."

John felt the stab of her pain as he had never felt wound of his own.

"Anne—don't!"

"It's true."

He could see that she was fighting for composure, and he got up and walked away a few paces to give her time to recover. If he stayed, he would touch her; and if he touched her, he did not know what might happen. So he walked away.

When he came back, Anne was standing. As soon as he came up, she spoke:

"I can't do it. You mustn't mind, but I really can't."

"Why can't you?"

"I really can't. You—you mustn't think I'm ungrateful. And I don't want you to think things—things—about Jenny." His face hardened, and she put a hand on his sleeve. "You mustn't—*really*. You don't understand—and I can't explain. Jenny—Jenny has offered me half."

She said the words with such a painful effort that his heart cried out in him. Jenny, to make her suffer like that! *Jenny!* Some day Jenny Marr should pay her utmost farthing.

He put his hand down roughly on hers.

"So Jenny has offered you half? Are you taking it?"

The hand under his throbbed. She tried to pull it away, but he held it close.

"No. I can't take it. Please let me go."

He let her go then, and stood wondering what to say. Everything that he said hurt her. How was he to help hurting her? She was like a bird in a net, fluttering and bruising itself against the hands that are trying to set it free. What did one do? Leave the bird in the net for fear of hurting it? Or just go blundering on?

"I've made a hash of it!" he said aloud.

"*You* haven't."

"I've made a beastly hash of it. I knew I should. Look here, Anne, for the Lord's sake, let's start fresh. We're cousins. I want to be friends. Oh, hang it all! Don't you see that you can't possibly go on with that Fossick-Yates woman?"

Anne did not know what she had expected—not Mrs. Fossick-Yates' name. She hastened to shelter behind her.

"Why do you hate the poor thing so?"

"She isn't a poor thing—she's an arrogant, bullying, rostrating henpecker. I wouldn't be poor little Fossick-Yates for a million."

"Nor would I. But then he can't give notice—I can. I shall stay six months to get a character and then I shall be able to take a really decent place." Anne's voice died suddenly on the last word. What had she said? What had she told him? How much did he know? He had accused her of looking upon him as a stranger. But the trouble was that she couldn't look upon him as a stranger. She found herself talking to him easily, intimately, and without taking any heed of what she said. What had she said now?

With a look of distress that went to his heart she faltered out another lame sentence or two. John broke in on them:

"You can't possibly go on for six months."

Anne was silent. One could manage a day at a time; but a month has thirty days, and July and August would have thirty-one. Six times thirty, and some odd days added in, was a hundred and eighty-three. She saw herself struggling through a hundred and eighty-three stuffy nights in a little stuffy room, with Mrs. Brownling breathing heavily beside her, and Mrs. Brownling's bed creaking every time Mrs. Brownling turned over in it; a hundred and eighty-three breakfasts with Mrs. Brownling, and a hundred and eighty-three dinners in the littered, dirty kitchen; a hundred and eighty-three suppers of bread and margarine, with an occasional piece of stale cheese thrown in; a hundred and eighty-three days of saying "Yes, madam," respectfully to Mrs. Fossick-Yates.

"I *can* do it—I *can*!" she said to herself.

She faced John with her head up and a little smile on her lips.

"It's no good," she said. "You see, you don't understand. You said just now that we were cousins. Well, we're not. Anne Waveney's dead. She was your cousin. I'm Annie Jones, and I haven't any claim on you at all. I've got nothing to do with the Waveneys; and none of the Waveneys have anything to do with me—they haven't any responsibility. I'm Annie Jones. I'm earning my living, and I mean to go on earning it; and I can't have friends outside my own class. You said you wanted to be friends. But we can't be friends. You can't be friends with Annie Jones." She stopped, breathing rather quickly.

"Is that all?" said John.

"Yes."

"Then do you mind being Anne Belinda, just till we get back? I mean it would prevent you feeling how improper it is for me to be out with Annie Jones."

Anne looked hard at him. He wore a grave and submissive air. His eyes met hers with a simple and earnest expression.

"You see, we're about forty miles from London, and we might just as well enjoy the drive back. We had quite a jolly time coming, didn't we?"

"You've been frightfully kind," said Anne.

"I've got a kind disposition. I expect it runs in the family. I expect you could be kind if you really gave your mind to it."

There was a slight pause. Then for a fleeting instant he smiled, a wide friendly smile.

"Come along, Anne Belinda!" he said.

Chapter Twenty-Six

THEY TOOK the road again, with John in a new mood. He seemed, for some reason, to be in very high spirits; and he talked so much that Anne hardly had to talk at all. Her vehement protest had left her rather shaken. She experienced a reaction. Why had she said all that? Perhaps he was laughing at her. Perhaps he thought—

Suddenly she felt that she did not care what he thought of her. She pushed the whole thing away and shut the door upon it. It was such a lovely day; the trees and the green slopes slid past. Why should she bother about anything? Why not just enjoy herself?

John told her about Rudolphus Peterson, and about crawling through swamps to photograph a foot or two of deadly snake. He was very friendly and cheerful. Once he told her an instructive anecdote about a gentleman called Red Pete, who was so proud that when an uncle left him fifty dollars, he tied it up in an old bandanna handkerchief and slung it over Niagara. And once he sang, cheerfully and unmelodiously, a ditty referring to a different aspect of the same vice, as exemplified by an incident in the life of a certain Mr. Page:

"Where the tram-lines run on Kingston Hill,
And fares are penny-a-ride,
Mr. Caractacus Emery Page
Drives forth in a car of pride.
"He drives in a Rolls or Daimler,
Or some other expensive bus;
And oh, how Caractacus Emery Page
Looks down on the likes of us!"

"I met a toad called Caractacus once," he added. "I saved his life. Perhaps he'll leave me fifty dollars, and I can throw them into the Thames off Waterloo Bridge, if it hasn't fallen down by then. Toads live to be frightfully old."

They came home in the dusk, and stopped at the corner of Malmesbury Terrace. As they drew up, John said in brisk, businesslike tones.

"If you'll send me a list of what clothes you want, I'll see Mrs. Jones gets them for you."

"Oh!" said Anne, a good deal taken aback. "Please don't."

"I never met anyone who said 'don't' so often. It's the sort of thing that gets into being a habit; and then you can't stop."

"I don't think—"

"You don't need to think. You want a coat, because it won't always be so warm as it was to-day. I suppose your clothes are somewhere. If they're at Waterdene, Mrs. Jones can just go down and dig them out. If they're at Waveney"—a brilliant idea struck him—"if they're at Waveney, we can run down there and you can get what you want yourself."

"I couldn't do that."

He had hurt her again. One couldn't move without hurting her.

"All right, Mrs. Jones can go."

"No, I don't want—"

"There you go again! Of course you want your things. Make a list and send it to me. Mrs. Jones shan't know where you are, if that's what you're afraid of. She'll simply pack a box and send it to me; then I'll send it on to you by Carter Paterson. It's as easy as mud."

He was dreadfully, perseveringly obstinate. It would be nice to have her things. These two ideas entered Anne's mind together.

"You won't tell anyone where I am?"

"Same terms as last week," said John firmly. "If you murder the Fossick-Yates woman and run away, you'll let me know where you've gone to."

Anne laughed just a little tremulously. Her lovely, lovely day was over. There were lights in all the houses; the sun that had shone upon the pine-scented moor was gone. She put her hand into John's and said, as lightly as she could:

"Thank you for my nice tea and my lovely drive."

He held her hand for a moment, and then let go of it rather suddenly.

Anne was a yard away when he called after her:

"Good-night, Miss Jones."

Mrs. Brownling let Anne in with a warning gesture in the direction of the drawing-room, the door of which was ajar.

"Is that Jones?" said the voice of Mrs. Fossick-Yates as they passed.

"Yes, madam."

The hundred and eighty-three days began to rise up in front of her.

"I'm glad you are punctual. I expect punctuality."

"Yes, madam."

The kitchen was untidier than ever. Anne had slipped into doing quite half Mrs. Brownling's work. During the hours that she had been away an incredible number of dirty plates seemed to have accumulated. A game of patience was in progress amidst the débris of tea and supper. Something with a pungently unpleasant smell had been spilt upon the stove.

"Good thing you weren't late," said Mrs. Brownling, shutting the door. "Didn't I tell you she'd sit there with the door open waiting to catch you? In a way, she'd be in a better temper if you was late, because then she'd get it off her chest, so to speak. It's to-morrow you've got to look out for now, and don't you forget it. There's a drop of soup I saved for you in the far saucepan. She don't allow supper on your evening out; but I've saved it, for I know what it is to go off to your bed feeling hollow. So you just drink it up."

Anne was glad of the kindness, if not of the soup.

"I wouldn't mind her temper if she wasn't so mean," pursued Mrs. Brownling. "Drat the cards! What's come to them? There isn't an ace in the pack to-night, and that I'll swear. 'Lucky at cards, unlucky in love,' is what they always say. And I'm sure if it was true, I'd be the Queen of England; for worse cards than what I've always had you couldn't imagine, let alone see. But there, I suppose I've had my share, when all's said and done. Did I tell you about the Italian Count that I was engaged to?"

"No—not that one."

"Didn't I? He was a very handsome gentleman—if you don't mind them black, which I didn't, being so fair myself.

She patted her light fuzzy fringe complacently. The colour of it reminded Anne vaguely of parsnips.

"Fair ladies prefer dark gentlemen as a general rule. And, of course, his manners were *lovely*. It was my poor father who came between us. He was a very violent-tempered man, though a perfect gentleman and very highly respected at the Board of Trade—I think I told you what a lovely inkstand he had given him on his twenty-fifth anniversary. Well, it was he that came between us. He said he didn't hold with marble halls, and curling hair, and a diamond ring on a gentleman's finger. And when he called the Count an organ-grinder's monkey to his face, there was quite an unpleasantness, and nothing for it but for me to send him back the lovely real mosaic brooch he'd given me for my birthday.

On Saturday Anne received a parcel. It contained a writing-pad, envelopes, an indelible pencil, a stylographic pen, five shillings worth of stamps—and a letter from John Waveney.

The letter ran:

"DEAR MISS JONES

"I think I'd better practise calling you Miss Jones. I feel as if it would need a good deal of practice. Are you going to practise calling me Sir John? Or shall I be a Jones too? I don't mind being one if you'd rather. But John Jones sounds pretty awful—doesn't it? Of course you could call me Mr. Jones if you liked. You had better think it over and let me know on Sunday—you do get out this Sunday, don't you? I'll be at the same place at half-past two. I'm sending you some things to write with, because you haven't written yet, and I thought perhaps you hadn't got a block, and couldn't get out to get one. I think you owe me five letters.

"Will you make out the list of the clothes you want and bring it with you on Sunday?

"Yours,

"J. M. W. *alias* Jones."

Anne looked helplessly at this epistle. He was a dreadfully unsnubbable young man. She told her conscience that she really had tried to snub him. And if he wouldn't be snubbed, what on earth was she to do?

Anne's conscience, in a voice of austere severity, immediately provided her with an answer: "You can stop seeing him, and you can return his letters unopened."

Anne was rather haughty with her conscience. She said: "How rude!" and then, with rather less certainty, "I—I couldn't be *rude*."

"Don't go out with him to-morrow," said the severe, unpleasant voice.

"But I want to."

"You oughtn't to want to."

Anne tossed her head.

"I won't be bullied," she said.

Chapter Twenty-Seven

THE WEATHER HELD. Sunday was as fine as Thursday had been, and about five degrees hotter. There was a shimmering haze over the distance, and a deeper, fuller green on trees and hedgerows.

"Why did you send me writing-paper?" said Anne.

"I told you why. Have you brought that list?"

"I've written to Nanna. I don't know where my things are."

"She'll know," said John cheerfully. "Look here, Anne, how much money have you got?"

Anne laughed.

"How frightfully sudden you are!"

"Yes, I know. I haven't got any tact. I hate crawling round on egg-shells. It's really ever so much better just to crash into the middle of what you want to say—it saves a lot of trouble in the end. How much money *have* you got?"

"Sixpence," said Anne.

They were passing through a little emerald wood. In the middle of the wood there was a pond. The reflections in the pond were the greenest things that Anne had ever seen. They were like green flames.

John scowled at all this beauty. He said: "Ridiculous!" in a loud, hectoring sort of voice.

"Why is it ridiculous?"

"It's the most insensate thing I've ever heard of. Sixpence!"

Anne fairly bubbled over:

"Oh, my sixpence—my pretty little sixpence!
I love sixpence better than my life.
I spent a penny of it, I lent a penny of it,
And I took fourpence home to my wife.

"Having only sixpence is a most valuable moral lesson—it trains one in habits of strict economy."

"When will you get any more?"

"Not for ages."

"Why?" The word was jerked at her.

Anne decided that he looked exactly like a cross schoolboy.

"Because I hadn't any uniform, and Mrs. Fossick-Yates had to get the things. And as far as I can make out, it'll take me about three months to work them off."

John was restored to cheerfulness by the bright thought that this obligation would prevent Anne from running away. He spent the rest of the afternoon in being very nice to her.

They were nearly back, when Anne said firmly:

"You mustn't write to me."

"Was I going to write to you?"

"I don't know. I'd rather you didn't."

"Why?"

"She looks at the post-marks."

"Let her."

"And she says what a lot of letters I get."

"Do you get a lot of letters?"

"Only yours—I don't think she likes it."

"Tell her they're from a cousin who is a most respectable young man."

Anne exclaimed in horror:

"She doesn't think any young man can possibly be respectable. You won't write—will you?"

"Wait and see," said John.

On Monday there was no letter. It is very depressing to be taken at one's word. On Tuesday there was a fat letter all about Mrs. Jones, and Anne's clothes, and plans for Thursday.

"Do you play golf? I forgot to ask. Write by return. And if you do, I'll bring clubs and we'll go somewhere and play. I'm frightfully keen, and frightfully bad. My last handicap was about fifty, I think. You'll knock my head off, and then you'll be prouder than ever. You remember Red Pete I told you about the other day? After he threw the fifty dollars into Niagara he got engaged to a girl called Maud Matilda Caroline Blenkinsop. She was a very pretty girl. I don't know why she got engaged to him. He jilted her because he found out that she had three hens and a cottage piano in her own right. I thought you'd like to know what pride leads to—though in this instance she was well out of it."

Anne's box came on Wednesday. All the things that she had asked for were there, and some that she had not remembered to ask for. She went through everything very carefully. Only a very few of the things had a name, or even initials on them. She destroyed all the marks there were, and felt an odd pang as she did it. It seemed to put Anne Waveney clean out of mind amongst nameless and forgotten things.

Here were the handkerchiefs that jenny had given her for Christmas—little transparent things made of sheer linen lawn with a slim "A" embroidered in the corner. The "A" could stay where it was; but Mrs. Fossick-Yates would disapprove very heartily of a parlour-maid who possessed handkerchiefs so much finer than her own.

There was the blue and silver frock she had worn at the Hunt Ball. Ronny Carstairs had proposed to her halfway through the evening, after telling her that she looked like a blue flower on a silver stalk. Ronny had published his first thin volume of poetry a few months earlier, so what he said didn't really count. Still, it was rather nice to remember now. Only what on earth was Nanna thinking about to put in blue and silver tissue and silver shoes? Anne had certainly not asked for them.

She packed them hastily away at the very bottom of the box. Then she wrote to John. The letter consisted of a single line without beginning or ending.

"The box has come. I don't play golf."

John had a visitor that morning. "A lady to see you, sir," brought him down into the lounge posthaste. It couldn't possibly be Anne, but if it were—

It was Jenny Marr, in the thin, smart black which she always wore in town, and which set off her fair skin and bright hair so perfectly. The chain which Nicholas had given her took the light as if its carved crystals were diamonds.

John said: "How do you do?" But even as Jenny's hand touched his, she was saying in an anxious tone, "Where can we talk?" and he realized that she had not just looked in to play some light game of make-believe.

He led the way to a small room that opened out of the drawing-room, and they sat down on a stiff upholstered couch. Jenny pulled off her gloves and tossed them down between them.

"Nanna came down yesterday," she said. "I couldn't get away before. Where is Anne?"

John was conscious of satisfaction. He had had them all against him, lying themselves stiff; and now the tables were turned, and it was Jenny who had to come to him and say "Where's Anne?" He smiled quite pleasantly.

"Why do you ask me?"

"Nanna said you'd sent her to fetch Anne's clothes. She said you'd given her a letter from Anne. Where is she, John?"

"Why do you want to know?"

Jenny tried to smile.

"I've been most terribly anxious. I should think you would know that. Where is she? It would be such a relief to know she's all right. You can't think—" Her words died under his hard stare.

"Can't I? I think I can," he said.

"What do you mean? How funny you are! I want to know where she is. *Of course* I want to know."

John let himself go a little.

"Haven't you hurt her enough?"

Jenny flushed brightly.

"Why should I hurt her? Why should you think—What has she been saying?"

He looked at her with contempt.

"When you offered her four hundred a year on condition that she kept out of your way, weren't you hurting her?"

"Oh!" Jenny was very pale. "She didn't say that!"

"She didn't say anything. It was Nicholas who told me. He said you'd offered Anne the money her father left away from her on condition that she left you and Nicholas alone."

"Oh!" said Jenny, shrinking back.

"That's why I said 'Haven't you hurt her enough?'"

"John, you don't—you don't understand. You're angry because of Anne. I love you for being angry and for taking her part. But you don't understand."

"Don't I?"

She put her hand to her wet eyes for a moment.

"No—you can't. It's not your fault. It's all such a horrible tangle! Don't you think I love Anne? Don't you think I want to have her with me? We've got all tangled up so that I can't do anything. It's for Anne's own sake as much as anything else. If she would take the money she could travel—she'd make new friends. I'd give her more than half—I'd give her six hundred—I could get Nicholas to let me do that."

"It's not what you'll give; it's what Anne'll take. And you know as well as I do that Anne won't take sixpence if she's got to take an insult with it. What's the good of saying 'Oh!' and crying? It *is* an insult, isn't it? What would you feel about it yourself if Nicholas—yes, *Nicholas*—were to say to you: 'I don't want to see you any more, or have anything to do with you, but you can have an allowance if you'll undertake to keep well out of my way'?"

Jenny's voice failed her. She put out her hands and she tried to say "Don't!" but only a little dry, whispering sound came from her lips. John's words had called up visibly before her face that very secret inward terror which sometimes whispered to her in the dead of night when she couldn't sleep.

John got up and walked away. There was a table at the far side of the room with papers on it. He stood there and turned the leaves of an illustrated weekly with angry fingers. The leaves turned. There was a picture on every page. He did not see one of them. After a moment he went back and stood by the end of the sofa.

Jenny had a handkerchief crumpled up in her hand; she held it in a hard, trembling grip.

"You don't understand," she said. "Why are you so angry? Why won't you tell me what I want to know?"

"Look here, Jenny," he said, speaking slowly, "it's no good. You can't have it both ways—you can't push Anne out of your life with one hand and hold on to her with the other. You told her to go away. Well, she's gone. The least you can do is to leave her alone."

Jenny looked at him in silence. Then she said hesitatingly:

"Is she well? Is she happy?"

"She's got such a lot to make her happy, hasn't she?" said John with so much bitterness that Jenny caught her breath.

"Why do you care so *dreadfully*?" she said.

And that was the moment that it came home to John just how much he did care for Anne. His anger, his bitterness, his determination—these he knew; but, until this moment, he had not known that they were the reverse side of love, the love he had for Anne. He felt as if he had always loved her, with an immense, protecting tenderness.

The sudden knowledge must have showed in his face, because Jenny said quickly:

"John, you can't!"

"Can't what?"

"Care for Anne—like that."

"Can't I?"

"You know you can't. You know it's impossible. What's the use of making it harder for yourself, and for her, and for everyone?" She put her handkerchief to her mouth and whispered: "You know—Nicko said he told you—she's—been—in—prison."

Just for a moment John went on looking at her. Then he laughed.

"What difference does that make? She's Anne."

A piercing stab of jealousy went through Jenny. It was not for John—she didn't want John, or anything of his; she wanted Nicko.

But she wanted a Nicko who would look as John looked just now; she wanted a Nicko to whom nothing would make any difference. If she were in Anne's place would Nicko have said what John had said? Would Nicko feel that nothing made any difference? She didn't know. She didn't know; and she was dreadfully afraid. She leaned back in the corner and closed her eyes. She didn't cry. It would have been easier if she could have cried. Her secret terror whispered to her of dreadful and unendurable things.

After a moment John said gruffly:

"I say, don't look like that."

Then she opened her eyes.

"Do you mean that you care for Anne—*really?*"

"Yes, I do."

"Do you mean you want to *marry* her?"

"What do you think?" His colour had risen. He looked her in the face and laughed.

"Is she—going to—marry you?"

"I hope so," said John cheerfully.

"Oh!" said Jenny. She dabbed her eyes and got up. "I'm lunching with Aunt Jenifer—I must go."

She did not offer to shake hands, but went over to a wall-mirror and stood there, touching her face with a little powder-puff which she took out of her vanity-case. When she had finished, she wrapped the puff in a rose-coloured handkerchief and put it away. Still standing there, with her back to John, she drew on her white suede gloves. Then she went to the door. But just before she reached it she turned and came back.

"You won't tell me where she is?"

"No—she wouldn't want me to."

"Will you take her a message?"

"I'll tell you when I know what it is."

"My love," said Jenny, "—and little Tony's love." She said the words as if they took all the breath she had. Then, without waiting for him to answer, she turned and went out of the room.

Chapter Twenty-Eight

JOHN WALKED UP Bond Street that afternoon, took a side turning, and entered a jeweller's shop. It had the usual large plate-glass window, with a little grill in the middle to shield a display of diamonds and emeralds. One side of the window showed some fine specimens of antique French and Russian jewellery; in the other there were Georgian candelabra and a few more pieces of old silver. The name over the window was Levinski.

It was not John Waveney's first visit to the shop. He had come in a week before to buy a cigarette case, and a day or two later had dropped in again and talked for half an hour to Mr. Levinski himself about old silver. He was received now with a beaming smile, and the candelabra were fetched from the window and displayed.

"From Mr. Herzheimer's collection," said Mr. Levinski in a whisper. "Yes, indeed—*the* Mr. Herzheimer whose collections were so famous. I think myself lucky to have secured this pair. Look! They are fine—isn't it?"

Mr. Levinski was a short man, with a plump, sallow face, wistful dark eyes, and a distinctly Jewish nose. He spoke with as heavy an accent as if twenty-five years had not gone by since he first wrote himself an Englishman. What he did not know about precious stones and old silver was not worth knowing.

John encouraged him to talk about the candelabra and about Mr. Herzheimer.

"I tell you truly," said Mr. Levinski, "Herzheimer had nothing bad in his collection. If you buy these you invest your money; you do not spend it—no, truly. It is an investment—yes, and better than Government stock. Pieces such as these, they have their value. It does not shoot up one day and drop the next like the franc—it is safe."

"There is always the risk of having things stolen."

Mr. Levinski shrugged his shoulders.

"The finer the piece, the less is the risk. There is so small a market; so many people who know; and the Customs, and the police, and Heaven knows what more. In the end, is it worth it? No, indeed."

"I suppose jewels would be better worth while. Didn't you lose some pearls a while ago?"

Mr. Levinski spread out his hands.

"Pearls? *Ah! There!* Pearls—yes. You cut the string, and—pfft! Who is going to say, 'This is mine; this is yours' unless there is something in the colour, or the shape, or the size—something distinctive?"

"You did have some pearls taken, didn't you? I remember seeing it in the paper. As a matter of fact, that's what brought me here. I saw the name and remembered it; and when I saw it again over your window I thought I'd come in. You got your pearls back, didn't you?"

"Yes, I got them back. I was lucky—all through I was lucky, except at the very beginning."

"How on earth did they get away with them at all?"

"You may ask!" Mr. Levinski lifted his hands. "Yes, indeed, you may ask. See, I will tell you. I was here, myself, as I am with you. A couple, newly affianced, are with me. They looked at rings, and the lady, first she will have a ruby, and then a sapphire, and then again she thinks a diamond is better than all; so I am bringing out rings one after the other. And whilst I am bringing the rings I bring out a parcel I have just received—five strings of pearls, very fine, very well matched. I thought perhaps the fiancé would take an interest. For a wedding present there is nothing better than a string of pearls. So I lay them out. Whilst I am doing this I see there is a lady talking to my assistant. Afterwards he tells me she asks the price of something in the window. She is young and very chic, in a grey costume and a black hat. All at once I hear her say: 'What lovely pearls! May I look at them?' and my assistant comes over to me, and I give him the parcel of pearls. I look down the counter and I see the lady slip off her gloves. I think to myself 'She is a lover of pearls—she will only touch them with her hand.' You see that—isn't it? One does not touch the thing that one loves with a glove on the hand—no? I see she has on a very valuable ring; and that gives me the idea that perhaps she will not only look and touch, she will buy. I see that, and then I cannot see any more, because I am attending to the ring of my fiancés. They buy the best of my diamond rings, a very fine stone—not the largest, you understand, but the finest stone. I am pleased that they have such good taste, and I am busy because there is to be an inscription in the ring. And by the time I have finished with all that the young lady in the grey costume is gone."

Mr. Levinski paused.

"I go to take back the pearls, and I say to my assistant, 'She did not buy, then?' and he shakes his head. And I say: 'Will she perhaps come again?' And he says: 'I do not know.' And then I take the pearls, folded over in their cotton wool and I see the middle of one string hanging out—no more than two pearls, but it is enough for me. I open the parcel, and I say, 'What is this—what is this— what is this?' And there is my assistant as white as paper. And there are four strings of pearls, and a string of pearl beads such as may be bought for thirty shillings. I run out into the street. I say: 'Which way did she go?' I look everywhere. I run into Bond Street. I look up and down. There is no grey costume; there is no chic young lady thief. I come back, and I telephone to the police, and I tell my assistant just what sort of a head he has to let beads be changed for pearls just there under his nose. I lose my temper, and he weeps. And the police say what I know already, that there is very little hope. There has been much snatching of pearls for two, three months past—the papers are full of it—and no one has yet the luck to get anything back."

"But you got yours back, didn't you?" said John. He was fingering the base of the nearest candelabrum.

"Yes—I have the luck. It is beyond belief what luck I have. Next day I go out to the front of the shop to take a look at the window, and there goes past a taxi; and there looks out of the taxi that young lady thief, in her grey costume and her black hat. The taxi goes quick round the corner into Bond Street. I run. I see it before me. I fling myself into a taxi that sets down a lady at a lace shop. I say:

'Do not lose them! I am Levinski—I have been robbed! You shall have five pounds if I catch her!' We follow. I see them in a block a hundred yards ahead. I jump out—I run. In a minute I see the grey costume—she has also jumped out—she runs. I call out. She turns the corner—I turn the corner. I cry, 'Stop thief!' and a policeman catches her by the arm. We go to the police-station. My pearls are in her bag. She does not say anything—she does not even weep. At her trial she says her name is Annie Jones, and she pleads guilty, and she gets a year's imprisonment because there have been so many of these robberies."

"Well," said John, "you were very fortunate. She had a nerve—hadn't she? What was she like?"

"Very chic—that was what I noticed in the shop."

"On the films," said John, "ladies who steal pearls always have dark hair and flashing eyes. Was she like that?"

Mr. Levinski smiled.

"Her hair was dark, but I do not think that her eyes should flash much when she is standing in the dock—isn't it?"

"Well, I suppose not. But in the shop, when you first saw her—you might have noticed her hair and her eyes then."

Mr. Levinski's shoulders rose to the level of his ears.

"As for that, in the shop I see only a pretty, chic young lady. I do not think about her hair or her eyes. I see her chic grey costume, and I see that she has a ring with a stone in it that I would gladly buy."

"What sort of stone?"

"It was an emerald," said Mr. Levinski—"and of the finest. If it had a flaw, I could not see one. I should have liked to see it close. Emeralds like that are rare. Afterwards I wonder from whom she has it stolen, and where she has it hidden—for it was not any more upon her hand when I catch her next day. The pearls are in her bag, but the emerald ring is not anywhere at all."

"Then in the shop you didn't see whether she was dark?"

Mr. Levinski suddenly fixed his wistful gaze on John.

"Have you then an interest in this young lady, sir?" he said.

"The story interested me—yes."

"And the hair of the young lady—that interests also?"

"I think you didn't notice it at all in the shop—only afterwards. Isn't that so?"

Mr. Levinski nodded.

"Yes, that is so."

"I'll take the candelabra," said John. "How many ounces did you say they were?"

Chapter Twenty-Nine

ANNE TOOK OUT her prettiest dress next day. She felt as if she would like to burn the grey coat and skirt—but a penniless parlour-maid has to restrain this sort of feeling.

It was a day of soft wind, racing cloud, and brilliant fitful sunshine. She put on the thin crepe frock, with its blue ground that matched the blue of her eyes, and its pattern of green and blue, which she had always loved because it reminded her of bluebells in a green spring wood. The dress was rather thin, and she slipped a blue coat over it. She did wish she had a new hat. Mrs. Jones had put in one of those little hats which roll up. It was rather faded, its blues and greens a little dim; but it was still becoming.

"Well, dear, you do look gay!" said Mrs. Brownling. "He's going to meet you, I suppose. I had an aunt who always said you could tell whether a young lady was going to meet a gentleman friend by the time she took to dress—and anything over half an hour means business, is what she said. She'd been fairly larky in her day, though very well married at the time I'm speaking of—something high up in the Navy her husband was, and they'd a lovely house in Plymouth. My father's sister she was, and of course that inclined her, to the Navy, as you may say. I told you, didn't I, dear, what a handsome watch my father had given to him by the other officers on his last voyage. Chimed the quarters something lovely, and had his initials on the back in diamonds. Well, so long, dear—and have a good time."

Anne walked down Ossington Road making good resolutions. After to-day she wouldn't let John come and call for her any more. This resolution so satisfied her conscience that she was prepared to enjoy the dangerous indulgence of "just once more" to the full.

John seemed very pleased to see her.

"We're going to Wisley," he said. "I say, that's a topping dress! Did it come out of the box?"

Anne nodded.

"Where's Wisley?"

"It's the Horticultural Society's gardens. Mrs. Courtney was talking about them; she said the azaleas were a dream, and anyone who hadn't seen them ought to go and boil their heads, or words to that effect. And she said I could have her ticket any day I liked; so I went and fetched it this morning. Do you like azaleas?"

"They sound lovely. I haven't seen any flowers since I don't know when."

"Not in Spain?" He rapped out the question, and looked at her sideways with a malicious gleam in his eye.

Next moment he was penetrated with remorse, for Anne drew a quick, pained breath and said, with a forced steadiness of voice:

"I think you know very well that I never was in Spain."

"Why should I know, when you've never told me?"

Anne did not speak. Jenny had told him she had been in Spain. And it was quite evident that he had not believed what Jenny said. How much did he know? What did he think? What did it matter what he thought? To-day would pass; to-morrow would come. And when to-morrow came she would have shut the door on John Waveney for good and all. Meanwhile, why not enjoy to-day? What a fool she was to let any skeleton come out of its cupboard, clanking and posturing between her and this one last day of pleasure!

She turned to John, suddenly gay and brilliant.

"Let's pretend!" she cried, with a laughing catch in her voice.

"What shall we pretend?"

"Oh, anything! That we haven't a care in the world; that I'm not Annie Jones; that I'm just all the things that I can't ever be again. Are you good at pretending, John?"

They left the car under the pine-trees and came into the gardens. The rock plants in the little sunk garden before the house were still gay with rose- and rust- and primrose-coloured rock roses; there were blue water-lilies coming into flower on a little square pond. They went down some steps, past a row of glass-houses, then down again by a damp and winding path that brought them out into the wild garden in the valley bottom.

A sheet of blue irises moved in the breeze like deep blue water just flecked with foam. A little farther on the large plum and white and purple Japanese irises were coming out one by one with their feet in the stream where pale moon-yellow water-lilies floated amongst smooth, flat leaves. A towering bush of double mauve rhododendron looked down on the water, the lilies, and the irises. It stood on the far bank, a sheeted mass of lilac bloom; behind it the steep rock slope rose up a hundred feet, hung with a brilliant arras of orange and scarlet, carmine, violet, blush, and burning blue. Everywhere between the brightness of the colours there were infinite shades of living green, from bronzy black to the colour, which has no name, that is like a flame burning in still air.

"Topping, isn't it?" said John.

Anne stood looking at the flowers. She did not speak, and she was pale. When John slipped his hand inside her arm she let it stay there. She felt as if she had escaped into a very beautiful, very fragile dream, an enchantment which would fade if she so much as breathed.

She was still standing like that when someone spoke her name.

"Anne! Good gracious! Anne!"

Anne came out of her dream with a startled leap of every pulse. As John's hand fell from her arm, she turned from her vision of enchanting loveliness and found herself face to face with Aurora Fairlie, very large, very red in the face, very hot in her thick rough tweeds. She wore a deer-stalker hat pushed well back on her head. And she was not alone. A middle-aged man with a lined, clever face; a thin, elderly woman, very limp, in grey georgette and ostrich feathers; and a golden-haired flapper, bare-headed, in the smallest possible quantity of blue organdie. These, grouped around Aurora and obviously of her party, all looked at Anne—and looked with recognition.

John saw Anne's hand close tightly upon itself. Then she smiled at Miss Fairlie and said:

"Hullo, Aurora!"

Miss Fairlie regarded her with a large smile.

"I ought to cut you dead," she began—John saw Anne's knuckles whiten—"never coming near me once since we got back! Is that all the thanks I get for taking you to Spain a wreck and bringing you back in the pink? You're a monster of ingratitude! By the way, you know Clement Moore and Janet, don't you? I'm sure you've met. But Casilda's only just left school. Grossly unfair I call it. How old are you, you little wretch?" She turned to the flapper, who made a face. "Seventeen? Can't think what Clem and Jan are thinking about! I had to stare at a blackboard till I was nineteen, and then only escaped going to college because I failed six times running in matric."

Anne shook hands with the Moores.

Mrs. Moore asked her if she felt quite strong again in the most uninterested voice in the world, whilst Aurora, in hearty tones, introduced "my cousin—no, not really my cousin—Anne's cousin, Sir John Waveney." After which she dropped a heavy ungloved hand on Anne's shoulder and patted it.

"We're going up through the rock garden. Yes, Jan, you've got to! Clem and I can walk behind you and prod. Anne, have you and John seen the azaleas? Turn down that path and you'll walk slap into enough colour to make you drunk for a week. They smell like pre-war beer—but it's more high-toned not to mention that. Come along, Jan, there's quite a good seat at the top for you to feel faint on."

She swept the Moores before her over a little rocky bridge that spanned the stream and led straight into a bewildering tangle of Osmunda fern and yellow iris.

Casilda Moore followed them for a dozen steps, then whisked round and ran back. She had round, blue eyes, as bright and hard as china beads. Her impudently cocked eyebrows were artificially darkened; they looked quite black against her fair skin. Her bright, uncovered hair shone in the sun. She came quite close up to Anne and said:

"Did you like Spain? Were you *really* there? We met Lady Marr at lunch last week. She *said* you were." Her voice was as impudent as her eyebrows. She lifted her chin at John and went on with a giggle: "Did you live in a castle? A castle in Spain sounds so romantic! '*Chateaux en Espagne*'—we had it in our French idioms; only I'm so stupid I never can remember what it means. Something imaginary, isn't it? I hope your castle was a real one. Was it?"

Anne laughed.

"I never aspired to a castle."

Casilda giggled again.

"I'll tell Lady Marr we met you," she said, and ran across the bridge.

John took Anne roughly by the arm and turned with her down the path which Aurora Fairlie had pointed out.

"Little beast!" he said.

Anne said nothing. The path turned at right angles, and they were out of sight of anyone. A very high bank of azaleas rose before them, orange, apricot, flame, and white—orange that shaded to vermilion, flame that melted into rose, and white that passed through half a dozen shades of ivory, cream, and primrose into deepest chrome. A single rhododendron stood amongst the azaleas like a high rock in a sunset-coloured sea; its mass of pale purple bloom was the last enchanting note in the rainbow chord.

Anne saw none of this beauty, or saw it only as a blur through a film of stinging tears. John saw her pale, and felt her trembling. High walls of leaf and bloom were above them. To be alone with

Anne and feel her tremble; to be so near that when she trembled he was shaken, too; to see how white she was—these things moved him into rash and unpremeditated action.

He said "Anne!" in a choked voice, put both arms round her very tight, and kissed the wet eyes. And when he had kissed her eyes, he kissed her soft, trembling mouth. And, just for an instant, Anne let him kiss her.

As the instant passed, she said "Oh!" in a little shocked whisper, and pushed him away. Even then he had one arm about her shoulders.

"Oh!" said Anne again; this time there was a little real anger in her voice.

John's arm dropped to his side.

"Anne darling! Don't cry!"

Anne snatched a handkerchief from her sleeve and pressed it hard against her eyes.

"I'm *not* crying!"

"Anne—don't! Someone might come!"

"I'm *not*!"

She withdrew the handkerchief for just long enough to inflict a glance into which she put all the angry reproach that she could summon. The fact that she was still crying rather spoilt the effect, and John was only conscious of an insane desire to kiss her again. He wanted to bang Casilda Moore on the head with a stone, and spank her as she ought to have been spanked for years. And he wanted to kiss Anne until she stopped crying and kissed him back.

He said, "Anne darling!" and Anne stamped her foot.

"I'm not! You're not to! I never said you could!"

"I can't help it—you are—how can I help saying it?"

"You're not to say it!"

She pushed the wet handkerchief back into her sleeve and began to walk away, keeping well in the middle of a very narrow path. With every step she took she became angrier with John. How dared he kiss her? How dared he touch her? How dared he think that she would let him kiss her like that?

A bright scarlet spot began to flame in either cheek. Her eyes were quite dry now, and very nearly as hard as Casilda's. The sweet heavy air, warm and moisture-laden, the scent of the flowers, the shade and sunshine, the colour and the bloom, all passed her by. It was she and John and burning anger who walked together on a straight path that led to nowhere.

They passed the azalea bank in silence, and found themselves on a broad, damp path under deeply shadowing trees.

"I want to go home," said Anne.

Chapter Thirty

THEY DROVE in silence out on to the London road and presently turned off to the right.

Anne went on telling herself how angry she was. She found it necessary to do this, because she kept thinking of things to say— the sort of silly, trivial things which were not at all in keeping with being aloof and dignified and very, very angry.

Through the tall, straight trunks of the pine-trees on either side of the road a pale glimmer of water showed. The shadows between the trees were very dark, but there were sun-spilled pools and streams of light, and hot, slanting golden beams that pierced the shade. The trees met overhead.

Anne found it fascinating to be carried so swiftly and smoothly from cold shadowed air into summer heat, and then back again to cold. It was like flying. If you shut your eyes, you could forget everything except that enchanted flight through the air.

"I am very angry with John," she said firmly to herself.

There was a faint, delicious scent of wood-smoke.

"Aurora's a brick—isn't she?" said John. "I should think she was absolutely unique. I love her passionately; but the Casilda flapper wants shipping off to one of the countries where young women are made to work, and get beaten every day by a sinewy mother-in-law if they don't come up to sample."

Anne looked haughtily at her own reflection in the wind-screen; she could see herself almost as well as if it had been a mirror. The little faded hat was undoubtedly becoming, but she was annoyed at detecting a faint quiver of the lips, which were meant to be severely set. By looking to the right she could see John's reflection. If he had looked in the least crushed, she might have relented a little; but the wind-screen offered her the picture of an entirely cheerful young man with a twinkle in his eyes. Anne therefore said nothing to John, but assured herself once more that she was very, *very* angry.

The road began to climb. The trees were no longer pines but beeches, emerald-green in the shadow, and gold-green in the sun. It was like driving up the aisle of some vast cathedral which had come alive and was praising God with the voice of all the green things upon the earth. It sang, "Praise Him and magnify Him for ever," so loud and joyfully that Anne forgot to be angry any more; the sheer beauty of the place came in on her like a flood and made her joyful, too.

It was some time before John spoke again. Then he spoke quite suddenly:

"Have you many rings?"

Astonishment made Anne turn and look at him.

"Rings!"

"Rings."

"What sort of rings?"

"Just rings," said John. "What the catalogues call dress rings. I can't think why, but they do. I once got landed in a commercial hotel where the only literature was jewellers' catalogues. There were six of them. And I gathered that you began at the top with dress rings at anything from five hundred pounds to fifteen, and finished up with gem rings, which ran from fifteen pounds to thirty bob. *Have* you many rings?"

As she had forgotten about being angry, Anne laughed.

"No, I haven't."

"Have you *any*?"

"Why do you want to know?"

"Well, we didn't seem to be talking much, and I thought we might as well talk about rings. Did you say you hadn't got any at all?"

"I've got two or three of my mother's, but I don't very often wear them. I mean"—her colour deepened—"I don't wear them at all. I suppose Jenny's got them."

"What are they like? You ought to have them if they're yours."

Anne's smile was so sad that he didn't know how to bear it.

"They're no good to me."

"You ought to have them. What are they like?"

"There's an opal, and a little old pearl ring, and one with two diamonds and a ruby. I'll ask Jenny for them some time.

"You've never had an emerald ring? Emeralds are topping stones. Don't you think so?"

What was he driving at? He didn't think—he couldn't possibly imagine—that she would let him—

At this point in her thoughts Anne blushed scarlet, and John saw her blush.

"Did you ever have an emerald ring?" he asked in a laughing voice.

"No. Why should I? I don't like emeralds a bit."

"Jenny does," said John. "She has an emerald ring, hasn't she? I've seen her wearing one."

"Her engagement ring."

"Yes, I thought so." He looked at Anne's reflection in the windscreen. "Did you ever wear it?"

"Jenny's engagement ring?" There was no mistaking the surprise in her voice.

"You might have. Don't girls wear each other's rings?"

"Not—" Anne stopped short and put one hand quickly over the other. After a moment she said, in a different sort of voice: "Why did you ask me that?"

"Perhaps I wanted to know whether you liked emeralds." He had been slowing down; he stopped the car now by the side of the road and swung round in his seat. "Perhaps I wanted to know what sort of ring you would like for an engagement ring."

Anne's left hand, which lay uppermost, closed hard on her right. Without any effort at all, she was angry again—angry and rather frightened, not of John nor of herself, but of something which seemed to be pushing them both. She tried to look angrily at John, but the something that was frightening her would not let her look at him at all.

John's hand came down on hers.

"Anne, are you still angry? You can't go on being angry."

"Yes, I can." The words were defiant, but the voice that carried them was a trembling traitor.

"Why are you angry?"

There was no answer.

"You know I love you very much. You must know that."

Anne shook her head. She was not angry with John any more; she was frightfully angry with herself. To have such a beating heart, to lose voice and words, to feel herself upon the edge of tears, just when she needed all her self-possession and all her nerve—it was unspeakably humiliating. She must say "No," and she must say it with a dispassionate calm that would convince him that it was all quite hopeless. She must send him away in such a manner that he would never come back. And how was she to do this, when she could neither look at him nor steady her voice to a single word?

It was when she felt his arm about her that she gave a little sobbing cry and shrank into the corner of the seat.

"No! Oh *no*!"

"Anne darling—don't! Look here, I won't touch you if you don't want me to. Only it's so frightfully hard when you look like that. Do you mind—I mean really mind—if I hold your hand?"

Anne didn't mind at all—that was the devastating part of it. She wanted to catch tight hold of the warm, strong hand that covered hers; she wanted him to put his arm round her again and hold her against the world. With a very great effort she lifted her eyes and looked at him through a mist of tears.

"Please."

John took his hand away at once and sat back.

"All right. But we've got to talk. I love you."

"You mustn't!"

"What's the good of saying I mustn't? I do."

Two of Anne's tears fell down into her lap. They did not soak into the rough crepy stuff, but lay on the blue and green pattern like shining drops of rain. Now that the tears had fallen Anne could see how obstinate John looked. He didn't look in the least as if he were making love; he looked quite frightfully determined, and his chin stuck out.

"It's no good," she said rather shakily.

"Nonsense! I mean you don't love people because it's good, or because it's bad. You don't plan to do it—it happens. And when it's happened it's no good saying 'don't' any more than if you'd fallen off the top of a house."

Anne looked for her handkerchief, failed to find it, and blinked hard.

"So you see it's not the slightest use saying that sort of thing. I love you. You can't stop me loving you. I can't stop myself. I don't want to stop—I like it—I like it frightfully—I want to tell you all about it from the very beginning."

Anne pulled herself together. It was like pulling something that was much too heavy to lift out of a very deep ditch; but she did it. She sat up straight and set herself to say what she had to say:

"You mustn't tell me. I can't listen—I don't want to listen."

Right in the middle of the last sentence her voice faltered because John looked at her with eyes that gave hers the lie direct.

"I think you might listen," he said with suspicious mildness.

"No, I can't—it's no use."

John sighed.

"My dear child, what's the good of talking nonsense? I'm not being useful; I'm being purely ornamental. I'm making love to you because I like making love to you."

Anne shook her head.

"You mustn't."

"Why?"

All at once she was composed; the mist was gone from her eyes, and the lump from her throat. The relief was very great. She was able to look at him, and she was able to say:

"John, how much do you know?"

"I know I love you, and I know that I can make you love me."

She lifted her hand as if to brush that away.

"You know I don't mean that. I mean how much do you know about me?"

John caught the hand and held it for a moment.

"You're Anne Belinda—that's enough for me."

"No, John, it's not enough. Don't play with me. Tell me how much you know."

"I think I know everything," he said very gently.

"Then"—she pulled her hand away—"I needn't say any more. If you know everything, you know that I can't listen to you."

"No, I don't. Now, look here, Anne, what's the matter with you is that you're too highfalutin. And there's no need to be highfalutin at all. I love you like anything and I want to marry you, and there's no reason on earth why I shouldn't, or why you shouldn't. It makes me mad to think of you cleaning that Fossick-Yates woman's spoons and laying her beastly table—every time I think of it it makes me feel madder. If you don't want me to go absolutely off the deep end, you'll let me take you right out of it all before anything happens. Hang it all, you can't *want* to stop with a woman like that! Marry me good and quick! I'll be nice to you, Anne Belinda."

"John, don't! It's impossible. No—wait! You say you know everything; but I don't think you do—or you wouldn't think I could marry you. I don't know what you've heard—I don't know what people are saying. Jenny's been telling them that I was in Spain with Aurora, and that I was ill. I wasn't ill, and I wasn't in Spain. I was in prison for stealing."

As she said the last word, she opened the door of the car and jumped out. She had thought that she could say it. Well, she had said it. But she couldn't stay there, so near, almost touching him, and wait for what he would say. The impulse to run away and never see him again was so strong and sudden that she was out of the car and running before she knew what she was going to do.

She stopped herself with a great effort when she had run no more than a dozen yards. John found her leaning against a tree. Her hands were behind her pressing the rough bark; her head, in its little close cap, was thrown back. She looked as if she were held by invisible bonds.

John put his hands on her shoulders.

"Anne darling, I knew! Why did you run away? I told you that I knew."

"Not *that*."

"Yes, *that*—and everything else—*everything* else. Do you hear? Now will you come back to the car and talk about really interesting things for a change?"

"I don't know what you mean," said Anne in a desperate voice.

"Don't you? I think you do; but I don't mind explaining. I've known about your being in prison for quite a long time. Nicholas told me the day after you went down to Waterdene and Jenny sent you away. He told me you'd been in prison, and he told me why. I can't think now why I kept my temper so beautifully. Every time I think about it I wonder why I didn't knock him down, but at the time I was so taken up with wanting to find you that Nicholas didn't seem to matter."

Anne actually laughed. "Why should you knock Nicholas down? It was true."

"Was it? I mean I know you were in prison all right. But I know something more than that—I know why you were there and who you went there for. You see, I've had some very interesting talks with Mr. Levinski."

"Oh," said Anne. Her lips just parted to let the sound come through; they were very stiff.

The tree against which she leaned seemed to be moving upwards, for she could feel the rough bark scraping along the palms of her hands. John saw her waver and begin to fall.

Before she quite lost consciousness she felt his arms close round her.

Chapter Thirty-One

ANNE CAME BACK to the sound of her own name: "Anne—Anne—Anne—Anne." It was like hearing a wave break. It was her own name, but it sounded strangely. She opened her eyes. John's face was so near that she shut them again immediately. Her left hand was resting on something rough and dry. Beech leaves—she was sitting on the ground on the drifted beech leaves. John's arms were round her, her head was on his shoulder, his face touched hers, he was saying her name.

She said, "I'm all right," and pushed with her right hand against his arm. It was not a very strong push.

"I'm all right, John."

Instead of letting go, the arm that was round her tightened.

"Let me go," said Anne in an odd, shaken voice.

"Aren't you comfortable? Is that better?"

Please let me go."

"You'd much better sit still for a little. You gave me a most horrid fright, and it would have been worse if I hadn't always been sure that that beast of a woman doesn't give you enough to eat. Look here, I've got some milk in the car. Can you lean up against the tree whilst I go and get it?"

He propped her against the tree and departed. Anne watched him through her eyelashes. She ought to be thinking what she was going to say to him. What did he really know? How much did he really know? When a person says they know everything, how are you to find out whether their everything is the same as your everything? She must find out—she must say something. It mattered tremendously what she said, and she couldn't think of anything to say.

John came back, very cheerful, with a thermos and two cups.

"It's not milk; it's coffee. Coffee's not too bad out of a thermos, but tea is simply foul. There are some egg sandwiches in the packet."

He tossed it on to her lap, poured out the coffee, and gave her a cupful. It smelt delicious, and Anne became aware that something hot to drink was what she really wanted.

"Next time you're going to faint from want of food, I do wish you'd say so first. It's all right for you, but it startles me no end having to catch you like that without any warning."

The word "Levinski" slipped through Anne's mind like a snake slipping through grass. John was talking and behaving as if nothing had happened at all. Was she to leave it at that? Or was she to say now—yes, now, between this sip of coffee and the next—"What did Levinski tell you?"

She set down the cup. There was a moment of dreadful endeavour. Then she lifted the cup again and drank.

Not now. Why should she speak? She couldn't speak—she couldn't.

"Look here, I was going to go over Leith Hill and have tea in Dorking, but I expect that's too far. We'd better just dawdle along. What do you think?"

Anne didn't know. In the end they carried out the original programme, and John beguiled the way with a great deal of cheerful conversation, and not a single word about Mr. Levinski.

When they were driving back to town he asked Anne quite suddenly what sort of engagement ring she would like.

"I haven't thought. Does one think about it when one isn't engaged?"

"I don't know; that doesn't apply. What sort of ring would you like?"

"John, I am not engaged to you."

"Aren't you?"

"Of course not."

"Oh? That makes it so complicated, because if I'm engaged to you I don't see how you can help being engaged to me."

"I'm *not* engaged to you."

"I think you must be. I don't see that there's any way out of it. Would you like a sapphire and diamond ring? Or only diamonds? Or a big sapphire with little diamonds all round it?"

"John, I'm not—"

"I know. You said that before. I do wish you wouldn't keep repeating yourself; it makes it so frightfully difficult to get anything fixed up. You see, it isn't as if I could just blow in and talk about rings whenever I wanted to. I mean we've simply got to get it fixed up now, or else I shall feel I've got to ring you up. And if I do that miserable Fossick-Yates woman will probably overhear your end of the conversation. She's got an eavesdropping sort of nose, and if she were to hear you say 'Make it rubies,' or diamonds, or whatever you did want to make it, she'd boil up no end of a scandal on the spot. I shouldn't like to let you in for anything like that. So you see it's absolutely necessary to fix it all up now. You do see that, don't you?"

Anne said nothing.

"I like blue stones best myself. I'd like you to have one of those lumpy sort of sapphires. And I think it would be a good plan if we went and chose it together, because then I could match your eyes."

John went on talking about rings until they reached the corner of Malmesbury Terrace.

Anne went on saying nothing. She listened to stories about precious stones, and apocryphal anecdotes about engagements and engagement rings. Sometimes she wanted to laugh, and sometimes she wanted to cry; but she managed to refrain from uttering a single word.

John left the car at the corner and walked up Ossington Road with her. It was a cloudy evening and dark. There were not a great many lamp-posts; midway between one lamp-post and the next there was practically no light at all. It was as they passed through one of these dark patches that Anne felt John's arm come round her. His voice, softened and eager, spoke at her ear:

"Are you still angry?"

Anne was not angry at all, but she said "Yes."

"Because I kissed you at Wisley?"

"Yes."

"I don't see why. Anne, you let me—you know you did!"

"Oh!" It was a shocked breath of protest.

"Anne—you did! I wouldn't ever kiss you if you didn't want me to. You know that—don't you?"

"Oh!" said Anne again.

John put his hand very gently under her chin, turned her face up, and kissed her as he had done before—two kisses for her eyes and one for her mouth.

"Oh!" said Anne again. Then she pushed him with all her might and ran up the road.

When he had seen her cross the lighted space outside the block of flats and disappear through the arched doorway, he turned and walked back to where he had left the car.

As he came into Malmesbury Terrace he was singing just above his breath:

"The world is full of crueltee,
Mr. Mulligan's gone from me;
Mr. Mulligan's gone to sea.
Cruel Mr. Mulligan!"

Chapter Thirty-Two

MISS FAIRLIE CALLED John up next day before he had finished his breakfast.

"Is that you, John Waveney? Oh, it *is*? You're about the thirtieth person I've spoken to since I got the hotel. I want you to lunch with me. I want to talk to you. If you're engaged, throw 'em over."

"I'm not engaged."

"One-thirty, then. I've left my hotel because Muriel Deane has gone to Scotland and lent me a flat. Take the address. You'd better write it down—110, Rigola Mansions."

At one-thirty he found Aurora most incongruously surrounded by gimcrack gilt furniture and delicate water-colours, her massive feet firmly planted on a rose-coloured Aubusson carpet. She wore heavy brogues and the same thick nondescript tweeds in which he had already seen her twice. He wondered vaguely whether she slept in them; they had that sort of look.

She shook him very heartily by the hand, and spoke over his shoulder to the maid who had shown him in.

"Lunch, Horrocks!" Then, as the door closed, "Stupid fashion calling a girl by her surname! Pretentious. Done to make believe you've got a butler when you haven't. Muriel's like that. Come along in—I had breakfast at half-past seven, so I want my lunch."

The dining-room was next door, a little white room with ebony furniture, black carpet, black curtains, and a black bowl in the middle of the table, in which floated an artificial white water-lily, rather dirty at the edges.

"Funerary—isn't it?" said Aurora briskly. "I told Muriel I should probably break her black-and-white china whilst she was away and give her something cheerful instead of it. She droops, you know—gold hair and transparent hands weighed down with immense diamonds; looks as if she'd never been out in the open air in her life, poor thing. The room gives me the pip, but the food's all right. Droopy women always have good cooks. Look here, everything's cold, and we're waiting on ourselves because I want to talk to you, and Horrocks has got a way of sliding in and out of the room that drives me wild. There's salmon, and beef, and a sort of salad that the cook fancies herself at. Help yourself."

When John had helped both of them, Miss Fairlie ate in silence for about five minutes, at the end of which time she got up, took another, and a larger, helping of salmon, and then began to talk:

"So you found Anne after all. Where is she?"

"She doesn't want anyone to know."

"I never heard such tiresome rubbish in my life! Why doesn't she want anyone to know?"

"She doesn't."

"Abominably stupid! Give me her address, and I'll see if I can't put some sense into her."

"I'm afraid I can't."

Aurora ate salmon rapidly.

"How did you find her?"

"By accident."

"What's she doing?"

"Parlour-maid," said John.

"Nonsense!"

"She is."

"My good man, why on earth?"

"To earn her living."

Aurora's small grey eyes darted a sharp question. She went on eating and looking at John, but she finished her salmon before she spoke. Then she said:

"Cut the beef, please. And don't give me the sort of skimpy helping you did before. I'm hungry. What's Anne doing earning her living? Didn't Anthony Waveney leave her provided for?"

"He altered his will."

"Why?"

John had his back to her. He added another slice to her plate and did not answer. When he had handed her salad and potato, and filled up her glass, he began to carve for himself.

"Sir Anthony left everything to Jenny," he said as he came over to the table.

Aurora, knife and fork in hand, was frowning portentously at the rather *passé* water-lily.

"We've begun at the wrong end," she said.

John agreed with her.

"The bother is," said Miss Fairlie, "that I don't know where I ought to begin." Her frown deepened and focussed itself upon John. "You see it's a question of how much you know, and how much I know, and whether we both know the same things. What do you know about Anne, John Waveney?"

John considered.

"A good deal," he conceded. "I know, for instance, that she wasn't in Spain with you last year. Do you mind if I ask what Jenny said to you when you turned up at Waterdene that evening? Did *you* know that Anne was supposed to have been travelling with you in Spain?"

"No, I didn't."

John nodded.

"I thought Jenny seemed a bit nervous. What did she tell you?"

Aurora ate beef. Presently she said:

"I can't tell you."

"All right—then I'll tell you. One of us has got to put his cards on the table, or we shan't get any forrader. Jenny told you that Anne had been in prison?"

"Yes—she did. Who told you?"

"Nicholas Marr told me three weeks ago. Anne told me herself yesterday."

Miss Fairlie's deep complexion had become several shades deeper. She produced a plum-coloured bandanna handkerchief and wiped her brow with it.

"Anne told you herself!"

John nodded.

"She got a year. The charge was stealing pearls."

"How many people know?" said Miss Fairlie roughly.

"Nicholas and Jenny, Mr. Carruthers, you, and me—also Mrs. Jones, who was Anne and Jenny's nurse. Anne gave her name as Annie Jones."

"No one else knew?"

"Sir Anthony."

"What a mix-up!" said Aurora. "What an infernal mix-up! And Jenny—I say, you don't mean to say Jenny takes the money!"

"That's too crude." John's tone was very dry. "Jenny isn't in the least crude; she's all affectionate generosity. Anne can actually have half—on conditions."

"What conditions?"

"The conditions are dictated by Nicholas. She's not to go there; and she's not to see them; and she's not to write to Jenny, or annoy her in any way."

Miss Fairlie laid down her knife and fork. She got up and helped herself to more salad. Then she sat down again.

"I see. What's your position in the matter?"

"I'm going to marry Anne."

"Sportsman!" said Aurora. "When?"

"As soon as she will. She's still saying 'No.'"

"Yes—she would. Look here, John Waveney, what's behind all this? I've known Anne since she was three. She's straight—dead straight. Why, bless my soul, I do know when a woman's straight and when she isn't. I'd bank on Anne!"

"So would I," said John. "You're a brick, Miss Aurora!"

"Drop the Miss! Well? What's behind it?"

"I can't tell you."

"I'd bank on Anne. But I'm not so sure that I'd risk anything I really cared about on Jenny. Is that it?"

"I can't say."

"H'm. I'll have some gooseberry tart. And you can put the cream and sugar on the table. Handed sugar is one of the economies of the rich. Muriel hasn't got a self-respecting sugar-bowl in the house; but such as it is, we'll have it between us and finish it. Jenny had the impudence to tell me I oughtn't to take cream on account of my figure—Yes, go on. Don't be afraid of it; I like lots—and I just said to her 'My good girl, when you're already forty round the waist, you won't let a matter of another five inches or so come between you and your cream and sugar.' By the way, Anne's too thin by half."

"She's with a beastly woman who doesn't give her enough to eat."

"She'd better come and stay with me at once."

"I say, you are a brick! I'm afraid she won't, though. Look here, Aurora, how much talk is there?—about Anne, I mean. Are people really saying things?"

"People always say things."

"What are they saying about Anne?"

"They come and ask me what was the matter with her, and say what a pity she couldn't be at Jenny's wedding. Some of 'em have the impudence to ask me whether she was really in Spain with me. I'm not going to forgive Jenny that in a hurry. I don't like telling lies. I wasn't brought up to tell 'em, and I don't like it. It's demoralizing. Every time I do it, it comes a bit easier. I'm beginning to take a pride in it. Disgusting I call it! And all because Jenny pitched on me!"

John laughed.

"You did it awfully well yesterday."

"That's what's so demoralizing. Look here, the whole thing's got to be put a stop to. Let Anne come here at once, mug up Spain—I've loads of photographs—go about with me, show herself. Then she can go and stay with Jenifer Courtney for a week or so. You can hang round until people begin to talk about you. Then the engagement is given out, Anne goes down to the Marrs, and you're married at Waterdene. That'll give 'em something else to think about. How's that for a plan?"

"There are only three objections."

"Objections? Nonsense! What are they?"

"Anne won't. Jenny won't. And Nicholas certainly won't. I don't know about Mrs. Courtney, but I should think she'd do what Jenny wanted her to."

Aurora snorted.

"Jenifer's a downright fool about Jenny—a hen with one chick, and would like everyone to believe it was the one and only bird of paradise. Change the plates and give me some cheese. There's gorgonzola and a marrowless cream thing suited to infants in arms. I'll have gorgonzola—I like to taste what I'm eating. Why did you bite my head off when I asked you if you were in love with Anne?"

John helped himself to cream cheese and grinned.

"You were so sudden. I'd only met you about an hour before. Besides, I didn't know myself—nor did Anne. You don't generally go about telling other people before you know yourself."

"Pass me the butter. I do wish I could cure Horrocks of skimping the butter—I think Muriel must be afraid of getting fat. I like butter and biscuit, not biscuit and butter. Does Anne know you're in love with her?"

"She ought to," said John with an odd fleeting smile.

Chapter Thirty-Three

JOHN GOT A LETTER from Anne that evening. It made him very angry. It had no proper beginning, because after writing "Dear John" twice, and "John dear" once, Anne had wasted three good sheets of paper by tearing them into small pieces and putting them into the kitchen fire. For this she was rebuked by Mrs. Brownling.

"Nothing chokes a fire like paper. Why, I've known a love-letter or two keep a family on loo-warm water for a week."

Anne might have retorted that there was nothing like never cleaning flues if you really wanted to keep your water cold; but she was too cast down to retort at all.

This was the letter that John read:

"I mustn't go on meeting you. I oughtn't ever to have met you at all. I blame myself very much. You mustn't come again. I really mean this. It puts us both in quite a false position. I can't be Annie Jones and Mrs. Fossick-Yates' parlour-maid and Anne Waveney at the same time. I'm not Anne Waveney any more—I want you to understand this; I'm Annie Jones, and Annie Jones can't come and meet you. I ought to have realized this before. I think I did really. When we met Aurora to-day, it showed me what a false position I was in. Please don't meet me any more, and please don't write or anything."

The letter ended just like that, without a signature.

When he had read it through twice, John sat down to answer it with the light of battle in his eye:

"DEAR ANNE,

"I'm beginning this way, because I don't feel in the least like saying 'Darling Anne' at the moment. However, you won't get this letter until to-morrow morning, so if I've stopped feeling angry by then, I will send you a telegram. Your letter is an infuriating one. I can't think why you wrote it. It's a frightful waste of time for one thing; and it's a frightfully bad letter for another. I don't think you know how to write letters. You ought to begin in the left-hand corner with 'Darling John' or 'My darling John.' Or, if you were in a nasty standoff sort of temper, which I'm afraid was the case, you might at least have put 'Dear John.' I knew a man once whose name was Macgregor Dennison—we used to call him 'Grigs.' He couldn't write letters either. But he knew he couldn't, and always used a *Polite Letter-Writer*. It tells you how to write to everybody. He was engaged to three girls at once when I knew him, and he wrote to them all every week. And they all said they'd never had such letters in their lives. They simply lapped them up and asked for more. The letters were very affectionate, but quite proper. I think you'd better have a *Polite Letter-Writer*. I will see if I can get you one. I will come round on Sunday at the usual time. Please don't be late, or I shall think you're not coming; and then I shall have to come and fetch you, and perhaps that would be a shock for Mrs. Fossick-Yates. I am not very fond of her, but I should not like to give her a fatal shock.

"Please be punctual. I shall be at the corner at half-past two, and I will wait there until three. After that I shall be obliged to risk giving Mrs. Fossick-Yates a shock.

"JOHN

"P.S.—I am still frightfully angry."

Anne got this letter by the early post. She changed colour several times whilst reading it. Finally she laughed. It was undoubtedly pleasant to have made John Waveney angry. Her spirits rose to a dangerous degree.

Presently the telephone bell rang. Anne flew to it. Suppose he had really sent a telegram. Suppose Mrs. Fossick-Yates—

She clapped the receiver to her ear, and caught the words: "A telegram for Jones."

A muffled sound broke from her lips. It was really an imprecation directed against the absent John, but the operator took it to indicate an uncertainty as to the name of the person to whom the telegram was addressed.

"J for Johnny; O for—"

"No—no—*no!*" said Anne, her voice smothered but desperate.

"J for Johnny; O—"

"No," said Anne. "I mean I've got that. Please give me the telegram."

"The telegram is for J-O-N-E-S—Jones."

"Yes, I know. Will you give it to me?"

"For Jones, 183, Ossington Mansions, Ossington Road. Are you taking it?"

"Yes. Do go on!"

"I am going on."

"To Jones, 183, Ossington Mansions, Ossington Road—"

"Yes, yes."

"Handed in at Vere Street at eight a.m. Are you taking it?"

Anne heard a door open behind her. She did not dare look round. Despair descended on her. She said, "Yes, I am," and felt her knees shake.

"This is the telegram: 'Second reading admissible.—J. M. W.'"

Anne hung up the receiver with a limp hand and turned to find Mr. Fossick-Yates regarding her with interest.

"Was that for me?" he questioned.

"No, sir."

"Thank goodness!"

Anne moved away. Was he going to ask her any more questions? Apparently he was not. She drew a breath of thankfulness, and took refuge in the kitchen.

At ten she received a parcel. It contained a small book bound in bright red. On the cover there appeared in gold:

THE ART OF LETTER WRITING

BY

A PEERESS.

Anne pushed the book well down inside her box and turned the key on it with a vicious click. Then she went into the kitchen to polish silver. Her colour was so bright that Mrs. Brownling commented on it.

"Haven't been rouging, have you, dear? It's fashionable enough, as everyone can see—and I won't say it don't brighten some faces up a bit—but in my young days, if you said rouge, you said the scarlet woman, and that was all about it. I remember when I was engaged to a gentleman of the name of Higgs that was in a soap-chandler's business and afterwards did very well in the wholesale, there was a very handsome lady that lived no more than three doors down from us. It was when my poor father was on the staff of the British Museum and overworking something shocking. They were nice little houses, though steep in the stair and a wicked basement. Well, Mr. Higgs put his foot in it—and I must say he might have had more sense. Right in the middle of Sunday supper he comes out with 'What a handsome neighbour we've got! A fine woman,' he says, 'a dashed fine woman—dashed fine eyes, dashed fine complexion!' You should have seen how my father looked. I told you how strict he was. He opened his mouth; but my mother got in first. She was a Miss Smith from Brighton, and very quick with her tongue. 'The lady's eyes may be her own, but her complexion isn't,' she says. And my father says: 'Silence, Matilda!' And then he says to Mr. Higgs: 'Profanity and immorality are disapproved of by me, sir.' And after that there were some unpleasant remarks passed on both sides, and in the end it came to my engagement being broken off which I dare say was all for the best, for he'd a shocking high temper, and it's better to find it out before than after."

Anne rubbed hard at spoons and forks and a coffee-pot. Part of her laughed and part cried, and a part of her was angry with John. She said "Wretch!" to herself, and rubbed the coffee-pot very hard indeed.

Chapter Thirty-Four

IT RAINED on Sunday. The sort of sky that looks as if it had been born grey and meant to die weeping hung low and dark over London; the rain came down with a hard monotony that never slackened or varied in the least; there was no wind. It was a very discouraging day.

"Can't say you're favoured, dear," said Mrs. Brownling, as Anne cleared away lunch. "Will he come and meet you? Some wouldn't. But I don't think much of a young man that's afraid of getting his feet wet; puts me in mind of a cat, and makes me feel like saying 'Poor pussy!' Will he come, d'you think?"

"I don't know what you mean," said Anne impatiently.

Mrs. Brownling put back a straggle of hair with a hand that left a black mark all across her cheek.

"Go *on*, Annie!" she said. Then she chuckled.

It annoyed Anne to have to put on the grey coat and skirt. She slipped her blue coat over it and, after a last disgusted look at the weather, pulled on her black felt hat. If John were a reasonable person he wouldn't expect her—especially after she had said she wouldn't come. She had made up her mind not to go, and she wouldn't go if it were not that John was perfectly capable of carrying out his threat and coming to the flat for her. With the drawing-room door next to the hall door, and Mrs. Fossick-Yates reading the Sunday papers on the other side of that door, the prospect of Sir John Waveney being overheard asking Annie Jones why she had failed to meet him was a really terrifying one.

Anne stamped her foot, put on her hat without looking in the glass, and then, when she had reached the door, turned back and put it on all over again, looking at herself carefully from every angle and making a number of minute adjustments. This took about ten minutes.

In the end she found herself hurrying down Ossington Road in a panic lest John should have got impatient and have started to meet her.

He was looking at his watch as she came round the corner.

"I suppose you know you're late. You're a frightfully unpunctual person. I can't imagine why I want to marry you. I haven't brought the car. We're going to pick up a taxi at the other corner. I rang up Aurora, and we're going to have tea at her flat."

Anne stopped dead.

"No—I can't!"

John took her by the arm and marched her along.

"I wish you wouldn't go out of your way to be disagreeable. Isn't the weather enough?"

"But—John—"

"Anne, you make me tired. Aurora isn't there. Have you got that? Aurora has gone away for the week-end; the flat's empty except for a parlourmaid called Horrocks, who is going to give us tea."

Anne allowed herself to be piloted to a taxi. After all, they must have it out some time. She must find out what John knew, and make sure of his silence.

When you are very busy from morning till night, and very tired when you go to bed, it is possible to shut and lock away the things which don't bear thinking of. Anne had made herself think about her work, about Mrs. Brownling, about the untidiness of the kitchen, and the harshness of Mrs. Fossick-Yates' voice, and about how angry she was with John. These things, which had really no form or substance, could be made to fill her thought and keep it busy. Now all these pretences vanished away and left her with an empty space in front of a locked room in which were things which she was afraid to look at.

She sat quite silent in the taxi and stared through the window at the rain and the drenched streets—black umbrellas all wet and shiny, pavements like shallow running streams, a pillar-box scarlet as the book which John had sent her.

Aurora had coerced Horrocks into lighting a fire in the pale drawing-room. Horrocks didn't hold with fires in May, especially with a coal strike on; but Aurora had prevailed.

John switched on the light in the tall gilt candlesticks with rose-coloured shades which stood on either side of the fireplace.

"Aurora says this is the least uncomfortable chair," he said; and Anne was betrayed into a smile.

"How nice to be in a drawing-room again!" The words slipped out just above her breath.

John said "Damn!" with some violence. And then: "I'm sorry, Anne, but you'd make a hen canary swear."

Anne's dark blue eyes flashed a quick mischievous look at him. It made his heart jump. He stood on the hearthrug with his back to the fire, looking down.

"Now, Anne."

"Well?"

Anne felt singularly disinclined to accept his challenge. Why couldn't he let her dry her feet and sit peacefully by the fire with pink cushions at her back?"

She said "Well?" in a very half-hearted voice.

"I want you to leave Mrs. Fossick-Yates at once. I want you to come here and stay with Aurora whilst I arrange about our getting married."

Anne drew a long sighing breath.

"We're not going to get married."

"Oh yes, we are. I'm not joking, you know—I'm dead serious."

"So am I. I can't marry you, John."

"You know I love you—" He paused, and added, "Very much."

Anne did not speak. The last two words had touched some secret spring of joy and pain; she could not trust herself to speak. If John would be angry, it would be so much easier. It was when he was so dear that she could not find the words to send him away.

"Anne, get up!"

He put his hands on her shoulders and pulled her out of her chair.

"Now look me in the face and tell me, don't you love me, too?"

Anne found courage. She looked him straight in the eyes and said "Yes."

"Then—"

"I can't marry you."

"Yes, you can."

He put her back in her chair.

"Sit down and listen."

He knelt by her, one arm round her shoulders.

"Anne—darling—just listen, and you'll see how easy it's going to be. You'll come here and stay with Aurora—it's all fixed up. Any talk there's been will die away as soon as you show yourself. Aurora said that at once. Most people think you've been in Spain with her as it is. It'll all be quite easy. Then Nicholas and Jenny must play up; and you must put your darling pride in your pocket and stay with them just long enough for us to get married from there. That'll stop everyone's mouth."

Anne felt herself at bay before her locked doors. She shook her head.

"I can't—they won't."

John laughed harshly.

"Won't they, by gum! I think they will. And if they don't—"

"No—John!"

"If they don't, I shall want to know who really took Levinski's pearls."

Anne wrenched herself from his arms and leaned back against the far corner of the chair.

"I took them—I told you I took them."

"Did you? The girl who took them wore an emerald ring—Levinski noticed it particularly. It was such a handsome ring that it made him think the girl really wanted to buy pearls, not merely to look at them. Where's your emerald ring, Anne?"

"I haven't got one. You know that. I borrowed Jenny's ring."

"That's a lie."

Anne's eyes blazed.

"Why shouldn't a thief tell a lie? I borrowed Jenny's ring."

"And she lent it—her engagement ring?" He laughed. "Did she lend you her hair, too? Levinski didn't notice her hair; but his assistant did. I found him day before yesterday—rather a susceptible young man with a noticing eye. He explained his carelessness by saying that the young lady had taken his fancy like. He said he was always struck on fair hair, and you didn't often find it with brown eyes. Have you got fair hair and brown eyes Anne?"

"You're making that up. He gave evidence."

"Yes, I know he did. I think you took care that none of your hair showed that day; and I don't suppose you looked at him. Did you? Anyhow, he was all of a doodah and only concerned with himself by that time. You see, he'd got the sack. No, Anne, you can't get away with it. It was fair hair and brown eyes and an emerald ring that took the pearls. Fair hair and brown eyes and an emerald ring. Well, Anne, is that you? Or is it Jenny?"

Anne strained back in her corner, her face colourless, her eyes frightened—*frightened*. John put his arms about her and pulled her close.

"Anne darling—Anne *darling*, don't look like that! Tell me about it. Won't you?" Quite suddenly he dropped his head on her shoulder. "You can't lie to me—I can't stand it! And there's no need to—I want to help you—Anne—" The words were all low and muffled.

She felt his shoulders shake. Her hand came up and began to stroke his hair. She said:

"John!"

He lifted his head. His face was wet.

"Tell me the whole thing, and we'll find a way out together. There's always a way out if you look for it. You haven't been looking you know; you've just settled down to being a darling idiot of a martyr."

"Oh! I haven't!"

"Yes, you have. You've tied yourself up to your stake, and piled up lots of slow combustion fuel all round you, and settled down to being grilled for the rest of your life. And I won't have it. You've got to come right off it and stay off it. I won't stand any more of it. Now, will you tell me the whole story from the beginning?"

Anne was silent. Her hand had dropped back into her lap. She looked down at it, steadily, seriously.

John's arms tightened about her.

"You've got to tell me. It won't hurt Jenny, if that's what you're afraid of. I've got proof against Jenny already. Look here, Anne, I'm not keeping anything back. I've seen pretty red about Jenny once or twice, and I've wanted her to be punished; I've wanted her to pay the last farthing; I've wanted her to feel everything you've felt, and suffer everything you've suffered."

Anne set her hands against his shoulders as if to push him away.

"You mustn't—you won't."

John bent and kissed the hands.

"I've got past that. I didn't tell you, but she came to see me."

"What did she want?"

"She wanted to know where you were."

"You didn't—"

"No, of course not. She gave me a message for you."

"You didn't give it to me."

"I think I'm a fool to give it to you now. I didn't want to undermine you—you're soft enough about Jenny as it is."

"What did she say?"

"She said to give you her love—and little Tony's love."

"Oh!" said Anne. She put her hands to her face for a moment, then let them fall and looked at John with a shining look of happiness. "You don't know—you don't know what a difference that makes."

"You're easily pleased! Oh, Anne, what a blessed little fool you are! You've given Jenny everything, and you're in the seventh heaven because she sends you her love!"

Anne laughed.

"You don't understand."

"Yes, I do. It's because I understand that I've stopped wanting to punish Jenny. You're *such* a little fool that I couldn't hurt her without hurting you. I don't want to hurt her; but I won't have her hurting you. She and Nicholas have got to play up and make things easy for you."

"Nicholas doesn't know," said Anne.

John whistled.

Chapter Thirty-Five

"NICHOLAS DOESN'T KNOW; and Jenny's afraid—she's always been afraid." Anne spoke quickly.

"Yes, I can see that. Look here, Anne, tell me the whole thing from the beginning."

Anne looked past him into the fire. She had kept silence for so long that to break this silence seemed hard. She had never thought that she would tell anyone. Now she leaned against John's arm and found words.

"It began a long time ago. You won't understand unless I tell you from the beginning. I want you to understand so much because of Jenny."

"I'll try."

"Jenny's very loving—she's all sunny and warm and loving. People love her, and she loves them—easily. I'm quite different. But Jenny's always been like that—she's got a loving nature."

John's face hardened and his jaw stuck out.

"You forget I saw you after you'd seen Jenny at Waterdene. You looked as if she'd killed you. What was her loving nature doing then?"

"She was frightened. It was my own fault—I'd no business to go down there. You see, I thought she would have told Nicholas— and she hadn't. So naturally he wouldn't have me there, and she was frightened."

"Oh, naturally." His tone was very dry. "Well, let's get on. And, I say, darling, don't try me too high—about Jenny's virtues, or I shall say things. I can't stand more than a certain amount."

"Be good," said Anne. "I can't tell you anything unless you're good."

"I'm earning haloes all the time."

"Go on earning them. If you don't understand what Jenny's like you won't understand anything. I told you it began a long way back. It began really the last year of the war, when we were sixteen. Jenny was staying with Cousin Jenifer, and she got into a sort of love affair with a man she met at the canteen Cousin Jenifer worked in. I never saw him, so I can't tell you what he was like. He wrote to Jenny, and she wrote to him. And by-and-by, when he was coming home on leave, he"—she hesitated—"he wrote and wanted Jenny to come up and meet him at an hotel. I don't know how he dared; but people always thought Jenny was older than she really was, and—John, you will understand, won't you?—Jenny was the sort of girl who doesn't see any harm in anything. There *are* girls like that. It's not just being innocent; it's more like having a blind spot somewhere. She thought it would be just fun, and she wrote him three letters about it saying what fun they would have, and planning things to do with him. And then he was killed. I didn't know anything about it for years afterwards—not until Jenny was engaged to Nicholas. Then her picture was in all the papers. And one day she came back from town in a perfectly dreadful state of mind. She'd been up staying with Cousin Jenifer for a week, and she said a woman had followed her and tried to blackmail her. She was frightfully upset, and she told me the whole story. The woman had got the three letters she'd written to this man—they'd been sent home with his things. The woman said she was his wife, and she said that she'd show the letters to Nicholas unless Jenny bought them from her for five hundred pounds.

"John, I begged Jenny to tell Nicholas. I said he'd believe her, that any man who really cared for a woman would believe her. But she went off to town next day, and in the evening she came back with the letters, and we burnt them. She'd pawned the string of pearls which Nicholas had given her."

"Little fool!" said John.

"My poor Jenny! She was in the wildest spirits. She laughed and sang and made me dance with her—the relief was so tremendous. She cared—she *cares*—so very, very much for Nicholas."

"I can't think why."

Anne burst out laughing.

"Oh, *John*, how funny you are! You don't care for people because you've got a reason for it."

John said what he hadn't meant to say:

"You certainly haven't much reason to care for Jenny." Then, as Anne winced, he cried out: "I'm a brute!" and caught her close and kissed her.

Anne kissed him back, with soft, reproachful kisses.

"You're not being good. You promised to be good, and you're not being a bit good."

"It's just as well you don't love by reason," said John.

"Are you going to be good?"

"I don't know. I'll try. Go on."

"I don't know where I'd got to."

"That little ass Jenny had just pawned her pearls."

Anne pushed him away and looked at him with laughing eyes that were suddenly swept by a shadow.

"Yes, she pawned them. She got five hundred pounds, and she was most awfully pleased about it. And then—you know the way things happen—Nicholas wrote and said he wanted her to go up and meet him in town, and she was to bring the pearls, because he was having them valued for insurance. They'd been his mother's, and someone had just told him that the value of pearls had gone up tremendously. Jenny went all to bits when she got his letter. She'd bought a string of sham pearls to wear, and she'd had the real clasp put on to them. The pawnbroking man did it for her; he had the sham pearls in his shop, and he told her no one would know—I shouldn't have known myself. And Jenny thought she could wear them, and then after she was married she could save enough money to get her own pearls back. Nicholas was making what Mr. Carruthers called 'very handsome settlements.' She thought it was all going to be quite easy, and when Nicholas' letter came she couldn't bear it. She sat on the floor with her head in my lap and just cried and cried. She said she couldn't live if Nicholas found out. No, John—Jenny's like that. I don't mean to say that she'd do anything to herself; but I do think she'd die if the people she loved stopped loving her and thinking well of her and all that. She *depends* on it. I didn't know what to say to her except that if she couldn't tell Nicholas, couldn't she tell Cousin Jenifer?"

"Well, that was pretty sound. Why didn't she?"

"She said she couldn't. And *honestly*, John, I don't think she could. I don't know if you can understand, but if either of them had cared for her less, I think she could have told them. You see, they both thought her perfect—Cousin Jenifer always did think that Jenny was absolutely perfect—and Jenny simply couldn't bear them to think less of her. I went on talking and trying to persuade her and at last she said she'd try, and if she could tell Cousin Jenifer, she would. And next day she went off to town for a week. She wrote to me after she got up. She told me she'd seen Nicholas and managed to put off giving up the pearls for a week. She said she'd told him she must have them to wear in town."

"Well?" said John.

Anne pushed her hair back. She had taken off the little damp felt hat; her dark, short hair was ruffled.

"Nanna and I went up to town for the end of the week. I expect you know that."

"Yes."

"We stayed at an hotel. I was going to have my bridesmaid's frock fitted. We were up two days. The first day Nanna and I were to meet Jenny at the dressmaker's. She came awfully late. I could see there was something wrong, but she wouldn't tell me what it was. And then Nanna went to see her daughter, and Nicholas called for us, and we had lunch and went to a theatre. I can see now just how it was. Jenny'd got those wretched pearls." Anne's voice broke in a little dry sob. Then she drew a long breath and went on: "We dined out in the evening and danced. It's so funny to think of it now! Next day Jenny called for me to go for a last fitting on our way to the station. Nanna was going to take the luggage."

"What is it?" said John as she stopped. She was so pale that he was frightened.

"It's so *hateful*! No—I want to get it over—I'd rather go on—it's only—"

"I know—Anne *darling*."

"I'm all right. We took a taxi. The road was up; we went by a lot of side streets. I didn't know where we were. I said, 'Oughtn't we to be in Bond Street?' and I leaned out of the window. We were just opposite a jeweller's shop. There was a man without a hat looking in at the window. He turned round and he saw me, and he called out something, and Jenny pulled me back, and our taxi went on round the corner into Bond Street. I looked back, and I saw that the man was running. And then I looked round and I saw Jenny's face. John, she looked as if she was dying—she really did. She said: 'Save me, Anne, save me!' And then she said: 'Is he coming?' And I looked again and the man was getting into a taxi. I said: 'Yes—what is it?' And she told me. John, I thought she had gone mad. She said: 'I took his pearls yesterday. Is he coming?' I don't know what I said. She went on saying: 'I took them.' And then she said 'Prison' in a dreadful sort of whisper. She said: 'I can't go to prison.' I thought she was going to faint. I shook her, and I said: 'Where are the pearls?' And she pushed her bag into my hand. I made up my mind what I would do. The man thought I was Jenny—we had grey coats and skirts just alike, and little black hats—I'm wearing mine now, but I expect Jenny's burnt hers. She was wearing it when she took the pearls, but in the taxi she wasn't wearing it. She had an old blue coat on. The man saw my grey coat and skirt and thought I was Jenny."

"You're not so much alike."

"We used to be. I was fatter than I am now, and I'd more colour; and clothes do a lot. People were always taking us for each other when we dressed alike. That's why Nicholas didn't like it. Well, I felt sure that the man would follow my grey coat and skirt, and I made a plan. I told Jenny she was to drive straight to the station and go down with Nanna, and that, whatever happened, she wasn't to say a word or tell a soul. And then I looked out again, and, just as I looked, our taxi stopped in a block. I grabbed Jenny's bag, and I jumped out and ran round the back of the taxi so that the driver shouldn't see me." Anne stopped.

"Anne—you little plucky darned idiot! Go on."

"There isn't any more. I thought I might get away—then I could have sent the pearls back—but I didn't." Her voice trailed away, and a shiver shook her from head to foot.

For a long minute she went on trembling, her head on John's shoulder, his arms comforting her. Then she sat up.

"I *am* a fool!"

"Yes, darling Anne, why did you do it? No one has any right to a sacrifice like that."

Anne put her hand on his shoulder and pulled herself up. She had to move, to try and break the vivid memory of that one most unendurable moment when Levinski's voice had accused her and she had felt the policeman's hand fall on her shoulder. It was the worst moment of all; nothing that came afterwards was as bad as that—the crowd, staring eyes, someone laughing, the accusing voice, and that hand on her shoulder.

She went over to the fireplace and leaned there warming herself against those icy shudders, which came back even now when she let herself think about it.

John followed her to the fire, and for a moment neither of them spoke. Then he said roughly:

"You'd no business to do it. It was your whole life."

Anne leaned on the mantelshelf and looked down into the fire.

"I do want you to understand," she said. "I do, *do* want you to understand."

Her left hand hung at her side. He took it, held it strongly for a moment, and then let it go again.

"I'll try."

Anne began to speak in a low voice:

"I only had a minute to think what I was going to do, but I just seemed to see the whole thing, for me and for Jenny. Time didn't seem to come into it. I *saw* it."

"What did you see?"

"I saw Jenny." She turned a little and began to look at him as she spoke. "I saw what had happened to her. It was just ruin—Nicholas, her marriage, her friends, her whole life, smashed and done for. Jenny couldn't—ever have got up again—she *couldn't*. I could." The colour rose brightly in her face. "That's what I want you to understand. I saw the whole thing; I didn't go into it without seeing it all. And I knew I could do it. Don't you know? You have that feeling sometimes. There's something very hard. You look at it, and all of a sudden you know you can do it; you have the feeling, the strength. That's how it was. I knew I could do it. I knew I could make them think it was me. And I knew, if they sent me to prison, that I could come out of it and not be different. Jenny couldn't. That's why I couldn't let her; she'd have been smashed. I knew I could do it and be just the same in myself."

John watched her with a deep emotion, for which he could not find any words. With those shining eyes, that ebb and flow of sensitive colour, that soft appealing voice, she moved him to a passion of pity and love. He lifted her hand and put it to his lips. He wanted to speak to her, but he could not find his voice. He held her hand against his face and struggled into speech.

"I swear I'll make it up to you!" he said.

Chapter Thirty-Six

ANNE'S HAND pressed his cheek for a moment before it slipped away.

"I can't let you," she said.

"I'm not asking you to let me do anything; I'm telling you what I'm going to do."

Anne murmured something almost indistinguishable. He understood her to say that she didn't see how he could get married alone. When she had said this she blushed rather beautifully and looked into the fire again. John put his arm round her, and there was an interlude. When the interlude was over, John was very much himself again, and not in the least in a mood to stand any nonsense."

"Sit down on the fender-stool—it's nice and warm—and I'll tell you exactly what we're going to do. First of all, as I said, you're coming here to Aurora. And if Mrs. Courtney asks you, you can go to her for a few days. You want to go about and show yourself and go and see everyone you know. Aurora'll see you do it whilst you're with her. And then you'll go down to Waterdene and stay with Jenny until we get married."

"John—I can't!"

"I do wish you'd stop saying that; I'm frightfully fed up with it. You've got to. It won't be for long, because we're going to give our engagement out at once and get married in about three weeks. No, don't begin all over again and say you can't go to Waterdene because Jenny and Nicholas won't have you. You *were* going to say that, weren't you?"

"Yes, I was."

"I knew you were. Now, look here, I've had about enough of this. You've made the sort of sacrifice for Jenny that only about one person in ten million would ever dream of making for anyone, and the sooner Jenny and Nicholas get down on their knees and start licking your shoes, the better."

Anne looked at the point of her shoe, and her lips trembled. She said: "John—*dear!*" And then: "Nicholas doesn't know."

"Nicholas has got to know. No, Anne, it's not the slightest use. The people who think you took those pearls have got to know the facts. Jenny knows, you and I know, Aurora knows. The people who've got to be told are your old nurse, and Mr. Carruthers, and Nicholas."

Anne locked her hands together and gazed at him, pale and agitated.

"John—really!"

"I've thought it all out. It's what's right. I'm not vindictive; I'm not out to hurt Jenny. Mrs. Jones is devoted to her and as safe as a house. Your family lawyer ought to know, and must know. And Nicholas has got to know. Jenny can tell him herself—put it any way she likes. But he's got to know what Jenny owes you, and he's got to do what he can to put things right for you. He can do a lot. I won't have talk about you."

Anne lifted her head with a small, proud movement.

"You mean you won't have talk about your wife. That's why I won't marry you; there's bound to be talk."

"I don't mean anything of the sort. I do wish you'd stop talking nonsense! I mean I won't have talk about you—*you*. I don't care who you marry. I'm not thinking of your husband's feelings; I'm thinking about you—and you ought to know that by now. Anyone who's heard the lie about you is going to hear the truth. That lets Jenny down a lot more lightly than she deserves. I've written to her. You can read the letter if you like."

He produced an envelope from his pocket, extracted a large sheet of paper, and laid it open upon Anne's knee. She read, in John's firm, rather upright hand:

"DEAR JENNY,

"Anne and I are going to be married. I hope you will be pleased, because we are. Anne is going to stay with Aurora for a week, and then, I think, she ought to come and stay with you until we're married. I'm sure you will want Anne to be married at Waterdene. She need not stay with you for more than a fortnight, because we want to get married as soon as possible."

Anne shot him a chilly glance, met one that confused her, and went on reading:

"I think you had better tell Nicholas all about Levinski's pearls. It will make it easier for you to be nice to Anne. Besides, it will be really more comfortable for you when he knows—he's rather in a false position. Anne didn't tell me about Levinski. I found out. The old man noticed your emerald ring, and the assistant who served you admired your hair. Besides, I was sure of it all along. Don't get frightened—I'm not going to hurt you. Mrs. Jones must know, and Mr. Carruthers, and Nicholas; because they think it was Anne, and I can't have that. You'd better tell Nicholas at once, because I'm coming down to-morrow, Monday, afternoon to talk things over. You see, people have been talking about Anne and wondering where she's been all this time, and all that's got to stop. It can be stopped quite easily if we all rally round. But if you and Nicholas don't play up, people will go on thinking there's something wrong. So will you please tell Nicholas at once.

"Anne sends her love.

"Yours,

"J. M. W."

Anne lifted her eyes from the page, caught a glimpse of John's chin, sighed, and said:

"What a hurry you're in!"

"Of course I'm in a hurry."

He took away the letter, put it in its envelope, stuck down the flap, and rose.

"I'll just go out and post this."

"John, please don't!"

"I won't be a minute. I want Jenny to get it by the first post, because I've got to-morrow all mapped out. Directly after breakfast I shall go down and see Mrs. Jones. Then I shall do Carruthers. By the way, I'm telling him to open an account for you at Lloyds'. They'll want your signature, but we can see about that on Tuesday. Carruthers will pay in five hundred pounds to start with. Then I shall have some lunch and push off to Waterdene."

Anne gazed at him with an odd helpless feeling. With the letter in his hand he crossed to the door. At the door he turned.

"You'd better see Mrs. Fossick-Yates directly after breakfast tomorrow and tell her that urgent private affairs are tearing you away from her. Aurora will expect you here by tea-time. If you haven't come, she will come and fetch you. But I think it would be just as well if Aurora and Mrs. Fossick-Yates didn't meet. I don't think they'd get on very well, and Mrs. Fossick-Yates might get ideas in her head about Annie Jones going to stay with an explorer. So I think you'd better get here for tea. I'll roll up about seven. Aurora has asked me to dinner."

He went out and shut the door behind him with decision.

Anne put her chin in her hand and wondered why she wasn't angry. She felt that she ought to have been angry. She ought to say that she wouldn't have a banking account, or stay with Aurora, or be engaged. On the other hand, when she did say these things they did not seem to make any impression. She felt limp, and weak, and rather happy.

Horrocks opened the door and began, slowly and disapprovingly, to bring in tea.

Chapter Thirty-Seven

CAREFULLY MAPPED-OUT days do not always conform to plan. John interviewed a tearful, incredulous, protesting Mrs. Jones, and a silent and shocked Mr. Carruthers. After which he lunched and took the road.

Jenny would have had six hours in which to tell Nicholas the truth. He drove through a light drizzle, feeling cheerful and determined, and quite unconscious of the fact that his letter had not reached Jenny. It lay in the hall at Waterdene with half a dozen others awaiting the return of Sir Nicholas and Lady Marr from a week-end visit.

John drove up to the house five minutes after Jenny had picked up her letters and run upstairs to the nursery.

"Sir Nicholas is in the study," said the butler. And to the study John followed him.

Nicholas was pulling a spaniel's ears. He said, "Down, Jess! Steady, old lady!" and turned as charming a smile on John as if their last interview had never been. "She nearly eats me when I've been away."

John's cheerful confidence received a slight shock. Was it possible for a man who had just—well, in the last six hours—been told something which was bound to be a bit of a facer to look quite so unconcerned and easy as Nicholas was looking?

"What will you have?" said Nicholas with his hand on the bell.

"Oh, nothing, thanks. As a matter of fact, I've really come down to talk business."

"The last man who did that wanted to sell me some dud shares in a non-existent mine," said Nicholas.

"It's not money. By the way, I wrote to Jenny. Did she have my letter?"

Nicholas seemed to find this a little crude. His eyebrows rose.

"I really haven't any idea."

"I wrote to tell her that Anne and I were engaged," said John, and did not know that his voice held a challenge.

"Anne!" said Nicholas.

"Anne Waveney."

Nicholas lit a cigarette and flicked the match neatly into the waste-paper basket on the far side of his writing-table. He said, "Good shot!" and then, "Well, well."

"What do you mean by that?"

"I mean that I suppose you know your own business."

"I suppose I do. But I think this is your business and Jenny's as well as mine."

Between two puffs of smoke Nicholas said, "Hardly." He sat on the arm of a chair, cigarette in hand, and looked at the toe of his boot. His smile was still quite pleasant.

John had a moment of uncertainty. Nicholas didn't seem to know. Jenny hadn't played up. Well, she'd had her chance. Nicholas had got to know, only—The moment of uncertainty flickered out.

"It's certainly Jenny's business. Whether it's yours or not is just a matter for you and Jenny to settle. No, wait a minute, I want to get it off my chest, and I'd like you to listen. I thought Jenny would have spoken to you, but it seems she hasn't."

"Jenny knows my views. I haven't altered them. Perhaps it'll save trouble if I say straight away that I shan't ever alter them."

"I'd like you to listen if you don't mind. Anne and I are going to get married in about three weeks' time. And I think when you've spoken to Jenny you'll feel—"

Nicholas interrupted him:

"My dear John, I shan't ever feel differently about Anne Waveney. I don't want to hurt your feelings, but it'll save trouble all round if you'll realize that my decision about Anne is quite final."

"I think," said John, speaking mildly, "I think that when you know the facts you'll feel that it's up to you and Jenny—"

Nicholas interrupted again:

"I don't accept the slightest obligation."

John pursued his way:

"There's been a certain amount of talk; and there'll be more if you and Jenny go on cold-shouldering Anne. Naturally, I don't want there to be any talk."

Nicholas lit another cigarette.

"Anne Waveney took her own line. I told you what that line was. I haven't the slightest intention of allowing Jenny to have anything to do with her."

"I really think you'd better talk to Jenny about it. I wrote to her and suggested that Anne should come down here until we could be married. Of course, if Jenny hasn't spoken to you, you'll say 'No.' So I think you'd better talk to Jenny before you say anything."

Nicholas shot him an odd sidelong glance. He smoked in silence for a full minute before he said:

"Nothing that you've said to Jenny is going to have any effect at all upon the situation." A second glance said quite plainly: "Now, will you go?"

John took no notice of it. He was wondering where Jenny was. He said in rather a hesitating manner:

"I think you don't know all the facts. There were things which I had asked Jenny to tell you. I think when you know them you'll feel differently about Anne. That's why I'm not getting angry. I'd like to see Jenny, if you don't mind."

Nicholas shrugged his shoulders, got up, and walked to the bell.

"If you'd rather hear Jenny tell you that my mind is made up, I've no objection—Yes, I rang. Will you ask her ladyship to come down. Tell her Sir John Waveney is here."

Then, as the door closed behind the servant, he returned to his lounging attitude and to an expression of bored annoyance.

Upstairs Jenny was sitting on the floor with her baby in her lap.

"He knows me, nurse! I'm *sure* he knows me! Didn't ums, lovey? Didn't ums knows its horrid old deserting mum—going away and leaving him for two whole days? Nurse, I'm sure he's heavier— I'm *sure* he is!"

"He's got your letters, ma'am. He'll have them in his mouth in a minute."

Jenny laughed and kissed the pink clutching hands.

"Lie still, angel! Oh, he's sucked the corner of this one! Piggy Wiggy!"

She held it up, and then remained looking at the envelope. Her mind said quickly: "John Waveney! Why should he write to me?" She took the letter out, tearing it a little in her haste, and read what John had written:

"Anne and I are going to be married."

The words seemed to jump towards her, seemed almost to hit her. She felt as if she had been struck.

"Anne and I are going to be married. I hope you will be pleased."

Pleased. She took a sharp breath and called the nurse:

"Nurse, take baby."

She got up with the letter in her hand and went over to the window with it.

Little Tony gave a piercing shriek of disapproval. He was very comfortable on Jenny's lap; it was soft, not starchy; and he liked being cooed at and tickled. He voiced the most passionate disapproval. But Jenny did not hear him.

"I hope you will be pleased." This—*this* was what she had always been afraid of. She was so much afraid now that she did not know how to go on reading the letter. She felt as if she was standing on the edge of some frightful nightmare. If she read the letter, she would slip over the edge and become part of it. But she had to read the letter.

She looked at it and read on. Anne to come here—Anne to stay with her! Nicko wouldn't—And then: "I think you had better tell Nicholas all about Levinski's pearls." The letter disappeared in the mist that seemed to fill the room.

Jenny went on staring at the place where the letter had been. The mist got thinner. She saw a white oblong with streaks on it—black streaks, letters, words, that danced, shifted, steadied. She began to read the words: "You'd better tell Nicholas at once, because I'm coming down tomorrow, Monday."

She read on to the end of the letter. She was to tell Nicholas at once—tell Nicko that she was a thief; that she had taken Levinski's pearls and let Anne go to prison for it. She was to tell Nicko all this at once.

Her right hand held the letter. Her left closed hard upon itself, driving the pink pointed nails into her palm. She began to breathe a little faster. John—she must get hold of John. She must get hold of him before he saw Nicko. And she must make him understand that she couldn't possibly do such a preposterous thing. He couldn't ask her to do it—not really.

"If you please, my lady—" It was the nurse with little Tony, now pacified, in her arms.

"What is it?" said Jenny sharply.

"If you please, my lady, James came to the door with a message from Sir Nicholas; and he says will your ladyship please go down, as Sir John Waveney would like to see you."

Jenny took the blow without any outward sign; it hit her so hard that, for the moment, it took away her power to feel. She crumpled up the letter and pushed it down into the pocket of her white jumper suit. She had thrown off her hat when she came into the nursery. She put up the hand that had held the letter, and smoothed her fair wavy hair. The other hand hung down rigid.

She went out of the door and down the stairs with the fear in her rising to panic. It was coming; she couldn't stop it. John was there with Nicko. The worst of all her terrible dreams was coming true. And there was no Anne to save her now.

Halfway down the stairs she began to run. Then, with her hand on the study door, she stopped, leaning there, her head against the panel, breathless and quivering. She heard John speak, and the thought rushed into her mind: "He's telling Nicko *now*."

She pushed the door open and ran into the room.

Chapter Thirty-Eight

WHEN THE SERVANT had gone to find Jenny, John remained looking at Nicholas for a moment. Then he walked over to the window and stood there looking out. The clouds were very black on the far side of the river; the water ran like dull quicksilver through the wet green meadows. The lilac was over, and the crimson may.

John looked out into the drizzle of fine rain and settled what he would do. When Jenny came, he would ask her if she had had his letter; then he would leave her to tell Nicholas. He could go for a tramp and come back again. He felt sorry for Nicholas Marr.

"I'm sorry Jenny didn't get my letter first thing this morning. I didn't think of her being away. Have you only just got back?"

"Five minutes before you—blew in."

"I see."

Perhaps he'd better give them a little more time—clear off altogether and come down again tomorrow.

"Jenny'll want to talk to you," he said. "I'll just make sure she's had my letter, and then I'll clear off. I can come down again to-morrow."

Nicholas knocked the ash off his cigarette on to the carpet.

"Can you?" he said. And with that the door was pushed open and Jenny came in.

John turned, and received a shock. For the first time, the likeness to Anne was a real thing. And it was a likeness of suffering. Jenny's face, with the colour drained from it and the eyes staring, was terribly like the face Anne had lifted to him when he met her, dumb and beaten, in the drive at Waterdene.

Jenny was looking, not at him, but at Nicholas. She ran into the room, and stopped by the writing-table, holding to the back of a tall chair and looking at Nicholas.

"Nicko! What has he said? Send him away! It's not true! You won't—you won't believe him if I say it's not true! You won't believe him against me! *Nicko!*"

Nicholas Marr got up slowly. He threw the end of his cigarette into the fireplace. Then he went over to Jenny and put his hand on her shoulder.

"Jenny!" The word came sharp.

The hand on her shoulder was firm. Jenny clutched at him.

"Nicko—send him away! What has he said?"

Then, leaning back against Nicholas, she turned upon John:

"How dare you come here with your lies? Do you think he'll believe them?"

Then back again to catch at Nicholas with a desperate hand:

"Say you don't believe him! Nicko, it's a dreadful, dreadful lie! I didn't do it—I didn't! Anne confessed—you know she did. She took the pearls, and she confessed. Nicko, send him away!"

"I'm going," said John. He went to the door and spoke in clear, deliberate tones: "I haven't said anything, Jenny. Why did you think I had? It's up to you. I told you so in my letter."

Then he went out and shut the door behind him.

Jenny took a shuddering breath. She let go of Nicholas and stood back a pace. He hadn't spoken. How much had she said? What was she to say now?

As the thought went through her mind, Nicholas looked at her, and she had hard work to keep from crying out.

"Explain," he said.

"I—Nicko—" She put her hand to her throat.

"That is hardly an explanation."

"Nicko—I—"

"Your very tactful cousin having removed himself, I'm afraid I must ask you for something a little more to the point."

Jenny gazed at him dumbly. It was worse than the worst of her dreams.

"What does it mean?" said Nicholas.

"I—" Her voice failed.

"John Waveney wrote you a letter. Where is it?"

She moved her head very slightly, as if to deny the letter.

"I imagine it shed some light on the situation. Will you show it to me?" Again that very slight movement of the head. "I think you have it—pockets aren't meant to hide things nowadays. Will you give it to me?"

Sheer terror opened Jenny's lips:

"Nicko, I can't!" Then, as he reached forward and took the letter from her pocket, she gave a little broken cry and shrank away.

Nicholas straightened out the letter without looking at it.

"I shall not read it without your permission. But I think you can hardly refuse your permission. You see, I'm bound to have an explanation. You seem unable to give me one. There remains the letter—and your cousin. Either I read this letter, or I ask John Waveney to tell me its contents. It's whichever you prefer, of course."

Jenny went back a pace, struck against the writing chair, and sat down. The fight was gone out of her. There was no one to help her. Nicko would never forgive her. She felt a great longing for Anne.

She laid her arms on the back of the chair and dropped her head on them.

"Am I to read the letter?" said Nicholas in that icy voice.

Jenny just moved her head again. This time the movement said "Yes."

She had no sooner moved than she would have given all the world to recall that despairing consent. If she had said "No," he wouldn't be reading that dreadful letter—*now*. Her forehead was wet where it pressed against her arm. If she could only faint—if she could die, and escape from Nicko's eyes.

After a long, cold time, Nicko's voice, slow, measured, controlled:

"You're to tell me about Levinski's pearls. I'm waiting."

He waited.

Jenny's mind, strung to the extreme of terror, was swept clear of conscious thought. When she and Anne were small they had been taught verses from a book that had belonged to their grandmother. One of these formal, stilted verses repeated itself over and over in the empty places of her mind:

"Now, Jenny, I pray, put such feelings away,
And own that you acted amiss.
How sweet to be friends and make loving amends,
And end all our strife with a kiss!"

"Answer me!" said Nicholas in a voice that Jenny had never heard from anyone in her life.

The shock brought her head up and gave her back the power of speech.

"Was it you who took the pearls?" said Nicholas.

Of all the denials that had come so fast to Jenny's lips there was not one to serve her now. She said, "Yes. Why?" She put her hand to her neck as if she were feeling for the pearls that were not there. "Your pearls—you wanted them."

"Mine? What do you mean?"

"You wanted them. I hadn't got them."

"Will you explain?"

Jenny went on looking at him with eyes that saw nothing—blank brown eyes like shallow peat-water.

"I had to have some money. I couldn't ask anyone. I pawned your pearls."

When she had said this, Jenny shivered under the contempt in his eyes.

"You told me Anne took your pearls and pawned them. That wasn't true?"

Jenny shook her head.

"You pawned them yourself, and when I went on asking for them you took Levinski's. Were you going to pass them off on me as mine?"

"I don't know—I didn't think—it was so easy to take them—I just did it."

"I see. And you let Anne take the blame?"

"She did it," said Jenny. "Anne's always—always—" She broke off with a little bitter cry of "Anne!" and dropped her head on her arms again.

Nicholas stood quite still. He had never liked Anne. Jenny was his, and he would share her with no one. Anne's likeness to her was an offence; Anne's love for her a claim. In his intolerable humiliation his anger against Anne was a relief. There was murder in his heart for Anne. What there was for Jenny he didn't know—contempt, colder than anger; resentment, far more bitter than a blow.

He said, very low, "You rotten little outsider!" and went out of the room without looking back.

Chapter Thirty-Nine

NICHOLAS CAME BACK to Waterdene in the dusk. The rain had ceased; it was a clear, grey evening with streaks of saffron in the west. He had driven furiously for hours. He came home now for no reason except that one cannot go on driving for ever.

Emmot, the butler, met him in the hall, a comfortable, rotund man who had been for twenty years at Waterdene, and to whom Nicholas was still secretly Master Nick.

"Her ladyship—we've been a bit troubled about her ladyship."

For an instant Nicholas went cold.

"What's the matter?"

"Nurse wanted to send for the doctor, but I said better wait till you came home."

"What's the matter?"

"Her ladyship's been sitting in the study ever since you went away. Nurse can't get her to move—not even for Master Tony. She and Harman are very much upset."

Nicholas shed his coat.

"Her ladyship's had bad news—we both have. I'll go to her."

"Nurse did get her to take some tea. I didn't think you'd want the doctor sent for till you came home."

"No—quite right."

He came into the study with his mood violently wrenched. Public opinion—no getting away from it. Servants, friends, relations, Press—you couldn't live your life, meet tragedy or disaster, in a decent privacy."

He had thrown his bitter contempt at Jenny and flung off. He came back to Emmot's concern, to what nurse and Jenny's maid, Harman, were thinking—to public opinion in his own household.

Jenny was sitting just as he had left her. Harman, frightened and excited, was at the far end of the room. She went out as he came in, with just one scared look over her shoulder.

As the door shut Jenny lifted her head from her arms. She looked as if she had been crying for hours. The light from the reading-lamp upon the table touched the edges of her hair with gold. The curtains had been drawn, and the room was in darkness except for that one lamp.

Nicholas put up his hand to the switch and turned on the light in the ceiling.

"I thought you'd gone," said Jenny.

"I've come back."

He went to the fireplace and stood there, one arm on the mantelshelf, his face dark and expressionless. His eyes avoided Jenny.

"Why did you do it?"

"I told you."

"You wanted money. Why?"

The thought of the money had been like poison all those hours.

"I had to have it." Jenny's voice was very faint and exhausted.

"How much was it?"

"Five hundred pounds."

"You had to have five hundred pounds. You were being blackmailed?"

Jenny choked on a cry.

"You were being blackmailed?"

"Who—told you?"

"It was fairly obvious. Perhaps you'll tell me why."

Jenny pushed back her hair. Nicholas felt a strange, sharp stab. She had looked like that when they let him see her after Tony was born.

"Are you going to tell me?" he said harshly.

Jenny got up. All her movements were stiff and slow. She held on to the chair, and said in a whispering voice:

"It wasn't anything really. But you won't believe that. Anne said to tell you; but I always knew that you wouldn't believe me. So I had to have the money."

"I think you must tell me now."

"It's no use. But it doesn't matter—it wasn't anything really. There was a man. I didn't know he was married. He was at Aunt Jenny's canteen. He made love to me. When he went back to the Front I wrote to him."

"What did you write?"

"Just letters—nothing at all. He said he hadn't anyone to write to him."

"Well?"

Jenny hesitated.

"Nicko—there wasn't anything."

Nicholas said: *"Five hundred pounds."* His hand rose for a moment, and then fell again. There was a certain finality about the gesture.

"It was when he was coming home on leave," said Jenny quickly. "He wrote about our doing theatres and going to dances together. When I said Aunt Jenny wouldn't let me, he said she needn't know—I could stay at an hotel with him. And I wrote him letters about it. I didn't know, Nicko, I really didn't know—I thought it would be fun."

"And you went?"

Jenny shivered at his voice.

"No, I didn't. He was killed."

Nicholas was looking at her very hard.

"He was killed. And they sent his things home to his wife—they sent her my letters. Nicko, she was a most dreadful woman. She saw my picture in the paper after we were engaged, and she came to see me, and said if I didn't buy my letters from her she'd show them to you. And when I said I hadn't any money, she said, 'What about those pearls you're wearing?' That's what made me think about the pearls. Anne said I ought to tell you—she always said so. She said you'd believe me. But I couldn't do it."

"How old were you?" said Nicholas abruptly.

"Sixteen. Nicko, I *didn't* know."

"Why didn't you tell me?"

"I couldn't. I minded—so much—what you thought. I cared so much, I couldn't."

She sat down again as if the strength to stand was gone.

Nicholas found himself believing her. He said:

"Have you told me everything, Jenny?"

"I think so"—her voice sounded very tired—"I think I have." Then, after a long pause: "What are you going to do?"

"I don't know."

"Are you going to send me away?"

Separation, and a hundred tongues wagging over their affairs; a hypothetical lover for Jenny, or a mistress for himself; Jenny alone and lonely—there would be plenty ready enough to proffer consolation. Nicholas knew his world very well; he was able to see Jenny's future very distinctly. If their separation was to be final there would be only one result; if temporary, what was there to be gained except a liberal spattering of mud? His mind, working coolly, discarded these solutions. Something fine in him recognized a debt to Anne, whom he disliked, and an obligation to Jenny, whom he loved. He did not feel that he loved her, but he knew it in the clear, cold places of thought. He knew that he could not separate from her, because she had never needed him so much. The need irked him, but it compelled him too.

Jenny had been watching him with eyes in which hope had drowned. He would send her away. He would take Tony away from her. She had lost Anne; now she was going to lose Nicko and Tony. It was her punishment. No one would ever love or admire her again. Everything was going from her except the power to suffer. She thought then of Anne, who had lost everything and been alone.

She went on looking at Nicholas.

After a long time he came over to her, frowning.

"We must have Anne here," he said. "They must be married from here."

That was a strange thing for him to say. Jenny thought how strange it was. Anne would be here, but Jenny would be gone. She felt puzzled about it.

"We'd better do it with a splash," said Nicholas, still frowning. "Ask everyone, and go the limit."

Jenny put up her hand and touched his sleeve.

"Aren't you going to send me away, Nicko?"

"What would be the good? You're my wife. We've got to stick it out."

Jenny held his sleeve.

"Nicko—"

"We've got to make the best of things. You're worn out. We'd better have a meal."

He pulled away from her and went over to the bell.

Jenny sat back in her chair. Everything seemed to have come to a stop. She heard the door open and she heard Nicholas speaking:

"Emmot! We want something to eat. It's too late for dinner. I think something on a tray in here—soup and something cold. Her ladyship's a little faint."

The door shut again. Nicholas lit a cigarette.

Chapter Forty

JOHN CAME into the drawing-room of Aurora's flat at a little after seven o'clock. He found Anne alone—Anne rather pale, in a blue and silver dress. She turned to meet him with an anxious "What has happened?"

"You look ripping in that dress," said John.

Anne caught him by the arm.

"John—please—*please*, what has happened?"

"I don't know."

"Haven't you been down?"

"Yes, I've been down. They'd been away for the week-end—Jenny had only just got my letter. I cleared off because I thought I'd be in the way whilst she was telling Nicholas."

Anne's hands dropped.

"She won't tell him," she said in a low voice.

"Yes, she will. As a matter of fact she had practically told him. She lost her head a bit and said things, and I came away. You will hear from them to-morrow, I expect. Anne darling, don't look like that!"

"What will Nicholas do?" said Anne in a whisper. "John, he's proud. If he doesn't forgive her—Jenny—what'll happen to Jenny?"

John put his arm round her.

"Nicholas is very fond of Jenny," he said." I noticed it a good deal when I stayed there. It'll be a bit of a facer for him of course.

But there you are—Jenny did it; and in the long run it's much better Nicholas should know. It was pretty bad for Jenny going on telling lies and being everyone's blue-eyed darling. She'll be a heap nicer if she can stop lying every second word. I tumbled to it pretty quickly, and I used to want to spank her every time she did it."

"Oh, John!"

"You bet I did! I hope Nicholas gives it her pretty strong—it's what she wants. And you needn't be afraid he won't come round—Jenny's a lot too fascinating for that. What I'm afraid of is that he'll come round a good deal too soon. Jenny's like that; she gets round you. I've been absolutely mad with her myself, and then when I saw her somehow I didn't want to hurt her. And when she came into the room this afternoon I was downright sorry for her, though she didn't deserve it." He laughed a little. "No, you needn't be afraid. Nicholas'll put it across her, and she'll cry and be dreadfully unhappy for a bit; and then she'll get round him. If she can get round me, you bet she can get round Nicholas. There's something about Jenny."

"Yes, there is," said Anne. Her eyes were shining.

"She'd better stop telling lies though, or she'll land in a nasty mess. I hope Nicholas doesn't let her off too easy—that's all I'm afraid of. That's enough about Jenny. Kiss me. You haven't kissed me yet. Have you stopped being a parlour-maid?"

"Oh, John, it was dreadful!" said Anne in his arms.

"What was?"

"She was—Mrs. Fossick-Yates. She started by having me up after breakfast and saying a friend of hers had seen me coming home with a man. John, she must have had sort of X-ray eyes, because you *know* how dark it was."

"There are some lamps."

John became suddenly aware that Anne had a dimple.

"How stupid you are! It wasn't—I mean you didn't. John, she couldn't really have seen anything; but she said she did."

Anne had a very pretty blush.

"What did she see?"

"She didn't—she couldn't! But she told Mrs. Fossick-Yates she saw you kiss me!"

"How horrible!"

"It's all very well for you to laugh, but it *was* horrible for me. She talked in capital letters for about half an hour, and she said the most awful things. And as soon as I could get a word in edgeways, I said I thought I'd better not stay any longer. And then she began to think about not having a parlour-maid, and she said I couldn't go, because I hadn't worked enough to pay for the dresses she'd had to get me. John, it was horrid—like being in a street row. I hated it."

"What did you do?"

"I said I was going to friends, and I'd send her the money for the dresses. Then she said much worse things"—Anne was quite pale—"so I went and packed my box and walked out. My sixpence just got me here. Aurora was an angel. She made me write a letter, and she enclosed the money Mrs. Fossick-Yates said I owed her, and she sent a messenger boy to bring away my box. I shouldn't have thought of that. She was splendid."

John's attention seemed to be wandering a little.

"Could you get married in a blue dress like this?"

"No—I don't think so."

The dimple had returned.

"Oh—" A short pause, and then, "We shall be getting married in about a fortnight. I think to-morrow fortnight would be a good day. It's a Tuesday. I think I should like to get married on a Tuesday."

Anne laughed, and was kissed.

"There's nothing to laugh at. To-morrow we will go and buy your engagement ring, and your wedding ring. And if there's time before lunch, you can buy something to get married in."

Anne gave a little scream; and as she did so, Miss Fairlie came in. She was tightly upholstered in a pre-war black satin, and wore three rows of extremely valuable pearls about a brick-red neck.

"Is he beating you already?" she said. "He will if you're not careful. He's not a young man I should marry myself. You'll be a poor, miserable, down-trodden squaw—but I suppose you don't mind."

Anne looked rather demurely at John. She had two dimples now. There was a little sparkling something behind the dark lashes which lifted for a moment and then fell.

"I wonder," she said.

THE END

Lightning Source UK Ltd.
Milton Keynes UK
UKHW021110161219
355461UK00005B/136/P